ROYAL BOROUGH OF GREENWICH

PeL
and the
Picture of
Innocence

MARK HEBDEN

HOUSE OF
STRATUS

This edition published in 2001 by House of Stratus, an imprint of Stratus Holdings plc, 24c Old Burlington Street, London, W1X 1RL, UK.

www.houseofstratus.com

Typeset, printed and bound by House of Stratus.

A catalogue record for this book is available from the British Library.

ISBN 1-84232-903-0

Though lovers of Burgundy might decide that they have recognised the city in these pages, in fact it is intended to be fictitious.

one

'Why do people play boules?'

Chief Inspector Evariste Clovis Désiré Pel, of the Brigade Criminelle of the Police Justiciaire of the French Republic, considered the question. The small boy alongside him weighed in his hand the heavy steel balls they had been using and waited for a reply. But it was Pel's day off and he didn't relish having to think when he was supposed to be resting. However, Yves Pasquier lived next door, and the two of them were in the habit of meeting each morning by the hole in the hedge that separated their gardens and setting the world to rights. Yves Pasquier admired Pel because he was a policeman and Pel admired Yves Pasquier because he was *determined* to be a policeman. Yves Pasquier also had a pretty mother, and Pel knew he wasn't going to be able to dodge the issue.

Why *did* people play boules, he wondered. Come to that, why did people play *le foot*, or chase girls, or fornicate, or for that matter smoke? Pel frowned. He knew why *he* smoked. It was because he couldn't stop. He'd tried on many occasions, starting early in the morning, bright-eyed and bushy-tailed, his determination strong, and ready for any sacrifice in the search for health and a happy old age. By lunch time, however, dull-eyed and shifty in demeanour, he was invariably seeking the Gauloises hidden at the back of the drawer in his desk for just such a failure of will.

1

The boy bent to the shaggy black mongrel at his feet. It looked like an elongated mophead and it was always difficult to tell which was the dangerous end. 'Where did boules come from?' he asked.

'The Romans?' Pel suggested hopefully. 'Perhaps in those days they used them as weapons and hurled them at each other. After all, a bonk on the conk from a boule wouldn't do you a lot of good, would it?'

The boy giggled. 'Perhaps originally they were cannon-balls. Would they know at the Hôtel de Police?' To Yves Pasquier, police headquarters were the fount of all know-ledge.

Pel's view was different. Despite their extensive files, there was a lot they didn't know at the Hôtel de Police and a great many things they would have liked to know. The origin of boules, however, was not among those subjects which normally held the attention of the men who occupied the place. Girls, yes. Beer, certainly. Crooks, occasionally. But boules – only in passing, after an evening at a bar or after a Sunday with the relations round for lunch. He was still wondering how to reply when the telephone went and a head was thrust through a window.

'For you!'

It was Madame Routy, the housekeeper that Pel's wife had taken on with Pel when she had married him. For years Pel and Madame Routy had lived in the same small house and when Pel had finally married, his bride – fortunately with the money to sustain her whims – had decided to take on Madame Routy, too. Pel had been convinced it was the biggest mistake of her life – almost as big as marrying Pel – but Madame Routy had been tamed. Pel had never been able to understand how, because he had never been able to get her to do a thing for *him*.

When he picked up the telephone, the voice at the other end of the line was that of Inspector Darcy, his second in command. Pel greeted him sourly. He didn't appreciate being called to the telephone on his day off.

'Well?' he snapped.

He could have sworn he heard Darcy chuckle. Though always loyal, Darcy often found him amusing. After all – Pel had to admit it – he *was* inclined at times to be a little odd and in his old age fully expected to descend into eccentricity.

'Thought you'd like to know, Patron,' Darcy said. 'Maurice Tagliatti's around again.'

'Who? Say that again.'

'Maurice Tagliatti. Like me to spell it out?'

'I know how to spell it. When did he arrive?'

'June, Patron.'

'That's three months ago. Why didn't we know?'

'Because nobody told us. He's been careful to keep a low profile. So low, his nostrils must have been dragging in the dust.'

'It isn't Maurice's style to lie low. He must be up to something. Where is he?'

'He's got himself a nice little country hideaway. I thought I might go and find out what he's up to.'

Pel frowned. Maurice Tagliatti had started as an apprentice in a nickel-plating plant in the city and had been in trouble with the police more than once before suddenly appearing to have amassed money. Nobody imagined he'd come by it honestly, but since then he had gone into property speculation, bought a chain of grocery stores, a string of vineyards and garages, and was now said to be worth a bomb. He had moved away some years before and was reputed nowadays to be involved with casinos, extortion, brothels and blackmail. You name it, he was at it. So if he were back in Burgundy, so was trouble.

Pel didn't hesitate. 'Pick me up on your way,' he said.

Replacing the telephone, he returned to the garden to present his apologies. He did it gravely and with considerable concern. Yves Pasquier was only ten but Pel always treated small boys with great consideration.

'I'm afraid you'll have to excuse me,' he pointed out.

'Been called out?' Yves Pasquier asked.

'Something's come up.'

'A crime?'

'Not yet. But I suspect there might be one in the offing somewhere.'

'Can I come? I'll not get in the way.'

Pel wondered how Maurice Tagliatti would react to being interviewed by a small boy. 'I think', he said, 'that you'd better grow a bit first.'

Yves Pasquier sighed. 'I'll put the boules away,' he said. 'Then I'll slip in and have a slice of Madame Routy's cake before I go home. Don't forget to ask about the boules.'

Pel nodded solemnly. It had come as a surprise to find that Madame Routy was feeding the next-door offspring, especially since he had learned that the boy's slice of cake was invariably two and sometimes even three. As Pel never ate cake and had never seen his wife eat cake, he could only assume that Madame Routy made the cakes especially for Yves Pasquier. Which seemed to indicate that in her old age that lump of agate he had always assumed she wore in place of a heart had changed texture and was now suddenly capable of feeling.

Pel's wife was at her desk. It always pleased Pel to see his wife at her desk wearing her spectacles and with her account books open in front of her. She ran the most expensive hairdressing salon in the city and recently, assuming that her clients – being wealthy – would still have money to burn even after paying the exorbitant fees she charged, had opened the most exclusive boutique in the city to go with the most exclusive hairdressing salon. It was already making a fortune.

The thought pleased Pel. Even for a chief inspector, police pay didn't make old age a sinecure, and ever since he'd been a young cop he had dreaded shuffling off his responsibilities for the last time to find himself facing a poverty-stricken retirement. Since all his working life he had been stuffing money into the bank like a hamster shoving food into its cheeks, poverty had always been a most unlikely fate but, such was his uncertainty, he liked to feel his wife's money was there as a cushion in case he'd miscalculated.

'I'm going out,' he said.

Madame Pel looked up, her spectacles on the end of her nose. 'A job?'

'Daniel rang. Tagliatti's appeared in the area.'

'Tagliatti? Tagliatti? Isn't he the one who—?'

'Yes, he is.' Whatever crime Pel's wife had in mind, Tagliatti would have been behind it. He drove large and expensive American cars, lived like a millionaire, and ran a string of girls of surpassing beauty – all, to Pel's everlasting surprise, apparently thinking the world of him.

The only thing Pel could consider in his favour was that, although brought up in Burgundy, he had taken himself south to the sun. It was one of the few blots on the landscape of Pel's beloved province that Tagliatti had originated there. He was not one of Burgundy's most distinguished sons and Pel could feel nothing but gratitude to him for shifting his sphere of operations.

'Where is he?' he asked as he slipped into the passenger seat of Darcy's car.

'At his country estate.'

Pel's eyebrows rose. 'I didn't know he had one.'

'He bought that place that used to belong to the Mangy de Lordy family.'

'What happened to them?'

'Most of what they possessed went down their throats and ended up in the till at the local bar. They had to sell up.'

'And Maurice?'

'He's given himself a title.'

'God Almighty!'

'He doesn't aim *that* high. Just Chevalier de Lordy. It's unofficial, of course, but since he owns the Lordy estates, and they constitute practically the whole of the village of Lordy, I suppose he has a certain amount of right on his side.'

Pel gestured back towards his house. 'Lordy's not far from here,' he said indignantly.

Darcy grinned. 'You'll be able to have him in for drinks, Patron.'

Maurice Tagliatti was no longer young but he was still dark, Italianate and dressed in a way that made Pel feel like the man who'd come to mend the lavatory.

He was in the garden when they arrived, inspecting his roses, accompanied by a girl who might easily have been a rejuvenated Brigitte Bardot. They were surrounded by a group of dark-visaged, smart-suited men who were clearly his advisers, bodyguards and probably accountants. Why, Pel wondered, did people like Maurice Tagliatti always surround themselves with men who looked like bouncers in a night club? In the drive behind them was the big black Cadillac Maurice liked to use. It probably, Pel decided, made him feel like Al Capone or something from the New York Mafia.

Tagliatti himself wore a lightweight blue suit with a red handkerchief in the breast pocket, and a wide-brimmed white hat. He beamed at the policemen and held out his hand. 'Inspector Pel,' he said.

Pel glared. '*Chief* Inspector,' he corrected.

Tagliatti's smile widened and he gestured at the men behind him. 'You know the boys?'

'I expect they're on our computer,' Pel growled.

Tagliatti laughed. 'Always one for a joke, aren't you, Chief?' He indicated the girl. 'My secretary, Vlada Preradovic.'

The girl gave them a sullen look that might have meant anything and Tagliatti gestured again, this time at a tall man standing beside him, thin-faced, handsome and expensively dressed without Tagliatti's bad taste. 'That's Georges Cavalin. He's my manager.'

Cavalin greeted Pel with a refined accent. The son of some proud father and mother, Pel thought, who had doubtless spent money on his education but hadn't been able to handle him.

Tagliatti was gesturing dismissively at the others: 'Bernard Guérin. David Ourdabi.' He gave up after two.

They were all typical heavies, broad-shouldered, in their thirties, but Ourdabi was younger, hard-eyed and, like Tagliatti, looked Italian. He was leaning against the wall, cleaning his nails with a nail file and trying to look like Humphrey Bogart. He nodded at Pel who stared back at him hostilely. He didn't like people who tried to look like Humphrey Bogart. Sometimes they behaved like Humphrey Bogart.

Tagliatti indicated the house behind him. 'Like my new home?' he asked.

The house wasn't big enough to be called a château, though without doubt Maurice would call it a château. It was what might be categorised as a *manoir*, large, square, roomy, covered with ivy and with that aura of *grande famille* that Pel so much admired.

'Why did you buy it, Maurice?'

Tagliatti looked surprised at the question. 'Prestige,' he said. 'The wish to be somebody. It's good, prestige. Good for the image. Makes people admire you. Good for tick at the grocer's. Haven't you ever wanted a big house, Chief Inspector?'

Pel had always wanted a big house but he wouldn't have dreamed of admitting it to Maurice Tagliatti. 'More to it than that, I think,' he said. 'What are you up to here?'

Tagliatti smiled. 'What I'm doing here is nothing to do with the police.'

'It has a lot to do with us.'

'I don't have to tell you.'

'No. But I can always arrange to take you in to the Hôtel de Police and question you there. We've had a nice comfortable cell at Number 72 waiting for you for a long time.'

Tagliatti's mouth tightened. Numbered 72, Rue d'Auxonne was the charming name by which the local prison was known. 'You have nothing on me,' he growled.

'I've not the slightest doubt', Pel pointed out, 'that I could find something.'

Tagliatti considered the point and obviously decided Pel was right. 'I'm buying wine,' he said. 'I have a chain of stores in the south. They need supplying.'

Pel gave him a frozen look. 'Nothing else?' he asked.

Tagliatti shrugged his plump shoulders. 'Visiting old friends. Why are you here?'

'Same as you. Visiting old friends. Letting them know we're aware they're around.'

They sparred for a little while longer but, though they made it plain to Tagliatti that they were prepared to deploy the whole of the Police Judiciaire if necessary to stop whatever it was he was contemplating, in the end the interview was not very satisfactory. Tagliatti was always a match for them and they had nothing on him whatsoever. He certainly *appeared* to be buying wine. He produced bills from the vineyards and there was no reason to dispute them, so that they left unsatisfied and with Pel in a bad temper.

He knew that Tagliatti was in the vicinity for a good reason. His interests these days were mostly around

Marseilles, which was the crossroads for most of the villainy in France, so he wouldn't have come to Burgundy for no reason at all, especially since the wine he claimed he needed for his supermarkets could all have been bought by his henchmen. Tagliatti had a whole army of assistants these days, everything from strong-arm men to crooked accountants and lawyers with, in between, perfectly honest little men who did his business without being aware of what went on behind the façade they provided.

'The picture of innocence,' Pel observed as they climbed back into the car. 'He's not here for nothing,'

'That was my view,' Darcy agreed.

'Oh, well,' Pel said. 'At least, he'll know we have our beady eye on him. It might make him careful. It might even make him decide it could be wiser to leave empty-handed.'

'It could also make him all the more determined to take what he came for,' Darcy said.

As it happened, they were both wrong.

It started a few weeks later. Things were quiet except for the usual frauds, swindles, wife beatings, extortions, threats, attacks with offensive weapons, run of the mill rapes, and what have you, so that the news of a new assault was nothing to get worked up about. This time, it was in a sports outfitters. Among the footballs and rugby balls, among the tracksuits and running pumps, among the static bicycles and rowing machines. A shop assistant appeared to have been beaten up, and Darcy had never come across such a thing before. Most people who went in for sport were so busy wearing themselves out trying to become gold medal winners they hadn't any energy left to attack anyone. Sitting back with a brandy, his arm round a girl, he had often watched them on television arriving at the finishing posts black in the face and with their eyes sticking out like hat pegs in a restaurant cloakroom, and had always wondered why they did it. He had never heard of an athlete going in for crime and had always assumed they were too dedicated – or too exhausted – to make a habit of it.

The news of the assault was brought in by a middle-aged woman with a jaw like the prow of a battleship. To look at her you'd have assumed she might have been the guilty party; instead she turned out to be the mother of the victim.

'Beaten up?' Darcy said, studying her across his desk.

'Beaten up.' The reply came short, sharp and definite.

'Badly?'

'Badly.'

'What are the injuries you complain of?'

'Not me,' the woman snapped. 'My son.'

Darcy stared at her. Darcy's stare normally sent women into a tizzy because Darcy was handsome, immaculate and forceful and he had the sort of teeth that shone in the sunshine like jewels in a Disney cartoon. Normally they won over admirers in droves. But not this one.

'I'd better have the name,' he said.

'Julien Claude Roth.'

'Address?'

'Apartment 3, 7 Rue Philibert-Riou, Blaine.'

'Where is he? In hospital?'

'No, he's at work.'

'I thought he'd been beaten up.'

'He was.'

'So what's he doing at work?'

'He likes working. I'm making the complaint on his behalf.'

'Why?'

'He doesn't want to.'

'Why not?'

'He just doesn't.' Madame Roth stared hostilely at Darcy. 'I decided he should. So I came.'

'So I see, madame.' Darcy began to suspect that he was dealing with something that was going to prove pretty trivial. 'What's the nature of his injuries?'

'Severe bruising to the head.'

'Severe?'

'Severe.'

'Anything else? Any broken bones?'

'No.'

'No split lip? No black eyes?'

'No.'

'What was it? A fight?'

'No. Just a beating up.'

'Where?'

'At France Sport, the sports shop in the Rue Général Leclerc.'

Darcy began to imagine people beating each other about the head with rowing machines or Indian clubs.

'Who committed the offence? Do you know?'

'Of course. It was Fernand Léon, the owner of the shop.'

This one, Darcy decided, was beginning to sound as if it would need the attention of a social worker, not a cop.

'What with?'

'What do you mean, what with?'

'Well, what did Léon hit your son with?'

'Nothing.'

'Nothing?'

'Well, his hand.'

'How often?'

'Twice.'

'Open or shut?'

'What? The shop?'

'No, madame. The hand.'

'It was open.'

Darcy sat back. 'Is that all?'

Madame Roth glared. 'What do you mean, is that all?'

'I expected a savage assault, madame, with your son struck with an offensive weapon, but it seems to have been just a scuffle.'

'It was an unprovoked assault.'

Darcy drew a deep breath. 'How old is your son, madame?'

'Eighteen.'

'Is he a big boy?'

'Not very. He's shy, too.'

'So why was he assaulted?'

'I expect Léon was drunk.'

'Does he often get drunk?'

'According to my son, no.'

'Doesn't your son know why he was attacked?'

'He can't explain it. He was just about to complete a sale when Léon set about him.'

Darcy changed step. 'Where's your son's father, madame?' he asked. 'Why didn't *he* come in?'

'Because he ran off with another woman twelve years ago.'

'Ah!' There was a wealth of meaning in that 'ah'.

'What's that got to do with it?'

'Nothing special,' Darcy said, though of course it had and Darcy's questions were never pointless because he was a good cop. 'But I like to know the background.' He placed his pen on the desk. 'I'll see it's looked into. There certainly seems to have been an assault, and assault is always a chargeable offence, however slight it might be – '

'It wasn't slight. My son came home with his face red and bruised and with a cut on his cheek. There was blood on it.'

'I see, madame.' Darcy rose. 'Leave it to me. We'll deal with it.'

In Pel's office he discussed it along with the other cases on the books.

'Some sort of dispute with the owner of the shop,' he said. 'A couple of slaps.'

Pel sniffed. It didn't sound much. Certainly not the usual mayhem inflicted on a civilised country by its uncivilised inhabitants. It could easily be handled by subordinates. Nobody was dead, and he and Darcy had to keep their programmes clear of trivialities in case the President of the Republic chose to appear in the area and someone tried to assassinate, kidnap or otherwise embarrass him. Darcy's team could handle it.

'What do you intend?'

Darcy shrugged. 'Give it to one of the boys. If everybody's busy, I'll give it to Misset. He ought to be able to clear it up.'

Misset was the flaw in Pel's team. Handsome but with fading looks, Misset moved with the speed of hardening cement and was constantly in trouble for dodging work.

As Darcy left, Pel looked at his watch. Four-fifty. He wondered if anyone would notice if he slipped off a little early.

He looked at the list on his desk to see what his team were up to and who was free. Jean-Luc Nosjean, the senior sergeant, was away with Claudie Darel, the only woman member of the team, winding up the remains of an art swindle inquiry that had occupied his attention on and off for months. De Troq' was involved in what seemed to be a neat little fraud involving one of the city's lawyers. De Troq' had a title – Baron Charles Victor de Troquereau Tournay-Turenne – and the manner to go with it. His family were poverty-stricken but, being an Auvergnat, he still appeared to have a great deal more than most and they always used him on delicate cases involving prestige because his manner could quieten the most raging snob. Aimedieu. Brochard. Debray. Lacocq. Morell. Bardolle. All involved. Not much. Just a dozen or so cases apiece – nothing really to call them busy. Finally there was Didier Darras, Madame Routy's nephew, the cadet who ran the office; Misset, who, with blank eyes and brain in neutral, was fit for little else but answering the telephone; and Lagé, who was contemplating a retirement which grew nearer every day. Not a bad bunch on the whole. Good, bad and indifferent. If anything big came up they'd all be in it and the days off they cherished above rubies would be gone with the wind.

He decided it was safe to go home but it had been a hot dusty day and he first slipped across the road for a beer.

The bar behind the Hôtel de Police was called the Bar Transvaal. It had been the Bar Transvaal as long as anyone could remember – perhaps since the Boer War – but, since apartheid had raised its ugly head, the landlord had felt it should be renamed the Bar du Palais des Ducs de Bourgogne after the splendid edifice nearby which had once belonged to the Dukes of Burgundy in the days when they had disputed the right to rule with the kings of France. Unfortunately, he hadn't been able to persuade the brewery, which in addition to beer supplied him with the awnings and the umbrellas for the tables outside, that this was a good idea, and at that very moment one of their representatives was in the bar indignantly demanding an explanation.

'What's wrong with the old name?' he was asking.

'I've changed it,' the landlord said.

'So...' The brewery representative had a nice line in sarcasm. '...because you fancied changing the name, you expect us to provide you with new awning?'

'Well, it's that apartheid,' the landlord said. 'People don't agree with it.'

The brewery man shrugged. 'We don't mind. South Africa's not our country. So why should we shove our nose in? Do you realise how much those awnings cost? And with a name like that? Bar Transvaal. A nice tidy name. Twelve letters. One space. Bar du Palais des Ducs de Bourgogne. Twenty-nine letters. Six spaces. Letters are expensive.

They're sewn on separately, you know. Even the spaces cost money.'

As Pel stood at the bar, listening, he reached for his cigarettes. Just one last one, he thought, before he went home, so he could resist during the evening and not smell like an ashtray near his wife. If he stopped smoking, he thought, drinking would taste better. Come to that, he realised, if he stopped drinking, perhaps smoking would improve. And if he stopped both he'd live longer. On the other hand, life would be damned dull. Perhaps he should limit himself to one every two hours, though he could just imagine the temper he'd be in after an hour and a half.

Starting after this one, he decided, fishing for his cigarettes. As he did so, his eye fell on a pamphlet lying on the counter. STOP SMOKING, it said. NATURE'S WAY. NOT A NICOTINE SUBSTITUTE, A GENUINE HERBAL REMEDY.

Despite himself, he started reading it. After all, why not? His wife never complained, but he knew she lived in hopes that one day he'd give them up. *Absolutely unique course,* he read. *Completely new approach. Murot's Anti-Smoking/ Aversion Tablets. Once you commence a course you will be a non-smoker. If you are not 100 per cent delighted, your money will be refunded immediately.*

He was just wondering if he ought to try it when the landlord leaned on the counter in front of him. He was smoking a cigarette, and stank like an incinerator. 'It's rubbish,' he advised. 'If you can't stop without *that,* you're not worth your cigarette money.'

Pel nodded sheepishly, shoving the pamphlet aside. 'Of course,' he said stoutly. 'Nobody should need that.'

'But there's this government campaign to cut down smoking, the landlord went on, lighting a fresh cigarette from the old one. 'So I leave the pamphlets around. They don't do any harm. Nobody takes any notice of them, anyway.'

Pel did. He took notice of anything that might persuade him he was about to collapse with lung cancer. He patted his pocket where his cigarettes were. Firmly. The pamphlet had decided him. The pamphlet and the landlord between them. Only a fool couldn't give up smoking. He'd stopped. Never mind one last one. From that minute. He suspected that the following day he'd be about as amenable as an atom bomb and his staff would suffer, but this time it was for keeps. He'd given up smoking before – for an hour or two anyway. This time, though, he meant it. This time he really would refrain. If he could refrain for the rest of the night – Holy Mother of God, what a thought! – he might be able to refrain tomorrow. And if he refrained tomorrow, there was no knowing to what delights of forbearance he might be led. He was just seeing himself free of guilt, a non-smoker, fit to be seen in the company of haloed non-smokers, E.C.D. Pel, reformer *extraordinaire,* when the telephone went.

The landlord snatched it up, listened, then held it out. 'For you,' he said.

It was Darcy. 'Hold your hat on, Patron,' he said and Pel knew that this was it – the big one that would involve everybody. Without thinking, his hand reached for the packet of Gauloises in his pocket.

'Go on,' he said.

'You'll never guess.'

'I don't intend to. What's happened?'

'We've lost our best customer.'

'For the love of God, we're not playing guessing games. Spit it out!'

'It's Maurice.'

'Tagliatti? What's happened to him?'

'He's dead.'

Pel actually smiled. 'Heart?'

Darcy laughed. 'Sure. It stopped. A bullet or something stopped it.'

'I don't believe it! Who did it?'

'That I don't know yet. But it seems they got Maurice and the man who was driving him.'

'Where?'

'Near your house, Patron. Bottom of the hill that runs down from Lordy.'

Good God, Pel thought, they'd be killing each other in his back garden soon.

'We've just had a message from the brigadier at Lordy,' Darcy went on. 'I've ordered cars and informed Forensic, Photography, Fingerprints, Doc Minet, the lot. And I've sent Lacocq, Debray and Aimedieu off. I'll be waiting with the car as soon as you're ready.'

As he put the telephone down, Pel stared at it for a second. Avoid strain, cures for smoking always said. Fat chance of that, he thought. Bang went his good resolution. He flipped out one of the cigarettes and put it to his mouth only to find to his surprise that there was one already there – alight.

Why, he wondered, did God have it in for him so? He'd obviously been doomed from the day of his birth. The world had been waiting in ambush for him. When he'd appeared there had been a brisk rubbing of hands all round and a great shout of 'He's arrived!'

He tossed the unlit cigarette on to the counter in a fury then, being Pel and a bit mean, he picked it up again, dusted it down and replaced it in the packet. Couldn't waste things. Might make all the difference between poverty and luxury in his old age. No good Burgundian wasted things.

All the same, he wondered as he reached for his coat, how in the name of God had that lighted cigarette found its way into his mouth?

two

The car was a big Peugeot and it was angled into the side of
the road, its front wheel dropped into a deep ditch. When it
rained in that part of the world, it came down hard and
heavy and most of the roads in the hills had ditches along
their verges to allow it to run away; Pel had always been in
fear of dropping a wheel in as he rounded corners. It was
being studied by Lacocq, Debray and Aimedieu, who were
standing in a pool of bronze-yellow sunshine that slanted
through the trees and thick undergrowth and speckled the
road with bright moving spots.

Two policemen from Lordy, one a brigadier, with a small
white Renault van, were erecting a barrier and, even as
Darcy's car braked to a halt, another van arrived with two
more policemen, followed almost immediately by more cars
and vans containing the men from Photography, Forensic,
Scene of Crime and Traffic. Not far away, eyed hostilely by
the policemen from Lordy, was a group of spectators, and Pel
wondered for the hundredth time in his career where they
came from. This was a country road yet within minutes there
were people standing about with their mouths open. If there
were a murder on a desert island they'd turn up. It was a
French habit. A man changing a wheel on his car. A girl
hitching up her stocking. A dog trying to mount a bitch.
They all produced crowds, drinking it all in.

'Who reported it?'

The brigadier indicated a long-haired boy in a red shirt wearing ear-muffs round his neck. Just beyond, parked under the trees where Pel hadn't noticed it, was an ancient tractor.

'Gilles Roblais,' the brigadier said. 'From the farm up the hill. He's the son. I've got a statement. He was on his way down. He went to the farm to telephone then came back to wait for us.'

'Did he see anyone?'

'Nothing but what we're seeing now. Just the car and the bodies. At first I thought there was only one, but then we found the other.' The brigadier moved gingerly towards the stalled car. It was well and truly riddled with bullets. 'Twenty-seven holes,' he pointed out. 'I counted them. I found six of the bullets. I haven't touched them. I reckon there are around twelve in the bodies. It's hard to say. There's so much blood.'

The other policeman gestured. 'There are cartridge cases in the road. One or two in the grass. They're all marked.'

The man who had been driving the car hung half out of the door. He had been hit several times in the head, neck and throat and, despite the blood, Pel managed to recognise him as one of the men who had surrounded Maurice Tagliatti.

'Got his name?'

The brigadier produced a driving licence spattered with blood. 'It fell out of his pocket,' he said. 'He's Benjamen Bozon, burnisher. Address in Marseilles.'

Pel studied the car. The front portion where the driver sat was shattered by the bullets, but there seemed to be no holes in the rear portion where a passenger would have been sitting.

'I thought Maurice Tagliatti was one of them,' he said. 'Where, is he?'

The policeman gestured and then Pel noticed a line of blood, drops on the road. They led to a small copse containing a low stone hut once used by foresters but

19

allowed to fall into disrepair. Its walls bulged and the roof seemed to have been scattered for yards around, with scraps of wood and broken beams. In the middle of it, half covered with tiles and pieces of brick and timber, lay what was left of Maurice Tagliatti.

The policeman gestured. Among the ruins, they saw two guns, a Walther 7.65 and a Beretta 9 mm. Scattered around were cartridge cases. The policeman gestured again. Some distance away in a half-circle of trampled grass were more cartridge cases.

'What happened?'

'I think he was hit but managed to escape from the car and got to this place and held off whoever it was who was trying to kill him. They did for him, though. With that.'

The policeman stirred the grass with his foot so that they saw the ring and pin from a hand grenade. 'I think', he said, 'that when they couldn't get near him, they tossed that in the doorway. It finished him.'

'It would,' Darcy said gravely.

'It *is* Maurice Tagliatti, isn't it?' the brigadier said.

'Yes,' Darcy said. 'That's Maurice all right.'

'There's a bullet wound in his shoulder,' the policeman said. 'It didn't kill him, though. It was the grenade did that. I found at least seven wounds.'

Tagliatti was wearing a cap, white linen trousers and a heavily checked sports jacket, not the normal smart lightweight suit he preferred, with the white hat and the red handkerchief in his breast pocket.

Pel stared at the corpse for a while, unmoved. People who lived by violence couldn't complain if they died by violence, and, if nothing else, the death of anybody like Maurice Tagliatti couldn't do anything for the police but help them.

Doc Minet appeared. 'No need to tell you the cause of death here,' he said. 'In the case of the driver, gunshot wounds. This chap – fragments from a grenade.'

'That would be about it.'

Prélat, of Fingerprints, was going over the car when they returned to it. 'There's nothing here,' he said. 'Except the driver's dabs.'

Leguyader, of the Lab, held one of the cartridge cases with a pair of tweezers. 'Nine-millimetre,' he said. 'British. Probably from a Sterling.'

Pel called over the boy with the ear-muffs. 'You found them?'

The boy nodded.

'See anything odd?'

The boy shook his head.

'No strangers?'

Another shake of the head.

'What happened?'

The boy indicated the tractor. 'Going to the lower pasture. Found 'em.'

'Hear anything?'

The boy merely indicated the ear-muffs. He seemed to be suffering from oral constipation. Pel decided he'd leave him to Darcy.

As they talked, a white British Range Rover with dark windows came roaring down the hill from Lordy. It stopped with a screech of brakes near the crowd of spectators, sending several of them scuttling for safety.

Pel recognised the driver as Cavalin, one of the group he'd see with Maurice Tagliatti a few weeks before. One of the men behind him, large, fat and hostile-looking, held a gun. Seeing Pel, Cavalin gestured and the weapon vanished at once.

'Chief Inspector,' he said. 'What's happened?'

Pel indicated the stalled car and Cavalin's eyes flickered. 'That's one of our cars,' he said. 'Was Maurice – ?'

'He's not in the car,' Pel said. 'He's up there in what's left of the hut.'

Cavalin swallowed hard. 'Is he – ?'

'He's dead.'

Cavalin walked towards the wrecked hut. When he returned, his face was stiff. He glanced at the body of the driver hanging half out of the Peugeot.

'This is a terrible thing,' he said.

It might be terrible for Maurice's organisation, Pel thought, but it wasn't a terrible thing for the police, and he wondered instinctively how much Cavalin was involved. He was one of the linchpins of Maurice's organisation, possibly heir to the throne, and the thought crossed Pel's mind that he might even have been responsible. In Maurice's society, it wasn't unknown for the boss to be removed rather suddenly – especially if he grew lazy, old and too ambitious – so that someone with new ideas could take over. There were quite a few varieties of treachery in the world Maurice Tagliatti had inhabited and Cavalin was probably not as upset as he was trying to convey.

'You got here quickly,' he said.

Cavalin shrugged. 'I thought something had happened.'

Pel eyed him narrowly. 'Why?'

'Why?'

'Yes. Why did you think something had happened? You, couldn't have seen it.'

Cavalin shrugged. 'One of the boys heard shooting.'

'It might have been somebody after a rabbit.'

'It didn't sound like *that* sort of shooting.'

The large fat man with Cavalin was scowling. 'They should have let me go with Maurice,' he growled.

'Who should?' Pel asked.

The fat man lifted his head. 'Maurice should. I usually did. But this time he said he wanted to go alone. I knew he shouldn't have.'

'Why shouldn't he have? Was he in danger?'

'Maurice was always –' Pel detected a faint move of the head from Cavalin and the fat man stopped dead. 'No,' he said. 'He wasn't in danger. But I was always with him when he went anywhere. But not this time. I wish I could find the son of a whore who did it. I'd kill the bastard.'

Pel studied him mildly. 'How?' he asked. 'I noticed you had a gun.

The fat man studied him for a moment then he nodded. 'I've got a gun.'

'Which you always carry?'

'Yes.'

'You'd better let me see it.'

There was a long silence then Cavalin spoke.

'Let him see it,' he said.

The fat man handed over the gun. Pel studied it. 'Swiss ninemill.,' he said. 'I don't suppose you've got a licence, have you?'

The fat man looked as if he hadn't the slightest idea what a licence was, and Pel handed the gun to Darcy.

'Confiscated,' he said shortly. 'No licence.'

The fat man stared hard at him, then glanced at Cavalin and again there was that faint move of the head.

'Jim', Cavalin said, 'tends to go over the top a bit.'

'That his name? Jim?'

'Yes. Jim Peneau.'

'Thought a lot of Maurice, did he?'

'He gave me a good job,' Peneau said.

'Doing what?'

'Looking after him.'

'In what way?'

Peneau began to suspect he was on dangerous ground again and his hand moved dismissively. 'Fetching and carrying. Running errands. That sort of thing.' He scowled at Pel. 'Maurice had a lot of people who didn't like him,' he said.

Pel nodded. 'I'm sure he did. I was one.' He looked at Cavalin. 'What about Maurice's wife? I've heard she doesn't spend much of the year with him.'

'No,' Cavalin agreed. 'She skis in the winter. She has a chalet in Switzerland. She goes to St Trop' in the summer. She also goes to Deauville. She likes sailing and has friends there.'

'Where is she now?'

'Here. At the Manoir.'

'Why?'

'It just happened that way.'

'Who's going to tell her?'

'I expect I will.'

'How will she take it?'

Cavalin drew a deep breath. 'I doubt if it will break her heart.'

'Like that, is it?'

'Yes.'

'I'll be coming to see her. Inform her.'

'I'll tell her to hold herself in readiness.'

Pel looked quickly at Cavalin but his face was grave and serious.

'Did Benjamen Bozon always drive Maurice around?' he asked.

'No.'

'Why was he driving today?'

'Because', Cavalin said, 'the chauffeur who usually handles this car – Bernard Guerdon – was sick. Some sort of stomach upset. Asked if he could have the day off. Maurice gave it to him, of course. He liked his people to be happy. Benjamen often drove for us.'

'Where were they heading?'

Cavalin shrugged. 'Personal shopping? I don't know. Maurice didn't tell me everything.'

'Why wasn't Maurice using the Cadillac? He usually used the Cadillac.'

Cavalin shrugged again. 'He used any car that was available. Perhaps the Cadillac was being serviced. There are plenty of others.'

Pel scowled. People like Maurice Tagliatti *always* had plenty of cars to choose from while honest cops drove battered old Peugeots. Pel himself had driven a battered old Peugeot until he had managed to marry a wealthy woman who had insisted on him having a car with secure doors that wasn't likely to dump her in the gutter every time it went round a corner.

'Bit pointless, I suppose,' Darcy observed, 'asking if Maurice had any enemies.'

Cavalin shrugged. 'In business, there are always enemies.'

'Especially in Maurice's business,' Pel said. 'Any new ones just lately? Connected, for instance, with the move up here from Marseilles.'

He wasn't deluded. Somebody had bumped off Maurice for a good reason, and in the world Maurice inhabited, he felt, that reason could only have been vengeance. Somebody wanted him good and dead.

He glanced at the car again. The day was warm and the spilled blood had attracted flies. The air was already full of their hum.

'Where were you at the time?' he asked.

Cavalin looked surprised. 'What are you suggesting?' he said. 'I was up at the Manoir. At my desk. Attending to Maurice's business.' He gestured, apparently recovered from the shock already. 'You can leave all the arrangements to me, of course. I'll inform the relatives and arrange for the interment.'

Les Tarthes, the Roblais farm, was on the slope of the hill overlooking the valley. From the gate, you could see the main road winding up the hill as far as Perrenet-sous-le-Forêt. The farm was an old place with ancient buildings of huge stones and heavy timbers but a lot of it seemed to be falling into ruins. As if old Roblais, who owned it, hadn't a centime to his name. Pel suspected he was worth quite a bit, nevertheless. French farmers were a law unto themselves and were always far wealthier than their clothes and their sparsely furnished homes suggested. A peasant background led to a frugality of living that might not produce comfort but certainly produced money in the bank.

'Been here long?' Pel asked.

'All my life.'

'Father here before you?'

'And *his* father. And his before him. And his before him. Father to son.'

Pel indicated the valley. You could see the Manoir of Lordy, Maurice's place, down there, with its wide lawns, slate mansard roofs, and the windvane over what had once been the stables.

'New neighbours,' he observed.

Roblais nodded.

'Spoken to them yet?'

Roblais shook his head and Pel began to see where the son had acquired his taciturnity.

'City types,' he said and Roblais nodded.

'See anything going on down there?'

'Cars coming and going. That's all.'

'Any strangers in your fields? In the woods round here?' Shake of the head.

'Know anything about them?'

Roblais shrugged. 'Funny lot,' he said.

'Why?'

'Wear suits.'

Roblais was wearing corduroy trousers, heavy boots and an old windcheater greasy with dirt. A cap, so old its peak was fringed with wear, sat at an impossible angle on his skull, but Pel noticed it didn't move when he shook his head. Probably it was nailed on. Country types had thick heads. He decided to leave old Roblais to Darcy, too.

three

By this time the specialists were busy, the photographers, the scientists and liaison officers, the fingerprint men and the scene of crime men, all of them cataloguing the minutiae of death. The media had been fed their share of meaningless facts. Darcy, an expert at it, had faced the reporters and to half-baked questions had given half-baked answers. The main briefing had been held. Eventually over fifty men would be involved, both uniformed and plain-clothed, because, even though the victims were Maurice Tagliatti, known mobster, and his driver, they still had to hold a proper inquiry. Murders could not be allowed to occur in the Republic of France without an effort to track down the killers. Though the police had never had any love for Maurice Tagliatti and his kind, they nevertheless had to push that point from their minds and pick up the guilty parties.

The thought engaged Pel's mind quite considerably. What, he wondered, had been going on at the Manoir de Lordy? And how had Cavalin managed to arrive on the scene so quickly? Was he responsible? Had someone tipped him off about what had happened, so that he could appear, concerned and agitated about the death of his boss?

'He was *too* concerned, I reckon,' Darcy suggested. 'Too agitated. The only thing going round in his mind was "Are we safe? Is it safe to go on doing what we were contemplating?" Because they were contemplating *something*, Patron. They have something up their sleeve. They're still trying to look innocent.'

They stared at each other, frowning. It wasn't a conference. The conference would come later. This was a pause in the proceedings to draw breath, think up tactics and offer ideas, while the technical men cleared up the scene of the crime.

As Darcy pushed a packet of cigarettes across, Pel eyed them gloomily. 'I'd just given up,' he said bitterly. 'It must have been the shortest period of abstinence ever.' He helped himself, dragged the smoke down to his socks, went into a coughing session, and immediately felt better. 'We were dead right the other day,' he wheezed. 'To go and see Maurice.'

'It doesn't seem to have done a lot of good,' Darcy observed.

'So who was after him?'

'Cavalin? Had he ambitions to take over? They call him the Dauphin, don't they – the heir to the throne? Or is it Maurice's wife? De Troq' told me he saw Maurice dining out with his secretary in the city the other day. She's a Yugoslav or something. Perhaps Maurice had grown tired of his wife and she didn't like it.'

'We'll have Cavalin in.'

'You're wasting your time, Patron. He'll have an answer for everything.'

What Darcy said was correct. Cavalin would have gone over every detail of the killing by this time and be ready for whatever came up. Pel sighed. 'What about the other things we have on the books?'

Darcy opened the file he held on his knee. 'There's a new one. A woman advertising her house for sale. Some type appears and asks to look round it. The next thing she knows she's locked in the lavatory and he's ransacking her jewellery box. I've got Bardolle on it. De Troq's still with his fraud case. Nosjean's still tying up that art racket. I've told them not to get too involved in case we need them. Oh, there's one other case: some Italian who lives here – name of – ' Darcy glanced at a pad by his arm. 'Giovanni Soscharni – reported by the library to be damaging their books. They didn't know who it was so I got Misset to sit in the reference room. I expect he went to sleep but he seems to have wakened up in time to see this Soscharni doing a bit of scribbling and brought him in. He said he disagreed with what the book said.'

He ought, Pel thought, to be made an honorary member of the Bigots' Society. It was a newish organisation, with Pel as secretary, treasurer, president and only member.

'He'll go up before the magistrates,' Darcy said. 'Meantime, I gave the Lordy cops instructions to keep an eye on Maurice's place, and radio in if anybody leaves in a hurry.'

'They won't,' Pel said. 'They'll lie low for a while.'

'Not if what Maurice was up to was urgent,' Darcy suggested.

There was still the Chief to fill in. The Chief liked to know the facts. The Palais de Justice had already been informed. Judge Brisard was handling the case – much to Pel's disgust, because he couldn't stand Judge Brisard any more than Judge Brisard could stand Pel. It was a long-standing enmity and, with Pel ahead on points at the moment, he didn't worry about offering much in the way of information.

The Chief was a different kettle of fish. He'd been a working cop himself, a big man who'd once been a boxer and had had a reputation as a young policeman for settling minor criminals with a clout round the head. He'd gone off the previous day to a conference in Paris and had just returned. He was puzzled by the news about Maurice Tagliatti.

'It can't be Maurice,' he said. 'I saw him in his car – that big Cadillac he uses – sitting right outside the Hôtel de Police as I returned. There was a chauffeur and he was in the rear seat. Right opposite the door as I drove in. Sergeant Olivier on the front desk saw him too.'

Pel sat up, his eyes narrow. 'What was the time? Exactly.'

'Five o'clock.'

'It was five when I was called from the Bar Transvaal. Maurice had just been killed. So if Maurice were killed out at Lordy about five he could hardly have been here in the city.'

'It was Maurice,' the Chief insisted. 'Or, at least, it looked like Maurice. He wore that white hat he likes to wear. And a blue lightweight suit.'

'He was wearing the white hat and the lightweight suit when I saw him a few weeks ago,' Pel agreed. 'But it wasn't Maurice you saw. Maurice was lying among the wreckage of a hut near Lordy with a bullet in his shoulder and full of bits of hand grenade. He was wearing a checked jacket and a cap.'

The Chief looked puzzled. 'There seems to be more to this than meets the eye. What are you intending?'

'I could sit back and enjoy it,' Pel said. 'We could even insert a few lines in the *Thanks* column of *Le Bien Public.* "The Brigade Criminelle of the Police Judiciaire are grateful to whoever it was who bumped off Maurice Tagliatti near Lordy today..." '

The Chief grinned. 'All the same, a major crime's been committed,' he said portentously. 'We mustn't rest until the perpetrator's been found. No matter who his victim is. Maurice was obviously up to something.'

Pel had to agree. Somebody had wanted Maurice dead, but Maurice had been engaged in something shifty enough at the time for him to wish to appear to be elsewhere. Otherwise, why had the man the Chief had seen been wearing Maurice's suit and hat? The Chief was no fool and if he said he'd seen Maurice then, since Maurice was dead near Lordy at the time, what he had seen had been Maurice's double. And if he'd seen a double it must have been arranged by Maurice for some reason of his own. And it had worked. Or nearly. Only the fact that Maurice was being bumped off at Lordy prevented it being accepted that he was in town. Someone had known what was in his mind, however, and had tipped off the men who had killed him. And that seemed to indicate that the tip-off had come from among his own followers because no one else could have known his intentions.

The Chief was still frowning. 'I even mentioned it to Olivier,' he said. 'We talked about it because we'd both known him since he was a young tearaway. We both certainly thought it was Maurice.'

Pel nodded. 'It seems', he said slowly, 'that you were intended to.'

four

It was late when Pel reached his home. It had been a long day and it had now started to rain as if to let everyone know that summer was over. His wife said nothing as he appeared, simply handing him a whisky. He sat down with it, feeling like an early Christian martyr at whom the lions had just turned up their noses.

'I'm not hungry,' he said. 'I managed to snatch a sandwich at the Transvaal.'

'There's a cold collation if you fancy it.'

Pel didn't. What he did fancy was about fifteen more whiskies and three packets of cigarettes.

'I had a visitor,' his wife said.

Pel looked up. 'Cousin Roger?'

Madame Pel's Cousin Roger was the only one of her whole vast family he could get on with. Cousin Roger was an accountant who had cherished ambitions as a boy of being a policeman. His failure to become one had led him to drowning his sorrows in booze and smoking too much. Pel felt they were twin souls.

'No,' Madame Pel said. 'Not Cousin Roger. Madame Pasquier. From next door.'

'What did she want?'

'She says Yves wants to see you.'

'See me? Why?'

'He won't say. He says he has something to tell you.'

'Well, it'll wait until morning, I suppose.'

'She says it won't. She telephoned just before you drove in.'

Pel frowned. 'He'll be having one of his fantasies,' he said. 'He has them a lot.'

'She says he's worried.'

'It must be his exam for the *lycée* then. He takes it this year. We believe in terrifying our children early in France.'

The telephone went and Madame Routy put her head in the door. 'For you,' was all she said, but Pel knew at once that it wasn't for his wife. Madame Routy always managed to sound twice as polite with his wife.

The caller was Madame Pasquier. 'Chief Inspector,' she said. 'I thought I saw your car arrive.'

Pel wasn't feeling like talking and couldn't think of anything to say, so he said, 'Oh.' It was hardly snappy repartee but it was better than nothing. It set Madame Pasquier going.

'It's Yves,' she said. 'He wants to see you.'

'Isn't he asleep?'

'He says he can't get to sleep.'

'Won't it do in the morning?'

'He says not.'

'I'm a bit tired. It's been a long day. You'll have heard about the shooting?'

'Yes. I'm sorry, but he insists and he's so fond of you. Could you slip round? I'm sure it won't take more than a minute.'

The Pasquier house was similar to Pel's. On the gate was a notice – *Beware. Very enthusiastic guard dog* – a compromise between the wishes of a ten-year-old boy who felt that the tatterdemalion mongrel that accompanied him everywhere ought to have credit for something about the house, and those of his father who had been unable to think what.

Pasquier, senior, was waiting at the door.

'Pel,' he said. He had caught on to the fact long since that Pel didn't like his given names and preferred to be called by his surname, with which at least you couldn't muck about much. 'Have a drink. I had it ready as soon as I heard you were on your way.'

He handed over a glass as big as a bucket, full of whisky and water. Pel eyed it warily. It would mean indigestion, he knew.

'*Santé*,' he said, taking a nervous sip. 'I'll take it up with me.'

As he went up the stairs he could hear Yves Pasquier debating bitterly about having to be in bed.

'Why can't I see him downstairs?' he was asking.

'Because –' his mother's voice was low and fierce '– because you're already in bed and you're going to stay there.'

'I go to bed too early.'

'You don't go to bed early enough.'

'If I go any earlier, I'll be going to bed at lunch time.'

'Why don't you go to sleep?'

'I don't want to go to sleep. I have to stay alert.'

'Why?'

'Somebody's got to stay alert.'

The boy was sitting up in bed. His hair was on end and there were dark circles under his eyes. As usual, his face was covered with scratches, as if he had just been pulled backwards through a hawthorn hedge. It was a strange fact about Yves Pasquier. He always looked as if he'd just had a fight with a roll of barbed wire. He also had a plaster on his forehead. He usually had a plaster somewhere. For a small boy, he seemed to live a very violent life.

The 'very enthusiastic guard dog' was lying beside the bed. As Pel appeared, it rose shaggily to its feet and for the thousandth time Pel realised he'd greeted the wrong end.

He pulled up a chair. 'I understand you've got something you want to tell me,' he said.

'Yes, I have. That is...' Yves glanced at his mother and made disapproving signs.

'I'm staying here,' she said. 'I want to know what this is all about.'

'Well...er...' Yves looked uncertain. 'It's that business we talked about – you know – about chewing gum in your trouser pocket. It's a bit messy when it gets tangled up with string and things. What's the best way to get rid of it? You said you'd ask the Laboratory if they had any suggestions.'

Pel paused. The boy was obviously fencing for time, not wishing his mother to be present. What he had to say he wished to keep between himself and Pel. He was determined to make it important, even if it wasn't. Pel tried to go along with him.

'They suggested the best thing was to throw the trousers away,' he offered gravely. 'Or burn them. Taking care, of course, to take them off first in case you incinerated yourself.'

Yves giggled and his mother frowned. 'Is this what you've brought the Chief Inspector round for?' she snapped. 'Don't you know it's pouring with rain?'

Yves looked up, shining with cleanliness, his face solemn and troubled. 'I'd like a drink of water,' he said. 'Iced water – from downstairs.'

She looked as if she'd happily strangle him. Pel rose and edged her towards the door.

'Leave it to me,' he murmured. 'Never mind the water. He'll talk as soon as you've gone. I'll tell you when I come down.'

As the door closed, the voice from the bed piped up again in a final attempt to delude. 'Boules,' it said loudly. 'Did you think to ask about them?'

As the door closed, Pel sat down and took a swig at his drink. 'Right,' he said briskly. 'Never mind the boules and the chewing gum. Let's have it. What's worrying you?'

Yves stared at him for a moment and drew a deep breath. 'I saw it,' he said.

'Saw what?'

'That shooting.'

'What!' Pel sat bolt upright so suddenly he spilled the whisky.

'At least, I didn't. Not quite.'

'Did you or didn't you?' Pel brushed at his trousers with a handkerchief. 'Don't act the goat. Let's have the truth. I'm busy. I have a couple of murders on my hands.'

'I know. I saw it on the television.'

'But you didn't see it happen?'

'No. Well, yes. Not really. It's like this – '

'You're not making it up?'

'No. Honest. I was on my bike. It's a BMX. You can do things on it. I've learned to spin round on the back wheel and come down facing the other way.'

'Never mind that now. Have you really got something to tell me?'

'Yes. Honest.'

'About that shooting?'

'Yes. Truly.'

'Let's have it in a straightforward manner, then. You know how to behave in court, don't you? I've told you about it often enough.'

'Yes, I know. I saw *Perry Mason* on the television last week, too. It was an old one but it was in court as usual.'

'Right, then. No more fooling about. Let's have it in a straightforward Perry Mason fashion.'

'Yes, Chef.' Yves sat bolt upright. 'I was on my bike. I was going to see Jean-Pierre Luxe. He lives at Lordy. His father keeps the garage there. But he wasn't in. It was hot, you'll remember.'

'I do. No frills.'

'They're not frills. Because it was hot I bought a bottle of Pschitt at the *épicerie* before I set off home and I was sitting on the seat in the Place de Paris opposite the Mairie and was drinking it when I saw this car.'

'Which car? That's no way to give evidence.'

'Oh! Well, no. It was a Citroën. One of the big ones,'

'Number?'

'I didn't get it. I couldn't see it.'

'Pity.'

'But I got a bit of it. It was a Paris number. I saw the 75 and there was a 4 and a 6 in it.'

'That helps. Why did you bother to look at the number?'

'I'm training to be a policeman.'

'*Formidable!* Was that the only reason?'

'No. They were acting suspiciously.'

'Who were?'

'The men in it. There were two. It was parked near the bar and they were at the counter.'

'That's suspicious behaviour?'

'Not that. But what happened was. While I was watching, the telephone on the counter of the bar rang and one of the men picked it up. He must have been waiting for a call because the barman didn't try to pick it up. This type from the car did.'

'Did you hear what he said?'

'No. But he said something then they both came out of the bar in a rush and got in the car and it drove off – slowly.'

'Slowly? There's something strange about a car moving slowly?'

'There is these days.'

Pel admitted the fact. Most people liked to set off as if they were a posse after Butch Cassidy and the Sundance Kid.

'Perhaps', he offered, 'he was having trouble with the engine.'

'He didn't seem to be. He just seemed to be going – well – slowly.'

'It doesn't seem to be much.'

'Just a minute – '

'There's more?'

Yves sat up in bed, his eyes shining with excitement. 'Yes. Then this other car came.'

'Which other car?'

'This big Peugeot. It came down from Lordy.'

Pel was leaning forward again. 'Go on.'

'It passed, going fast. As it did so, the other car – the Citroën – speeded up. As if it was chasing the Peugeot. As if they'd been waiting for it. They both went round the corner towards the city, and then I heard this shooting.'

'You didn't see it?'

'It was round the corner and down the hill. But I heard it.'

'You're sure it wasn't just a car backfiring?'

'Cars don't backfire these days.'

Pel had to admit that it was a long time since he'd heard a vehicle backfire.

'It made this noise.' Yves made a violent noise with his mouth 'Like a machine gun.'

'And then?'

'I heard a bang. Tinny. Like you hear when a car hits something. Then more shots and a bang. Then nothing.'

'What did you do?'

'I didn't do anything. I went on sitting there. I wondered what it was all about, but then I thought maybe these two types in the car were crooks and had noticed me sitting there and might think I'd noticed them, so I thought I'd better be going home. Then – I nearly missed it because they were trying to force me to go to bed too early as usual – I saw it on the television. There was even a sort of plan to show where it had happened. It was only round the corner and down the hill from where I'd been. I thought I'd better tell you. It looked to me like a set-up. These two types in the bar. They were strangers. I've never seen them in Lordy before. Then this telephone call came and they came out to the Citroën. In a hurry. They ran. They got in the car. I thought they'd shoot off – like the cops do in *Starsky and Hutch* on television. You know – tyres screaming and all that. But they didn't. They went ever so slowly. I wondered why they'd run to the car as if they were in a hurry and then driven off slowly as if they weren't. Did I do right?'

'You'll make a good policeman,' Pel said, and the boy beamed with pride. 'Anything else?'

'No. That's all.'

'It's enough. We know to look for a Citroën with a Paris number with a 4 and a 6 in it. What colour?'

'Grey. They make a lot of grey ones.'

'What about the men inside it?'

'They wore caps.'

'What about the men in the Peugeot? Did you see them, too?'

'Yes.'

'Both of them?'

'All of them.'

'What do you mean, all of them? How many were there?'

'Three.'

'There were only *two* in the car. There were only two when we got to it.'

'There were three when it passed me. That seat at Lordy's up on the bank. I could see into the car. One in front. Two in the back.'

Pel frowned. 'That's interesting,' he said.

And so it was because, although Cavalin must have known there were two men in the car with Maurice, not one, he hadn't bothered to say so. He wondered why.

'What about the men in the Citroën?' he asked. 'Could you describe what they looked like? Noses, for instance? Chins? Colour of hair?'

'The one nearest me – the passenger – had a big nose.'

'Shape?'

'I don't know. Just big.'

'Never mind. I think you'd better go to sleep now. I'll come and see you again and get you to make a statement. I'll send someone along.'

'I'd rather go down to the Hôtel de Police and make it there.'

'All right. Hôtel de Police it is. We'll get you to describe what you saw of these men and have the artist draw it.'

'Will they give me a lie detector test?'

'We don't have lie detectors in France. We prefer to get at the truth by more subtle methods.'

'A punch on the nose?'

'It's not a method I advocate.'

'Will there be a reward?'

'At this moment there isn't. But something might be done. Even if it's only a ride in a police car.'

Yves looked up and gave a beaming smile. 'I could probably find out about boules while I'm there,' he said. 'Somebody might know.'

five

The Manoir de Lordy stood on a small knoll, almost like a fortress, and, like a fortress, it appeared to be well guarded. Barbed wire in three strands had been newly strung along its boundaries, and at the lodge gate there was a man with a shotgun who looked like another of the types Maurice had employed to make sure he wasn't bothered by hawkers, itinerant preachers or gangland enemies who wanted to kill him.

'Open up,' Pel said.

'You can't come in here,' the guard said.

Darcy flashed his identification card. 'We're the police.'

'You still can't come in.'

'If you don't open this damn gate,' Darcy snapped, 'I'll arrange to have it smashed down! With artillery if necessary.'

The guard looked a little bewildered. Clearly his orders were precise but he had never had to refuse admission to the police before. 'You're trespassing,' he offered in rather more conciliatory tones.

'We're on duty.'

Reluctantly, the gate was opened. Darcy stopped the car inside the drive and climbed out.

'Got a licence for that gun?' he snapped.

'It's all right. Maurice said it was all right.'

'Let's have a look at it.'

Reluctantly, the guard handed over his shotgun.

'Anything else?'

A Luger appeared from under the guard's armpit. Darcy studied it.

'Regular little armoury, aren't we?' he said, opening the door of the car and tossing the two weapons inside.

'You can't do that!' the guard yelled.

'I've done it.'

'They re mine!'

'Not any longer. You obviously haven't a licence so they've been confiscated. We seem to be doing it a lot lately. What's your name?'

'Edouard Shapron.'

'Live here?'

'Yes.'

'I'll arrange to have you charged with threatening police officers with an offensive weapon. Now get out of the way.'

Climbing back in the car, he drove past the startled guard, who stared after them, his mouth open.

'That's a good way to deal with armed men, Daniel,' Pel said admiringly.

Darcy shrugged. 'Sometimes it doesn't work,' he said. 'Then they shoot you.' He glanced in the mirror. 'He's gone inside the lodge. I expect he's telephoned the house to warn them we're coming.'

He had.

Cavalin was waiting by the door as the car crunched across the gravel.

'I'm sorry that idiot threatened you,' he said.

'He'd better not threaten any more of my men,' Pel said. 'There'll be a few around here from now on.'

They got down to business quickly and Cavalin made no attempt to dissemble.

'Of course there was another man in the car,' he admitted. 'Maurice often had two men with him.'

'Why?'

Cavalin shrugged, a hint of amusement in his eyes. 'Maurice lived rather an exciting life. Things had a habit of happening.'

'I want to see this other man,' Pel snapped. 'Why didn't you report it?'

They sat in the library of the Manoir, Cavalin smooth, immaculate and ready with the answers, as they had known he would be. The man who had been in the car when the shooting had occurred, another of Maurice's minders, was fetched, a thickset black-haired man called Antonio Sagassu who looked as though he originated from Corsica. He sat in an armchair with his arm in a sling, his face grey under its tan, a brandy alongside his good arm.

There were also two more of Maurice's heavies, together with the man who'd been introduced as David Ourdabi, standing in a corner, tossing a set of keys up in his hand and as usual trying to look sinister in the Bogart manner.

'I just never thought,' Cavalin explained. 'I thought you must have known. Confusion perhaps.'

Pel looked like a snake about to strike. He had returned from the Pasquiers' house the previous night full of whisky. There had been a second large glass waiting for him when he had appeared downstairs and his wife had had another ready when he returned home. He hadn't slept very well because of indigestion and the thought that Yves Pasquier's information had brought up something significant. But Cavalin had obviously been thinking of it, too, and was ready for him.

'After all,' he said, 'he was hurt.'

Pel looked at Sagassu. 'You better tell us what happened,' he said.

'I don't know,' Sagassu lied stoutly.

'Perhaps a week or so in a cell might help you remember.'

'I didn't see!'

'Charge him under Section 62 of the Penal Code, Daniel,' Pel said. 'For refusing to give aid and assistance to the police.'

'You'd better tell them what you know, Tonio,' Cavalin said quietly.

Sagassu looked sullen but eventually he started to talk. 'I didn't see,' he insisted. 'I was half asleep. It was warm and I'd had some wine. The next thing I knew I saw a car going past and heard shooting. I was hit in the arm and Maurice took one in the shoulder. Poor old Benno was just covered with blood. Then the car ran into the ditch and I fell out.'

'Go on.'

'Maurice shouted to me to get Georges.'

'Georges?'

'Me,' Cavalin said. 'I'm Georges.'

'What exactly did he say?'

' "Tell Georges," he said. "I'm going for the hut there." He had a gun in his hand.'

'This one?' Pel produced the Walther they'd found.

'Yes.'

Pel produced the second gun. 'And this, I presume, was in his pocket.'

'I expect so.'

'Did he shoot back at the men who killed Bozon?'

'No. He was having difficulty keeping his feet. I fell out of one door and he got out of the other. I saw the other car stop and two men running after him. I was in the ditch. There was more shooting and then a bang. He never thought they'd have grenades. I decided I'd better bolt. I went through the woods.'

'Did anyone give chase?'

'I don't think they knew I was in the car. Maurice was sitting up but I was half asleep and had slumped down. They probably never saw me so I thought I'd better do as I'd been told, and let Georges know.'

Pel turned to Cavalin. 'And that', he said, 'would be why you arrived armed to the teeth?'

Cavalin admitted it. 'We were supposed to look after Maurice,' he said.

'You didn't do very well at it, did you? What were you intending to do?'

Cavalin shrugged again. 'God knows. Something. I don't know.'

Pel stared about him, aware of Sagassu's hostile glare. The room had become silent and even Ourdabi had stopped fidgeting with his keys.

'There seem to be a lot of heavies round here,' Pel said.

Cavalin smiled. 'There are.'

'How many?'

'Including me, eight. Only I'm not a heavy. I'm a light. I look after the books. There's one less now, of course. Bozon's left. Unexpectedly. Sadly missed.'

Pel glared. When he was on a job, only one person was allowed to be funny. 'What are they all for?' he demanded.

'To guard, of course.'

'Who? Maurice?'

'Who else? Unfortunately, they seem to have slipped up. With the result that very shortly they'll all be out of a job. With no Maurice to guard, there isn't much else for them to do.'

'I'll have their names.'

'Just the survivors?'

Pel glared and Cavalin smiled. 'Me – Georges Cavalin. Jim Peneau. Bernard Guérin. He's the chauffeur. Edouard Shapron. Antonio Sagassu. Léonard Devreux. David Ourdabi.'

'Who else is here?'

'The cook. Madame Goriot. Two gardeners – by name Sérin and Mouiche.'

'Maids?'

'We look after ourselves in that department. There's also Sidonie, of course – Maurice's wife. And Vlada, Maurice's... er...secretary.'

Pel turned back to Sagassu. 'Who dressed your arm?'

'Some type Georges sent me to.'

'Some old friend of Maurice's?'

'I don't know.'

'Because *he* didn't inform the police either, did he? What's his name?'

'Dunois. Dr Alexei Dunois. 'Cavalin supplied the information.

'Did *you* tell him not to inform the police?'

'No. Perhaps he never thought.'

Pel turned again to Sagassu. 'Why didn't *you* inform the police?'

Sagassu shrugged. 'I told Georges. I thought *he'd* tell you.'

'So why didn't he?'

Cavalin smiled. 'It slipped my mind.'

'How? I mentioned you'd arrived quickly. Why not tell me then that you'd been informed by Sagassu what had happened?'

Cavalin shrugged. He was a great shrugger.

'You said you'd heard shooting and thought somebody had been after a rabbit. What with? A machine gun?'

Cavalin's smile came again. It came easily. 'You'd be surprised what people carry. I've seen them setting off after rabbits with everything but a cannon. We're a nation of hunters. It's a pity we so often miss the rabbits and hit each other.'

Pel scowled. 'You knew somebody had been shooting and that they'd shot Bozon and Tagliatti. You probably didn't know they'd ended up besieging Maurice in the hut and finally throwing a hand grenade at him, but you must have known he was being attacked. That's why you arrived armed like a set of paratroopers. But you didn't tell us that. Why not?'

'I was only concerned with getting down the hill to see what had happened to Maurice.'

'So why didn't Sagassu telephone us after you left? He must have known we hadn't been informed.'

'Perhaps he was scared,' Ourdabi prompted.

'Yes, I was,' Sagassu said quickly. 'I was.'

'Why didn't you remain with the car? Two of your friends had just been shot. Didn't you stop long enough to make sure they didn't need help?'

Sagassu looked shocked. 'Would you?' he asked.

Pel stared at him. 'Why did you come all the way back here to give your information? Why didn't you stop at Les Tarthes, the Roblais farm, just round the corner and up the hill? Why stagger all the way up the hill, with a bullet in your arm, to this place?'

'There was a telephone here.'

'There's a telephone at the farm. If you look, you can see the wire.'

'Well, I didn't look,' Sagassu growled. 'And I felt that someone needed to inform the police.'

'But nobody did inform the police, did they?' Pel snapped. 'The first the police heard of it was when they received a call from the Roblais farm. From Gilles Roblais, who found the car a good ten minutes after you'd left it and while, I suppose, you were on your way up here through the woods. You informed Cavalin, but Cavalin didn't inform the police. He got in another car and went down to see what had happened.'

'I intended to inform the police,' Cavalin said.

'You had a telephone. So why not use it at once?'

'I suppose I was like Sagassu here – shocked by what had happened. I was concerned for Maurice. Sagassu arrived in a bit of a state, covered with blood and with a bullet in the thick part of his upper arm. You'd be shocked, Inspector – '

'*Chief* Inspector.'

'Of course.'

'Are you sure he didn't come all that way back here just to warn you?'

Cavalin's eyebrows went up. 'Warn me of what?'

'That somebody had just shot Maurice.'

'Why would I need to be warned?'

'So that if there were anything that needed tidying up you'd have plenty of time to do it, before we arrived.'

'What would I have that needed tidying?'

'You *could* have had all the plans you'd made to have Maurice shot.'

Cavalin's eyes hardened. 'I think I ought to have my lawyer here, Inspector.'

'*Chief* Inspector. There's one other point. We've discovered why Maurice wasn't using the Cadillac. It was because it was already in use. Somebody was sitting in it in the city. Close to the Hôtel de Police. Where he could clearly be seen. He was dressed in Maurice's clothes and he was there a good half-hour, and he was seen. The man who saw him thought he was Maurice. What was all that about?'

'I don't know.' Cavalin's shoulders moved again. 'Maurice didn't tell me everything he got up to.'

'Who was it?'

'Well...' Cavalin hesitated. 'I've learned it was Léonard Devreux. He came back after you left. The driver was Bernard Guérin. He's been with us a long time.'

'I'd like to see him. Devreux too.'

When they appeared, Devreux and Guérin added nothing. Devreux was one of the bouncers they'd seen surrounding Tagliatti when Pel and Darcy had paid their 'courtesy' call. He was big and fat and looked vaguely like Maurice.

'Why were you wearing Maurice's suit?' Pel demanded.

Devreux shrugged. 'It's not Maurice's,' he said. 'It's mine. He gave it to me. I was the same size. He often gave his old clothes to me.'

'It wasn't old. He was wearing it when I last saw him. It didn't look old then.'

Devreux shrugged again. It was obvious he'd been well briefed. Pel could just imagine the hurried conference that had been called and the roles everybody had been given to play.

'He said he didn't like it,' Devreux went on. 'He took against it, he said. I don't know why. It cost a lot, I know. He said he liked it when he bought it but then decided he didn't. I'd once said I liked it. Perhaps that's why he gave it to me.'

'And the hat? Did he give you that, too?'

Devreux's shoulders moved again. 'It went with the suit.'

'Why was the car in the city at the time Maurice was being shot?'

'We just went in, that's all.'

'Why?'

'Personal business.'

'What personal business?'

'I had to see my lawyer. Arnaud Dugusse. He's Maurice's lawyer, too. But he wasn't in and we had to wait until he was.'

'Did you have an appointment?'

'It wasn't an appointment. I just went on the off-chance. My wife's been giving me trouble. We separated. There's a lot of fuss going on about the kids. I love my kids and – '

'Why were you using Maurice's Cadillac? Why was he using a Peugeot and you the Cadillac?'

'Maurice went off in the Peugeot. So we took the Cadillac. We always did that. We used whatever car was available.'

'You went *before* he did. Or you couldn't have been near police headquarters when he was shot.'

Devreux pulled a face.

'Why did Maurice go in the Peugeot?'

Devreux shrugged. 'I don't know. I just took the Cadillac. Bernard here said he'd drive me.'

'Don't you drive yourself?'

'I've never been good in cities.'

'It's his eyes,' Ourdabi said quickly.

'That's it,' Devreux agreed. 'It's a condition I have with my right eye, you know. I don't see out of the corner of it. I don't see cars coming from the right. They're a blur.'

Devreux was lying stoutly, Pel knew. 'Always?' he asked.

'Oh, yes.'

'Bad?'

'Very.'

'What about the other eye?'

'That's bad too.'

'Very bad?'

'Yes. Very bad.'

Pel had a malicious look in his eye. 'Have you a driving licence?'

'Yes.'

'Let me see it.'

He stared at the document silently. 'No indication here that you have bad eyesight,'

'Well, no...' Devreux fumbled a little. 'I took it out before it grew too bad.'

'And now it's very bad.'

'Yes.'

Pel handed the driving licence to Darcy. 'Hang on to that, Daniel,' he said. 'He's obviously not fit to hold a licence with those eyes of his. He'll be having an accident. Arrange with Traffic to have it cancelled.'

Devreux's mouth dropped open and Pel gave him a spiteful glance. Darcy grinned and so did Cavalin. They both knew Pel's game. He was just making things as difficult as he could for Devreux, as he always did for anyone on the wrong side of the law.

'So,' Pel said. 'You went into the city with Guérin here to drive you.'

Devreux nodded, looking faintly sick. 'Yes.'

'Good friends?'

'Always have been.'

'So why didn't you sit in the front with him where you could talk? Why sit in the back as Maurice did?'

Devreux thought hard. 'Bernard said, "Why not ride in the back and pretend you're Maurice?" So I did. That's all. He joked about it.'

'How? I've had a look at that Cadillac. It has a glass partition between the driver and the passenger. I expect Maurice had it put in so he couldn't be heard when he was discussing business.'

Devreux was unperturbed. 'Bernard had the window open. It slides backwards and forwards. We chatted through that.'

'And if I get in touch with Dugusse, I expect he can confirm that you saw him?'

Devreux nodded. 'I expect so.'

So did Pel. He knew Dugusse. He was a lawyer from the shiftier end of the legal scale. He'd represented Maurice on more than one occasion in the past and earned his income from defending crooks of various types when they came before the beaks. He knew every inch of the law and how to get round them.

'Where was Maurice when you left?'

'Looking at his roses.'

'So he *hadn't* left when you did?'

'Well, no. He liked his roses. He always said he'd like them for his funeral.'

'I expect he'll have them,' Cavalin observed. 'That's something we can manage. Not from here, of course. Bit windblown up here. We'll have to get them from Fleurs de Bourgogne in the city. Maurice's wife will want it that way.'

Pel looked up. 'What about Maurice's wife? How did she take it?'

Cavalin shrugged. 'As I thought she would. There were no tears.'

'Who benefits from Maurice's will?'

'She does, I imagine. I don't know. Maurice had his faults –' too right he did, Pel thought – 'but he has two children and he would have prepared for them and for his wife.'

'What about the other one? This Vlada. She was his secretary, wasn't she?'

'So he said.' Cavalin's face changed. 'I doubt if he'd got around to providing for *her*. But he might have done it in other ways. I wasn't privy to his family affairs.'

Outside the door, Pel paused for a moment, listening. When he reopened the door Devreux was just in the middle of a wild gesture, shouting at Ourdabi.

'You've lost me my goddamned licence, you stupid *con* –'

He saw Pel and smiled sheepishly.

'You can always appeal,' Pel said benignly. 'Of course, it might not work.'

'See that it doesn't, Daniel,' he rapped as he closed the door again. 'Make your report good and strong.'

It was a small victory but they were really getting nowhere. Cavalin did not have a police record but plenty had been turned up about him. As a young man he had considered going in for law and had studied it for a while until, doubtless, he had realised there was more money to be made from being on the wrong side of it. Certainly, like the late Maurice Tagliatti, he had proved himself a master of caginess. Nothing they had asked had startled or agitated him, his answers always as cool as those of a master barrister in a law court.

Sagassu *had* warned him. After he had escaped the blast of gunfire, his first thought had clearly been to warn Cavalin that whatever it was Maurice had been contemplating was off and, since he had just been shot to death, his alibi obviously had to be off, too.

'I have to see the Chief,' Pel said as they left. 'To let him know the developments. Go and see this lawyer, Dugusse, Daniel, and send someone to see the doctor.'

'There's only Misset available.'

'Well, even Misset ought to be able to take a statement, and the lawyer'll be much too bright for *him*.'

The lawyer, Dugusse, was a flashily dressed individual who could twist the rules until they squeaked. As they'd expected, he confirmed everything Devreux had said.

'Oh, yes,' he said. 'I'm handling his affairs. His wife's being very difficult so he has my permission to call on me any time he finds it necessary.'

He was full of confidence, arrogance even, certain he could field anything the police could throw at him. Dr Dunois was different. He was a shabby-looking man with a large moustache stained by nicotine enough to put a smoker off for the rest of his life. His surgery was a dusty place, full of books, and there didn't appear to be much going on there. His wife acted as his receptionist and, by the look of it, he didn't have many patients and probably had to live off shady cases like Sagassu's.

He regarded Misset nervously. Cadet Darras from Pel's office was with Misset as a witness to what was said – it was always wise to have a witness present – and Misset was showing off a little. He adjusted the dark spectacles he wore and put on his James Bond face as he explained why he was there.

Dr Dunois gave a nervous cough. 'Yes,' he admitted slowly. 'A man called Sagassu *was* brought here.'

'With a bullet in his upper arm?'

'That's correct.'

'You received him?'

Dunois nodded. 'Yes, I did.'

'And the bullet was extracted?'

Dunois' head jerked up. For a moment he was silent then he spoke quickly, almost as if he were glad to get the thing off his chest. 'Yes,' he said. 'He was given an injection of morphine and the bullet was extracted with scalpel and forceps and the bleeding points stitched up. Sulfa powder was applied as an antiseptic and the wound bandaged and a sling applied. He was given penicillin tablets. He was then taken away. I don't know where to.'

'Are you prepared to sign a statement to that effect and covering all this?' Misset asked.

Dunois seemed much more cheerful suddenly, 'Yes,' he said. 'I'll write it all out.'

'In your own hand?'

'Yes, yes. I'll do it now. How the wound was cleaned, the bleeding stopped and a bandage and sling applied. Is that what you want?'

'That ought to do it,' Misset said importantly. 'Let's get on with it. You realise, of course, you'll be charged under Section 60, don't you? As an accessory after the fact. You're in trouble, old lad, in case you don't know.'

'Yes.' Dunois nodded. 'I understand. What will happen to me?'

Misset smiled. 'Probably a thumping great fine,' he said. 'Unless you have a record. In which case it could be a lot more.'

That night the Citroën the assassins had used turned up. It was found parked among the trees in the Forêt de

Fougerolles. It was just as Yves Pasquier had said – grey, and its number was 8456-QZ-75. There was nothing wrong with the boy's eyesight. It had been stolen, of course – from an estate agent in Auxerre who was relieved to learn it had been found but indignant that he couldn't have it back at once.

'What do I use in the meantime?' he demanded.

'Haven't you another car?' Darcy asked. The estate agent was fat and looked prosperous. 'It'll take only a few days.'

'Well, my wife has a little Renault.'

'Won't she lend it to you?'

The estate agent pulled a face. 'I can't imagine my wife lending me anything,' he said. 'She says she needs it to fetch the kids from school.'

'Can't she arrange with a friend?'

'My wife', the estate agent said, 'never arranges anything that might add to my pleasure and comfort.'

The Citroën, of course, produced nothing. They could hardly expect much. People about to murder their friends and associates by spraying them with bullets from an automatic weapon were usually careful enough not to leave fingerprints around. There were no dropped visiting cards, no cigarette packets with addresses written on them, no smell of specially made after-shave lotion they could identify as belonging to some type who wanted to rule the world. It was easy in detective stories – not so easy in real life.

Their only real witness was Yves Pasquier and it occurred to Pel that it might be as well to keep that fact very dark. People who were prepared to commit a double murder might well be prepared to commit another to prevent themselves from being identified.

'It *must* be a gang assassination,' Darcy said. 'Maurice must have double-crossed somebody.'

Pel sat silent. 'I don't think it *was* an assassination after all,' he said after a while.

'He's dead, Patron.'

'Perhaps that was just a by-product. Perhaps they wanted him alive. But he was a bit too smart and got to that hut. And since they couldn't get him alive, they *had* to have him dead, because by that time he would know who they were and, since I imagine he couldn't report them to the police, he'd certainly have put his own mob on to them.'

'Why try to take him alive?'

'I don't know. But if they'd wanted him dead, they'd have directed their fire at him. But they didn't, did they? He was hit once. Bozon was hit seven times. This was a professional job and professionals don't miss. They wanted the car stopped and Maurice in it – alive.'

'Why?'

'Because he had something they wanted? That was why Devreux was in the city trying to look like him. So that anybody who might have been watching would have thought Maurice was there, instead of where he actually was. He was probably off to organise this "big thing" he was involved in. Whatever it was. Why otherwise disguise himself as somebody else? Why not go dressed in his normal get-up and in the normal car?'

'So what *was* this thing they wanted?'

'Loot Maurice had picked up? Information about loot? Perhaps whoever arranged it was a partner with Maurice in something, and Maurice had kept more than his share. In a case like that, they'd want to know where it was, wouldn't they?'

Darcy frowned. 'It must have been big to risk tangling with Maurice, Patron,' he said.

'It isn't all that hard if you've got a traitor in the organisation. And Maurice had. Somewhere. The type who telephoned the bar at Lordy where the killers were waiting. That call told them Maurice was on his way. That's why they ran to the car – to make sure they were ready – and why they drove away slowly, so he could pass and they could pick him up.' Pel paused, thinking. 'But Maurice was too quick for them and after that there was nothing they could do but kill him.'

Darcy gestured. 'Well, it doesn't look as though they found out where whatever they were after is hidden. Unless Maurice gave up and told them and *then* they killed him.'

Pel shook his head. 'He didn't tell them,' he said. 'If he had, they'd have taken him away with them and held him until they found it.'

'So what happens now, Patron? Do they give up?'

Pel shook his head again. 'If it was as big as it seems to be,' he said, 'I suspect that that's the last thing they'll do.'

six

The following day, Pel's wife announced that she had to go to Paris. Stocks at the boutique were running low and she had to see a collection at one of the Paris fashion houses. She also had to see her stockbroker – to arrange to stuff away, Pel imagined, a few hundred thousand spare francs where they would do most good. He was always impressed by the way she handled money and had long since handed over his own affairs to her. Not that they occupied much of her time. A cop's salary hardly made him a financial tycoon, but it was nice to know that what there was of it was being properly dealt with.

She was packing a briefcase by her desk when he sat down alongside her.

'How long are you staying?' he asked.

'I'm not staying. I'll be back in the evening.'

'Ah!' Pel didn't like Paris and this altered the situation. 'In that case, I'll come with you.'

Madame looked delighted. 'We'll have lunch together,' she said. 'I'll treat you.'

Pel's heart had thumped a bit at the mention of lunch. Paris restaurant prices were enough to make a man have a heart attack and he had had a feeling she wouldn't welcome a suggestion that they ate at one of the drugstores where he would normally have eaten. The knowledge that his wife would be paying out of the profits she made lifted his heart with joy. He had an excellent wife in full working order whom he loved, but he was still Burgundian enough to enjoy a bargain.

Madame Pel looked at him from the corner of her eye. 'I don't suppose you'd be interested in visiting a fashion house,' she said hopefully.

Pel avoided her glance. 'I'm on business,' he said.

'I thought you might be. Who is it this time?'

It was Pépé le Cornet.

Pépé was getting on in years these days and, wishing to appear legitimate, conducted his affairs with decorum and a minimum of guards – and then only to make sure someone with an old grudge didn't manage to get near enough to stick a knife in his back or drop a bomb in his soup. These days, however, the number of people with grudges against Pépé had diminished considerably. Most of them were in prison, dead or drawing the old age pension. Trying for a peaceful retirement, he was even willing to help an old enemy like Pel from time to time.

Feeling he had to make sure the Hôtel de Police hadn't fallen down during the night and that nobody had kidnapped the Chief or run off with the police funds, Pel was up early to drive to the city. His wife picked him up an hour later after he'd dealt with the major paper work and they set off for Paris where she dropped him outside the discreet set of offices Pépé le Cornet ran near the Luxembourg. It looked like a lawyer's chambers but it wasn't. The name on the polished brass plate was *Pierre Lamotte et Cie*. Pierre Lamotte was Pépé's real name. The old gangster greeted Pel cheerfully.

'You look well, Chief,' he tried.

Pel scowled. 'It won't last long,' he said.

'We're seeing too much of each other these days. People will begin to talk.'

Pépé gave a little laugh to indicate it was intended as a joke but Pel didn't respond. 'You'll have heard about Maurice,' he said.

Pépé tried hard to put on a doleful expression, as if Maurice Tagliatti were an old colleague. In fact, Maurice had troubled him many times by trying to muscle in on his territory, and it suited Pépé well that he'd been forcibly removed. He was even thinking of sending a wreath.

'Sad,' he said gloomily.

'Who was after Maurice?' Pel asked.

Pépé lit a large cigar and pushed the box across. Pel managed to refuse.

'Nobody I know,' Pépé said.

'That Belgian chap, Rykx, we sent down – '

Pépé looked alarmed. 'Not *we*, Chief,' he said hurriedly. 'Never say that. I had nothing to do with it.'

'You gave me information that was useful.'

'It would be more than my life's worth for people to know that.'

'Right, let's start again. Rykx – could one of his lieutenants have been after Maurice?'

'Rykx's sidekicks were small-timers, Chief. Rykx was a small timer, too, who tried to be big but hadn't got what it takes.'

'So who would want Maurice dead?'

Pépé shrugged and Pel probed again.

'So who's on the up and up, Pépé?'

Pépé considered. 'Type called Pierre Rambi. Calls himself Peter the Ram. But he's not big.'

'So who *is* big?'

Pépé considered for a moment. 'Ever heard of Carmen Vlaxi?'

'Who's she?'

'He isn't a she. He's a he. Mixed breed. Half Spanish, half Arab. Came up from Spain. Worked things round Toulouse for a time then got ambitious and came north. He's trying to forget his background these days and pretends to be Castilian. The boys call him Carmen the Bullfighter. He's building up. Operates across the east end of the city, out towards Lille and down towards the south.'

'As far as Burgundy?'

'Maybe.'

'Tell me about him.'

Pépé shrugged. 'Thirty-eight. He's done time. That was fifteen years ago, though, and he's kept out of trouble since. That doesn't mean he hasn't had trouble. It's just not been made public, that's all.'

'Powerful?'

'He took over Rykx's organisation when you sent him down.'

'Why didn't *you*?'

Pépé looked hurt. 'I'm legitimate these days, Chief. That ulcer I had. I thought it was cancer. It made me think. I decided I'd play it straight from now on.'

'Or was it that this Vlaxi, being younger, moved faster and had it organised before you got off your backside?'

Pépé scowled. 'The little bastard must have been tipped off,' he growled. 'I expect one of Rykx's boys told him. There's a type called Theophile Corro. I expect it was him. When he decided to move in, Vlaxi was there already. Everything worth going for.'

'I thought you'd gone legitimate.'

Pépé gave a weak smile. 'Well, you know how it is, Chief. The boys don't like just dropping everything. Not everything. They like to keep their hand in.'

'Had this Vlaxi ever crossed with Maurice?'

'Once or twice. But he always managed to hold Maurice off and Maurice never managed to put anything across him.'

'Nothing that might have made Vlaxi want Maurice dead?'

Pépé considered for a while. 'It's my opinion,' he said finally, 'that Maurice had come to the conclusion that Vlaxi was too smart and too young to tangle with. Maurice was one of the old school, like me.'

It was a protest Pel had heard before.

'Assassination', he pointed out, 'is a nasty business. Messy. Causes repercussions. What was Maurice into, that someone had to knock him off?'

Pépé shrugged.

'He must have been into something, mustn't he?'

'I reckon so.'

'But you've not heard what?'

'No idea. When I heard about it I thought of Vlaxi straight away, but I've had my ear to the ground and there are no whispers. Vlaxi wasn't interested in Maurice.' Pépé allowed himself a small smile. 'Of course, he might be now. Like he was with Rykx. Now that Maurice isn't around any more, he might muscle in.'

'It would make him pretty powerful, wouldn't it?' Pel said. 'Wouldn't you be interested in keeping him out?'

'I'm not ambitious these days, Chief.'

'*He* might be. And if he takes over Maurice's territory, he'd then be powerful enough to take over yours.'

The point had obviously not escaped Pépé. 'I'm keeping my eye on the little *con*,' he said sourly. 'But Maurice was being careful. He'd decided to stay on his own patch, and leave me in mine and Vlaxi in his. I think he'd got a new bit of fluff.'

'He had.'

'Well, I think he was all for a bit of comfort and preferred to stay where he could handle things – in the south.'

'So,' Pel asked, 'what was he doing back in Burgundy?'

There was time to put in a telephone call to Darcy.

'I'm wondering', Pel said, 'if somebody connected with that Belgian chap, Rykx, we sent down over the Barclay

63

kidnapping* is involved. Some sort of revenge. Something of that sort. Pépé says not but we'd better look into it. Contact Brussels and see if you can get a list of Rykx's associates.'

Meeting his wife for lunch, Pel found himself eating at a restaurant where the prices took his breath away. He was surrounded by elderly businessmen with high belly-holding trousers who looked set for the rest of the afternoon, and young whiz-kid types wearing with-it clothes that all seemed to be yellow, pink or pale blue. There were also one or two faces Pel had seen on television, and his wife enjoyed pointing them out.

'Everybody eats here,' she said. 'I always come here when I'm in Paris. Everybody knows me.'

Pel was touched by a whiff of jealousy but by this time he'd polished off the best part of a bottle of Fleurie and he was feeling pretty mellow. Since his wife barely drank and had expressed her intention of doing the driving, he went mad and had a brandy as well. It turned out to be the father and mother of all brandies. A tulip-shaped glass as large as a plant pot was produced and brandy was poured over it and set alight. When the flames had died, more brandy was poured inside. The aroma made Pel's head swim.

There was enough of it for him to fall asleep as soon as they set off and he didn't wake until they were turning off the motorway as the sun started to sink. Getting his wife to drop him at the Hôtel de Police where he'd left his car, he went to his office to make sure that the Police Judiciaire was still functioning as it ought. He noticed that Nosjean was back from wherever it was he'd been and was talking to De Troq' in the sergeants' room. The two of them had been as thick as thieves since they'd first met.

Claudie Darel followed him into his office with a report on what had happened during the day. A police car had been

* See *Pel and the Touch of Pitch*

sent to the Pasquiers' home to convey Yves Pasquier and his mother to the Hôtel de Police where the boy had been interviewed. Plied with Coca Cola and lollipops, he had thoroughly enjoyed himself, especially the session with the police sergeant artist who had endeavoured to draw what he thought he had seen. The sergeant was still around, and appeared with Darcy just behind.

'It isn't much, Patron,' he said, offering Pel his sketch pad. 'Nothing that could be put on Photofit, because he only saw them in profile. They never seem to have looked in his direction and the driver appeared only as a dark silhouette.' A page was turned over. 'That's him. We had several tries. All he could tell me was that he was a plump chap with a big chin and a fleshy neck. Do I have them printed and put out?'

'Let's make sure he's got them right first. I'll find out this evening.'

Immediately he arrived on the Pasquiers' doorstep, Pel was offered another large whisky. He feigned horror but he drank it just the same.

'Did he go to bed all right tonight?' he asked.

'No trouble,' Madame Pasquier said.

'Has he told anyone?'

The Pasquiers eyed each other. 'Only us.'

'What about at school? Has he told anyone there?'

'He didn't go,' Madame Pasquier said. 'He seemed a bit overexcited so I kept him at home.'

'Good. Anybody else?'

'His friend, Jean-Pierre Luxe from Lordy, telephoned. He wanted to come but I put him off.'

'Anybody here he could have told? The daily help, for instance.'

'Madame Rouot from Leu. He might have told her.'

'I'll see her.'

Madame Pasquier looked worried. 'Is it important?'

'It could be *very* important.' Pel explained the way he had been thinking and the Pasquiers' eyes locked.

'Is he in danger or something?'

'It was a double murder. And he's our only witness.'

Madame Pasquier began to look alarmed. 'Are you suggesting they might try to get him?'

'They don't know anything about him. And I shan't let it out. Just make sure he says nothing, that's all. I'll be keeping an eye on things, and you'll be the first to know if there's danger. I think I'd better have a word with him. Or is he asleep?'

Madame Pasquier gave a mirthless laugh.

The boy was sitting up in his bed, his right hand in the air, two fingers extended in the small boy's traditional way of pretending to hold a pistol. He was just taking aim at the door when he realised Pel was standing in front of him.

'Having trouble with gangsters?' Pel asked.

The boy grinned. 'I've just bumped one off.'

'Can I come in?' Pel sat on the end of the bed.

'Have you caught those types in the car?'

'It usually takes a day or two.'

'Did it help? What I told you.'

'Oh, it will. I thought I'd come and have a chat. It's secret, you see.'

'What is?'

'What you told me. There are some things policemen like to keep to themselves. Because if they get out, they warn the criminals we're after them. And the trouble is, if anybody says anything, in the end it gets to the newspapers and they publish it. And that means that *everybody* knows about it. Do you understand?'

The boy nodded. 'It's always best to keep something up your sleeve, isn't it?' he said.

'That's about it. And this information about there being three men in another car and you having seen them, that's one of these things. Nobody else knows you got a look at them.'

'They were talking.'

'Who were?'

'These men. If you remember, it was hot and the car windows were open. And it was going very slowly as it passed me. I could hear them. Ever so plainly.'

'Oh?' Pel sat up. 'What did they say?'

'I don't know.'

'I thought you could hear them quite plainly.'

'I could. But I couldn't understand them. They weren't speaking French.'

'They *weren't?*'

'I think it was English.'

'*English?*' Pel sat very still for a moment. What in the name of God had they got into? 'Do you understand English?'

'I'm doing it at school.'

'And – ?'

'I don't understand it.'

'Then how do you know they spoke English?'

'When they came out of the bar, one of them said, "We've got him!" That's English, isn't it?'

'Yes, it is.'

'Do *you* speak English?'

'A bit.' Pel had an older sister who had married an Englishman and he'd picked up enough to get by. 'Did they say anything else?'

'Well, I didn't get to hear them much. But the other one said, "Make it fast!" '

'That was all?'

'Yes. just then the Peugeot came past and the Citroën shot away. If they were saying anything after that I didn't hear it for the engine. I'm sorry, I forgot to tell you about it. I was so busy telling you what I saw, I forgot what I heard. After all, it wasn't much. Is it any use?'

'It might well be.'

If nothing else it seemed to indicate that Pel's visit to Pépé le Cornet had been pointless. If Maurice Tagliatti's assassins spoke English the chances were that Pépé *wouldn't* know them because all Pépé spoke was French.

He got the drawing identified as satisfactory and rose to go. 'You've been very helpful,' he said. 'More than you realise. But this makes it more important than ever that we keep it to ourselves. You mustn't say a word of what you know to anyone.'

'I told Maman. I told Papa.'

'I think they'll keep it to themselves.'

'Are they after me?'

'You're perfectly safe. But only if you keep it all a secret.'

'You can rely on me, Chef.' Yves grinned. 'Found out about boules yet?'

The daily help, Madame Rouot, lived alone and when Pel arrived she was just putting a scarf round her head to go to see her daughter at the other end of the village. Yes, she said, she had listened to what Yves Pasquier had told her but, no, she hadn't told anyone else.

'Daughter?'

'I haven't had the chance.'

'Neighbours? Postman? Grocer? Nobody like that?'

She had told nobody.

'Keep it that way,' Pel advised. 'I don't want it to get around. What about your husband?'

'I wouldn't tell him if the Archangel Gabriel arrived in the kitchen. I divorced him three years ago. That's why I have to go out to work.'

Madame Pel was also warned. 'Madame Routy doesn't talk,' she pointed out.

'She did when she worked for me,' Pel said.

'She doesn't now. If I tell her not to say a word, she won't.'

Pel couldn't understand how his wife could produce such loyalty in Madame Routy. He had never been able to.

'I had a check run on Vlaxi, Patron,' Darcy said. 'He was in Spain at the time. His mother died.'

'It wasn't him.' Pel explained what he'd learned and Darcy's jaw dropped.

'English?' he said. 'They were *English*?'

'That's not what I said. I said they were *speaking* English.'

'Same thing. They'd hardly be speaking English if they were Polish.'

'They might if they were Americans.'

Darcy conceded the point. 'If Maurice is involved with Americans, whatever it was he was in is big. Americans like things to be big.'

'We don't *know* they're Americans. They might be English.'

'Come to think of it,' Darcy admitted, 'it fits. I've been checking Maurice's telephone bills. He seems to have had a lot of foreign calls.'

'When?'

'April and May. I expect he was setting up whatever it was he was interested in. He'd also been to the States and the Middle East in the last month or two.'

The barman at Lordy confirmed what Yves Pasquier had said. 'I never saw them before,' he insisted. 'They came in and had a few drinks. They were foreigners and they asked if they could give our telephone number as they were expecting a call. It was no skin off my nose so I said yes. They turned up again the next day and were drinking at the bar.'

'What did they say?'

'Nothing much. Then the telephone went and one of them answered it. He said "Okay!" That's all. "Okay." Then they ran outside and I heard one shout something to the other. I don't know what it was. Then the car disappeared.'

His description of the car matched the boy's but he hadn't studied the men much.

'Well,' he said, 'they were medium height, medium build.'

'Medium faces, too, I suppose,' Darcy said sarcastically.

'Well, they both had noses and they both had eyes and ears. Two legs. Two arms. All the rest.'

'How were they dressed?'

It was like dredging a river for lost property. But they had learned that the men *were* foreigners. English, the barman thought, and they were dressed in trousers and lightweight windcheaters – the barman hadn't noticed the colour. One was blond – he'd noticed that – and the other was dark – he thought. And that was about it. Their faces seemed to have been so nondescript as to have been anonymous.

'I think', Pel said bitterly, 'that if Brigitte Bardot walked past some people they wouldn't notice. Let's contact Paris, see what they know about Englishmen and Americans in France.'

They didn't come up with much – just a few names that had popped up many times before. It certainly seemed that, in addition to the refugees from half the world's pogroms, France these days contained fragments – more than fragments, colonies – from every nation in the world. Most of the English, however, were middle-aged to elderly people who felt they could live a little more happily without the rigours of a northern winter, and there were no reports of the sort of people who would wipe out a couple of gangsters with a sub-machine gun.

Pel's conference had a subdued note. Prélat, of Finger-prints, had found dabs on the car that had contained the murderers of Maurice and Bozon. Most of them belonged to the owner or his family, but there were one or two others that couldn't be identified.

'Two men,' Prélat offered. 'One with a scar across the thumb. I've tried the national computer. Nothing.'

'Which means', Darcy observed, 'that they probably *are* English.'

Pel studied the photographs which lay on his desk showing the Peugeot with its two victims. He looked at Minet, who shrugged.

'Seven bullet wounds in the driver, Bozon. Throat. Head. Shoulder. Any of those in the first two places would have been fatal. The passenger, Maurice Tagliatti – one. But four other wounds. Three in the face, all of which would have been fatal. There were also several wounds in the chest, neck and throat which could have killed him. All commensurate with having been close to an exploding grenade.'

'The bullet wounds', Leguyader, of Forensic, said, 'were fired from a range of a metre or so. It looks as though the assassins' car drove up alongside and the man with the gun was in the back. He fired solidly, I think, at Bozon, the driver. The lines from the entrance holes to the exit holes were slanting as if the cars were moving. There were twenty-seven bullet holes in the car. The gun was a 9mm Sterling. British made. Same gun that hit Sagassu. It was an assassination.' Leguyader paused. 'Killing by violent means for political or religious reasons. In this case, doubtless for private reasons, connected with what they were engaged in – crime. The word derives from *hashishin,* a person who takes hashish. It was bound up with Arab politics in the eleventh and twelfth centuries. The original Assassins were members of a breakaway Moslem sect which adopted the practice of murdering their enemies as a sacred religious duty. They were alleged to take hashish to inspire them with visions of paradise.'

Pel glanced at Darcy. But Leguyader hadn't finished yet. 'Was it a conspiracy?' he asked. 'Persons joining forces in secret for an evil purpose, to make an agreement to commit an unlawful act?'

'I know what a conspiracy is,' Pel snorted.

'It *could* be a *crime passionnel*.' Leguyader had the bit between his teeth now. 'That's a defence plea that we recognise in France.'

'Who's supposed to have committed that?'

'Maurice's wife? She may have entered a conspiracy to have him murdered.'

'A conspiracy can't be a *crime passionnel*.'

'In certain circumstances it could be argued that it was.'

As Leguyader sat back there were several grins. Everybody knew his favourite reading was his encyclopaedia and that he spent his evenings with it so he could quote it the following morning at Pel's conferences to give himself an aura of knowledge.

Remembering Yves Pasquier's query, Pel tried it on Leguyader – sarcastically. The sarcasm rebounded.

'Boules? Of course. Played by two or three people. Or by teams. Known to the English as bowls. In Italy as *bocci*. The English play with bowls made of ebony weighted on one side. We use unbiased steel balls all apparently the same but each carrying different striations for identification purposes. In the south it's called *pétanque*. It's supposed to have been invented near Marseilles by a man who suffered from rheumatism and couldn't manage the game that required you to take three steps before bowling. He produced the shorter version and, as the local dialect for *pieds fixes,* or feet together, was *ped tanco,* from that came *pétanque*.'

They were all silent as Leguyader finally dried up. He could be overpowering when he got going. Pel studied him for a moment. Well, he thought, at least I've got something to pass on to next door.

seven

The funerals of Maurice Tagliatti and Benjamen Bozon took place in the city. There was no point in holding on to the bodies because there was no question about who they were or how they'd died – the only question was why, and who was responsible – and permission was given for the interments to be held.

The Rue d'Auxonne was full of people. The cortège consisted of two hearses, followed by the limousines containing the family mourners. It always startled Pel a little to learn that people like Maurice Tagliatti had families, even that they had fathers and mothers. He always felt that gangsters appeared suddenly from under stones or, like mushrooms, grew up and – usually – were bumped off violently, died in prison or simply faded away. How many of the people lining the grass verge were mourners and how many were there merely out of curiosity he couldn't tell as he stood by the parked police car with Darcy. It was an old trick watching the crowd, in the belief that the murderer was there, but it always seemed to Pel a vain hope and it was now. There was nobody he could see who would have been likely to be involved with Maurice Tagliatti.

There was a sung mass and the funeral cars were decorated with black and silver draperies, with more draperies round the door of the church inside the cemetery where the priest waited. The weather had become drizzly and dull and the low clouds made the surrounding tombs of the bourgeois dead of the city – all decorated with glass-covered photographs and plastic wreaths inside dirty glass domes – a grey wilderness of rectangular shapes reaching away into the mist. Inevitably there were far too many flowers. Like everything else about Maurice, it was overdone and there were enough to be vulgar. All morning men had been unloading wreaths. *With fondest memories of Maurice,* said one. *Never forgotten,* said another. Mother of God, Pel thought, they were going over the top a bit. He wondered if Pépé Le Cornet had sent one – *Yours in eternal hell, Pépé.* Or from more important sources – *With happy expectations, Mephistopheles.*

The chapel entrance was puddled where the drizzle had blown and its interior was full of the heavy scent of the flowers piled against the altar steps. As Pel moved inside, the only illumination came from the candles near the coffins in the body of the chapel.

There were two groups of mourners. Bozon's wife had two children with her. Perhaps Bozon had been nothing but a driver, one of the people surrounding Maurice Tagliatti who were largely innocent of what he was up to. Maurice's wife was an attractive woman with blonde hair who didn't appear to be fighting back the tears. Behind them came Sagassu, his arm still in a sling, Devreux and Guérin and several others, all trying to look as innocent as new-born babes in dark suits and black ties with mourning bands on their arms. In the grey light, despite the innocence they affected, their faces seemed heavy with menace. There were also a few women, drummed up, Pel felt, to make the funeral look respectable. People of Maurice's ilk set a lot of store by respectable funerals.

Behind the mourners the pall bearers laid the wreaths down, the choir sang a Requiem, the De Profundis was played and the choir started again. The strong smell of incense swept over everybody as they moved outside, the coffins in front, then a boy with a silver cross and the priest bent over his prayer book. Near Pel were the newspapermen, Fiabon, Sarrazin, Henriot and Ducrot. They had gone to town over the shooting.

MAURICE AND SIDONIE, *France Dimanche* had headlined. TRAGIC COUPLE'S HAPPINESS SHATTERED. Tragic couple! It made Pel want to throw up. *France Soir* had tried to equal the sob stuff. BURGUNDY LOVE NEST FOUND BY GUNMEN, they had said. Henriot, of *Le Bien Public*, which was a small provincial newspaper, hadn't been so ambitious. CITY MAN SHOT, he had announced. AMBUSH AT LORDY. Henriot was always less dramatic than the other newspapermen in case the conservative types who read the paper gave up their subscription in disgust and bought a bottle of brandy instead.

When Pel and Darcy returned to the Hôtel de Police, Misset was standing in the middle of the sergeants' room. He was doing nothing as usual and, moreover, was stopping other people working.

'Why is a woman like a horse?' he was asking Brochard.

'Go on,' Brochard said wearily. 'Why?'

'Because she's expensive to keep, difficult to mount and often needs new shoes.'

'Heard it,' Brochard said uninterestedly. 'At school.'

'There's another – '

'Misset!' Darcy roared.

Misset flushed and adjusted the dark spectacles he wore. Since his eyes had started to go, he had worn them dark to suggest instead of short sight the image of somebody who might be a menace to a man and a holy terror with women. Sometimes Pel wondered if he still had eyes behind them. As he shuffled off, trying to look busy, Pel and Darcy gestured to Brochard to follow them. The policeman stood in front of Pel's desk, wondering what was coming.

'Where do you come from?' Pel asked.

'Near Chatillon, Patron. North end of the Plateau de Langres.'

'What did you do before you became a cop?'

'Farming. For my father. But I've got an older brother, so the farm will never be mine. I thought I'd try something else.'

'Fancy going back to farming?'

'Driving tractors? Sloshing round in cowshit? No thanks, Patron.'

'Not up there. At Lordy. The Roblais farm.'

'You mean, to keep an eye on Tagliatti's lot?'

'That's exactly what I mean.'

'Fine, Patron.'

'It'll mean driving tractors. Getting manure on your boots. Dirty hands. Maurice Tagliatti's lot are pretty smart. They'll notice anybody who doesn't fit in.'

'They won't notice me, Patron.'

'Right. Arrange to be a cousin come to help. You'll have to do a bit of work, of course. They'd soon notice anybody wandering round the fields not working. Had you much on?'

'Nothing important, Patron.'

'Dump it all on Misset. It'll stop him telling funny stories.'

Misset watched sullenly as Brochard cleared his desk. 'Off out?' he asked.

'Yes.'

'What's on?'

'Surveillance.'

'Where?'

'A farm.'

'What sort of farm?'

'A farm type farm.'

Brochard had been told to keep his mouth shut and he was doing just that. Misset was intrigued. He was always alert for information. He'd been earning beer money from Sarrazin, the freelance, for years now for titbits of information he'd provided for the papers.

'I was due out tonight to play boules,' he said. 'Now I can't.'

Brochard smiled at him. 'Good job it's raining then, isn't it? They'll call the match off.'

The fingerprints on the car used by Maurice Tagliatti's killers had still not been identified and there was a lull in the investigation. Running his fingers through his thinning hair, Pel took out a packet of cigarettes and stared at it for a while as if it might attack him. Finally lighting one, he stared at the glowing end, deep in thought. It always irritated him to have to investigate the killing of a criminal. Much better, he always felt, to be thankful that someone had done their job for them.

He brought himself back to the present with a jerk. *Could it have been Pépé le Cornet?* He mentally shook his head. Pépé preferred these days to lie low and live off his ill-gotten gains. And these days he rarely left Paris. Pépé, he decided, was a spent force. But what about his lieutenants? From what he had heard, there was no one in the offing as a leader. Paris claimed that when Pépé went his organisation would split up into half a dozen smaller organisations which would eventually cancel each other out and that it would take ten years for such an organisation to grow again.

Other bosses? There was this type, Carmen Vlaxi. He hadn't made an appearance in Pel's diocese yet but there was always a first time.

Maurice's wife? Née Sidonie Thrénier. Once a minor actress without much future until she had caught Maurice's eye. Maurice had never been short of women, but somehow Sidonie Thrénier had managed to put a rein on him. The general opinion now, though, was that she had never been able to hold him and had turned her interest elsewhere.

Where?

Darcy had it that Cavalin, Maurice's heir apparent, had been seen around with her. Were they working together? To remove Maurice and leave the path clear for moonlight and roses and to put Cavalin where Maurice had reigned? It was an idea.

'Cavalin,' he said abruptly. 'See him in church, Daniel?'

Darcy looked up, signed his name at the bottom of the form in his hand, then sat back. 'He wasn't there, Patron.'

'I wonder why? Has he bolted? Was he the one who planned it? The Crown Prince, they call him, don't they? The Dauphin. I wonder if he'd started to get ambitions? I wonder if he was after Maurice's job?'

'Or Maurice's wife, Patron?'

'Yes,' Pel mused. 'Or Maurice's wife.'

As they were talking, Leguyader put his head round the door. Pel scowled. He never welcomed Leguyader into his office because Leguyader was pompous and self-opinionated, and in Pel's opinion there was room for only one self-opinionated individual in the Hôtel de Police. Unfortunately, Leguyader was good at his job and Pel knew it, so he made an effort to be pleasant. He gestured towards a chair but Leguyader ignored it and advanced to the desk. He was holding a small envelope which he laid in front of Pel.

Pel stared at it, then at Leguyader, then picked up the envelope and opened it gingerly. Inside were a few flakes of grey substance and a little powder of the same texture.

'What is it?'

'It came off Maurice Tagliatti's trousers,' Leguyader said. 'It's clay.'

Pel frowned. 'There's no clay round here.' He knew it was so, because he had heard his wife say so when she'd been discussing the garden with Madame Pasquier over the hedge.

'It's not that sort of clay,' Leguyader pointed out. 'It's modelling clay.'

Pel had never heard of modelling clay.

'It's made of potter's clay mixed with a little finely powdered sandstone,' Leguyader explained. 'They use it to teach art students to be sculptors – as a way of seeing things in depth. There's a clay modelling department at a lot of art schools, and in them there's usually a big tub of that stuff. It's kept pliable by adding water or, for a short time, by covering it with a wet cloth. I understand they model with their thumbs and fingers and with small scalpel-like wooden tools. I'm told that the head of Socrates is a standard exercise because he had a lot of beard and it has to be shaped into curls and curves with the thumb.'

Pel listened carefully. There were times when Leguyader's devotion to his encyclopaedia had its uses.

'Clay models are used for a variety of purposes,' he went on. 'If they're going to be large and likely to sag they use metal supports – wire, flexible tubing, iron rods – which they shape to the basic structural image and then lay the clay over them. For instance –' Leguyader demonstrated ' – that famous statue of Perseus by Cellini has an arm held at right angles to the body – like this – holding the head of Medusa. But for the fact that the arm was supported inside, it couldn't have been done. Perhaps –' Leguyader gave a little self-satisfied laugh ' – that's why the Venus de Milo hasn't any arms. Perhaps the sculptor forgot to support them and they dropped off.'

Pel gestured at the fragments of clay. 'And this was on Maurice's trousers.'

'I thought it was mud. I've been in touch with the Ecole des Arts Décoratifs. All modellers apparently get it on their clothes.'

Pel frowned. 'So,' he said, 'how did Maurice get it on his?' He ground out his cigarette, pushed his chair back and gestured at Darcy. 'Let's go and find out.'

As they appeared in the drive of the Manoir de Lordy, the wheels crunching on new gravel, workmen were moving about, as if Maurice's renovations were still going on despite his sudden departure, and a painter was up a ladder working on a window. The interior was newly enough garnished to smell of fresh paint.

Pel dispensed with the courtesies quickly. 'Maurice,' he said. 'Did he have any hobbies?'

Cavalin looked puzzled. 'Roses,' he said. 'That's all.'

'Nothing else? He didn't draw? Or paint? Or model with clay?'

Cavalin looked blank. 'Not to my knowledge.'

'How about his wife?'

'No.'

'Any of the boys?'

'No. Why?'

'How about Ourdabi?' For some reason, Ourdabi, with his Humphrey Bogart look, had caught Pel's attention and he was prepared to assume him guilty of every crime in the statute book. He was by no means given to introspection or self-analysis, and his judgement, he felt, was impartial – and, of course, always correct.

Cavalin was looking at him with an amused smile on his face. 'Don't you like Ourdabi, Chief?' he asked.

'I don't like any of you,' Pel snapped. 'How about him? What are *his* pastimes?'

Cavalin smiled. 'Chiefly tossing a bunch of keys up and down and trying to look like Humphrey Bogart.'

'Bozon, Benjamen. How long had he worked for Maurice?'

Cavalin shrugged. 'About four years.'

'What exactly did he do?'

'He was a driver-handyman. He was trained as a burnisher but he gave it up and came to work for Maurice.'

'What about you? What are you?'

'I'm a director of Maurice's companies.' Cavalin pushed across a sheet of notepaper. *Maurice Tagliatti et Cie,* it announced, with headquarters in Marseilles.

'So why are you here in Burgundy?'

'Maurice had ideas of buying up vineyards. It's profitable just now.'

'I thought since President Pompidou people in France were drinking less wine.'

'They are.' Cavalin smiled. 'But they're drinking more in England. We export.'

'Why would anyone want to murder Maurice?'

Cavalin shrugged. 'Can't think. Maurice was an honest – '

'Come off it,' Darcy snapped. 'We know what Maurice was.'

Cavalin shrugged again.

'What happens to his organisation?'

'Organisation?'

'He had one. You're part of it.'

Cavalin gestured. 'That's something we have to decide with the widow. There'll be lawyers to see. The will to read. We shall have to know what Sidonie wants. It's all in the air at the moment. We're just keeping everything going until we know.'

'What was your relationship with Maurice?'

'He was a good man to work for. He paid well. He left things to me.'

'It's a big organisation. Ever thought of taking it over?'

Cavalin stared at them for a moment, his face expressionless. He was as good at avoiding expressions as Maurice had been. 'I couldn't take it over,' he said slowly. 'I wouldn't want to. I haven't the skills. Maurice was good at what he did. I'd always rather be Number Two.'

Probably, Pel thought, because as Number Two he was less likely to be bumped off.

'I suppose you always knew what Maurice was up to.'

'Not always. There were things Maurice preferred to keep to himself.'

'What exactly were Maurice's relations with his wife like?' Cavalin smiled. 'Poor.'

'She's good-looking, isn't she?'

'Intelligent, too.'

'Ever fancied her yourself?' Darcy asked.

Cavalin stiffened and Pel thought for a moment he was going to become angry at Darcy's blunt question. Instead he smiled. 'I think we all like to have her around.'

'That wasn't what I said.'

Cavalin paused. 'Then, no,' he said. 'I haven't. It would have been most unwise.'

'What about now that Maurice is dead?'

Cavalin smiled. 'I've never been involved with women,' he said. 'It doesn't pay.'

'Never with Sidonie?'

'Never.'

Somehow they didn't believe him.

'Has she always been on the right side of the law?' Pel asked. Cavalin's face hardened. 'Always,' he said. 'You can look her up. She has no record. She wasn't very old when Maurice swept her off her feet with his Cadillacs and I think she's regretted it ever since. She stuck to him because of the children.'

'Did Maurice trust you?'

'Absolutely.'

'Even with his wife?'

'Of course.'

'Did you try to comfort her?'

'Of course. It was a situation none of us liked.'

'Maurice's killers were waiting for him. Could anyone have tipped them off?'

Cavalin's eyebrows rose. 'Who, for instance?' he asked.

'Let's stop playing, Cavalin,' Pel snapped. 'We're not dealing with ordinary people. We're dealing with one of the mobs. We ask the sort of questions that go with them. Could *you*?'

'I could, but I didn't.'

'What about Maurice's wife? Could she?'

'I can't imagine it for a moment.'

'Who would know that Maurice's car was going down the road at that particular time?'

'Only Maurice. Or his secretary. Or one of the boys.'

'Which one?'

Cavalin shrugged again.

'Was he playing square with the secretary?'

'I imagine not. Playing square wasn't a habit of his. He met her in London in April while he was on a visit there.'

'Was she a secretary in London?'

'No. She was an au pair.'

'So why did Maurice think she'd make a good secretary?'

Cavalin laughed outright for the first time. 'Because she has good legs,' he said. 'And a nice pair of boobs.'

'What was Maurice doing in London?'

Cavalin laughed again. 'Probably preparing to make away with the Crown Jewels. You say you know what he gets up to, Chief Inspector. If you do, you know more than I do.' Cavalin was thoroughly relaxed now. 'It's no good. I can't put you on to any plots. Sidonie wouldn't try to kill Maurice. Nor would I. And, I suspect, nor would Vlada. She's not bright enough.'

Vlada Preradovic was a small slight girl, barely into her twenties. She had blonde hair – Maurice seemed to have liked blonde hair – huge blue eyes and the figure of a film starlet, and the perfume she wore was powerful enough to make their knees buckle. Her looks were marred at the moment by a red nose and red eyes because she'd obviously been weeping. She had no idea who might have been responsible for Maurice's death, only that it had robbed her of what had begun to look like the chance of a good life.

'He looked after me,' she sniffed.

'Did you ever do any secretarial work for him?' Darcy asked.

'Of course.'

'Much?'

'No. Not much.'

'How often?'

'Not often.'

'When was the last time?'

She couldn't even remember.

'Did you really do secretarial work for him?'

'No. Not really.'

'What *did* you do for him?'

She gave them a sharp glance and said nothing. They didn't pursue the subject.

'Ever do any modelling?'

She nodded. 'Yes. Once. I've got the right figure. I did it for a shop in London. You can ask. Eve, it was called. In the King's Road. I used to do it in my spare time.'

'Not that kind of modelling. Clay modelling.'

'You can wear clay?'

'You make models with clay.'

Light dawned and she shook her head.

'Did Maurice?'

She laughed. 'You have to be joking.'

Pel tried a different line. 'You were close to Maurice. Did you ever hear anyone threaten him?'

'People didn't threaten Maurice.'

'Did you know of anyone who would want him dead?'

'No.'

'Did he ever talk to you about anyone wanting him dead?'

'He once said there were people.'

'Who?'

'He didn't tell me.' Her brows came down. 'He promised he'd marry me. Now look what's happened. She'll get all his money.'

'Who?'

'His wife. What about me? What do I get?'

Pel glanced at Darcy, who shrugged. It certainly looked as though Vlada Preradovic wasn't going to get very much.

Sidonie Tagliatti wasn't much help either. Her mouth was tight, not from meanness but to avoid saying too much. Her eyes had a dead look.

Like Vlada Preradovic, she had never heard of modelling with clay, she'd never known that Maurice was interested and didn't know anyone who was. Nor, she said, had she had anything to do with Maurice's death.

'I wouldn't have dreamed of setting it up,' she said. 'I often thought I'd like to see him dead – especially when he brought that stupid little creature, Vlada, here and expected me to be nice to her – but I wouldn't ever have dared to make a move in case it went wrong – as this one did.'

'What was this one about?'

'I don't know.'

'If you'd been up to something and Maurice had found out, what would he have done?'

She didn't bother to answer.

'I understand relations between you and Maurice were difficult? Was there anyone else you were interested in?'

'That's none of your business.'

'It's police business.'

'It might be, but I don't tell what I feel and think to policemen.'

Pel shrugged. 'Do you know anyone who would want Maurice dead?'

'I should think the world's full of people who wanted Maurice dead.'

'Anyone in particular?'

'I can't help you. I never knew what he got up to. I tried hard not to know. It was safer.'

'Who would tip off the killers that Maurice's car was about to pass down that road at that particular time?'

She gave a bark of laughter. 'Any of them. All of them. You don't think Maurice's boys loved him like a father, do you? They were all in it for what they could get out of it; they'd all like to take over from him.'

'Who? Cavalin?'

'No. Not Georges.'

Pel remembered Humphrey Bogart. 'Who then?' he asked. 'Ourdabi?'

She stared at them for a long time before she spoke. 'Particularly Ourdabi,' she said.

eight

The man who had locked the woman trying to sell her house in her own lavatory and then rifled her jewellery box had not been caught. Not only that. He'd done it again in a different part of the city and, with everybody else concerned with the late lamented Maurice Tagliatti and his henchman, Benjamen Bozon, the job had been handed to Lacocq. Lacocq was still fairly new to Pel's team and hitherto had been used just for leg work and asking questions. The fact that he was now working on his own made him grow ten centimetres overnight. Misset's book-defacing Italian, Soscharni, had appeared before the magistrates and, having no previous convictions, had been bound over to be of good behaviour.

Since they were all busy on their own inquiries, it was some time before it occurred to Darcy that he had still done nothing about the assault on the shop assistant, Julien Claude Roth, who, it seemed, was now employed by Sport Olympe, another sports outfitters in the Rue de la Liberté. As Darcy appeared, he was in the window arranging a bright pink track suit over a stand and attaching nylon thread to the sleeves and trousers with clips and securing the other ends to the display unit with drawing pins. He looked up as Darcy entered.

'Looks pretty,' Darcy observed.

Julien Claude Roth blushed. 'Not bad,' he agreed.

Darcy looked for signs of desperate wounds, but there was nothing beyond a small scratch high on his cheek. Julien

Claude Roth looked just what he was – a normal eighteen-year-old, pink and white, innocent, not too bright, and good-looking only because he was young.

Darcy flashed his identification. 'I'm Inspector Darcy, Police Judiciaire. We've had a complaint.'

'Oh, Dieu,' Julien Claude said. 'She came. My mother came.'

'Yes,' Darcy agreed. 'She did. She laid a complaint against one Fernand Léon, of Sport France, in the Rue Général Leclerc. She said he'd beaten you up.'

Julien Claude Roth blushed again. 'He didn't beat me up.'

'What did he do?'

'He hit me.'

'Well, that's an indictable offence. You can't go round clouting people. Is that what he did? Clout you?'

'Yes.'

'Why?'

'I made a mistake.'

'That's no reason to go round handing out clouts. We're a bit fussy these days about people clouting other people. There's such a lot of it about.' Darcy studied Roth. 'I don't see any signs of a beating up. No black eyes. No missing teeth. No limp. No cuts or bruises.'

'There aren't any.'

'What's that mark on your cheek? Did he do that?'

'Yes.'

'What with?'

'His ring, I think. But he didn't intend to.'

'But he did intend to hit you?'

'Oh, yes, he intended that. But not to cut me. It was just a clout or two. He was angry.'

'What did you do? Sell the Parc des Princes or something?'

Julien Claude managed a smile. 'I didn't sell anything. I was going to sell some sports equipment, that's all, but I didn't get around to it.'

'What had you in mind?'

'A set of boules.'

'And that deserved a clout?'

'Well, I got one, didn't I? He was out and I went into the cellar for something; and he came back and – paf! – that was it. But it was nothing to get worked up about. Not really. And, after all, he did me a good turn as it happened. When I left France Sport I got this job here and I get a better wage. Not much, but a bit. I've forgotten it. I don't bear any malice. It was just one of those things. Léon was a funny chap.'

'How?'

'He was on edge a lot. He was a nervous type.'

'What about?'

'Sometimes he worked late. Down in the cellar after I'd gone. I think he was crating things up. He bought and sold things with a type in Marseilles called Boileau. They exchanged stock. I expect what upset him was me going in the cellar.'

'There was something special in the cellar?'

'Not that I know of. Just sports goods. I had my eye on something I'd seen but he found me there and went for me. Paf! Wallop! It seemed to bother him.'

'But now you'd prefer we forget about it?'

'I didn't bring the charge, did I?'

It had been Darcy's intention to call on Fernand Léon at France Sport in the Rue Général Leclerc there and then, but the street was full of fire engines, firemen, policemen, the usual spectators, and smoke. Chief Lapeur, of the Sapeurs Pompiers, was just climbing out of his car. 'Dress shop,' he said to Darcy. 'Flimsy stuff. You know what women wear. Somebody left a fire on. It went up like a torch.'

Darcy decided to leave Fernand Léon for a more opportune time.

When he reached the Hôtel de Police almost everybody had gone home. Nosjean had just finished the reports on the art fraud he'd been looking into and was stuffing things into drawers and reaching for his notebook.

'Report of an attack on a woman at Talant,' he said. 'I'll handle it.'

'Haven't you got enough on?'

'One more thing won't hurt.' Nosjean was a good cop and never grumbled about extra work.

'Annabelle-Eugénie Sondermann,' he said. 'Impasse Chévire. Lives alone. Plenty of money. Cop at Talant reported it. Maid telephoned. She'd been out and when she returned she found her on the floor. The cop thinks she's been hit with a poker; looks like an intruder she disturbed.'

'Need help?'

'Misset's still here. I think he's had a row with his wife and isn't all that keen to go home. I'll take him.'

Heading for Talant with Misset grumbling behind him, Nosjean decided he wasn't sorry to be finished with the art fraud. It had tied him down in Lorne which was not at all the place he would ever choose to stay in long and was far from the flat he shared with Marie-Joséphine Lehmann.

His feeling for Marie-Joséphine Lehmann had come a little unexpectedly and had sprung from the fact that, as an art expert, she had accompanied him to Lorne and Nosjean had somehow found his way into her bed in the hotel where they were staying. Within twenty-four hours he had moved into her flat and given up his own.

So far, he hadn't introduced her to his mother or his three sisters who were a formidable trio who liked to keep a sharp eye on his morals, and one of these days there would have to be a confrontation. Under the circumstances he considered it wiser to put off the meeting until as late as possible, but that was something that wasn't going to be easy because Mijo

Lehmann had started to ask when she was going to meet his family.

He drove to Talant as if he were going to a bank that was about to fail and he was anxious to get his savings out before it was too late.

'It's all right,' he said to Misset who was bouncing about on the rear seat because the front passenger seat was stacked with books and papers. 'We have a good hospital and a marvellous rescue services. In half an hour you could be in bed with the top specialist to look after you. I have a special style of driving. No hands. No signals.'

The Impasse Chévire was at the end of the village. On one side there were houses, on the other side nothing but open fields. Half-way along was a half-circle of large houses, built round a grassed-over island so that they all looked inwards to each other, their gardens radiating outwards to the south like the spokes of a wheel. Annabelle-Eugénie Sondermann's house was smaller and its garden ran through an orchard to the long copse of trees that lay behind all the other houses in the Impasse Chévire.

When Nosjean and Misset arrived, Annabelle-Eugénie Sondermann had already been removed to the hospital and the daily help, a middle-aged woman who wore a pink dress and apron, was nervously making coffee for the cop on duty outside the door.

'What happened?' Nosjean asked.

The cop had hastily removed the cigarette he was smoking – you never knew when it might be Pel – but had relaxed as he saw Nosjean. Nosjean looked too young to be dangerous.

'The daily help had gone out,' he said. 'Doing a bit of shopping. When she came back she found her lying in the wreckage of the tea tray.'

'You know this Annabelle-Eugénie Thing?'

'Oh, sure. Not bad-looking considering her age.' The cop was twenty-two and anybody over thirty was geriatric. He decided to be clever. 'The help was doing a bit of shopping for herself. Knicker elastic. New suspender belt. That sort of thing.'

'Have you asked her?' Nosjean demanded.

'No.'

'Confirmed that was what she was after?'

'No.'

'Then let's stick to facts, shall we?'

The cop's jaw dropped. Mother of God, he thought, this one was formed in Pel's image! He dropped his cigarette and stiffened. 'She left the tray ready in the *salon*,' he reported. 'Annabelle-Eugénie likes an afternoon nap.'

'Is she old?'

'No. Forty-five. But she considers herself delicate. Minces about the place, looking after herself.'

'Married?'

'Never got round to it. From what I've heard she was scared of it. But she had boyfriends when she was young and she seems to have been pretty enough.'

'You know this?'

'I've heard it from my mother. She knew her.'

'Go on.'

'The help left the tea tray ready. Name of Simone Clément. Spinster like Annabelle-Eugénie. Cup, saucer, milk, sugar, biscuits. That sort of thing. When she came back, the first thing she saw was the tray on the floor. Milk and sugar everywhere. And Annabelle-Eugénie on her back behind the settee with blood all over her face. She telephoned us and we had her removed to the hospital.'

'How is she?'

'Touch and go.'

'Was it sexual?' It was a question you always had to ask these days. When Nosjean had started as a cop it didn't always follow, but in the last few years something seemed to have happened to the world.

The cop shrugged. 'Her clothing wasn't disarranged.'

'Found the weapon?'

'It's the poker. It's a heavy one. It was lying beside her. It's still there. I marked out where she lay. I used pink tape from the maid's work basket, held in place with weights from the kitchen scales. It's a thick carpet so there was no other way.'

Nosjean gestured at Misset. 'Take a look round outside. See if there's anything that might be interesting.'

'There won't be,' Misset said.

'Something might leap out and bite you in the leg,' Nosjean snapped.

Misset scowled and moved away. He resented the fact that Nosjean was younger than he was and had been at the job far less time. But Nosjean had ideas and drive while Misset contrived to avoid both. Nosjean gestured at the cop who had watched the exchanges with interest.

'Let's have the housekeeper, or whatever she is, in here. We'll take a look at the room. She'll know if there's anything missing.'

The cop jumped to it. He'd realised that Nosjean's youthful demeanour didn't mean a thing. This one, he decided, could be nasty.

Simone Clément, the help, was a stringy little woman, her eyes still red with weeping. The room was wrecked as if Annabelle-Eugénie Sondermann had put up a good fight. The teapot was in pieces and the cups, saucers, milk jug and sugar bowl seemed to have been smashed to small fragments, as if the feet of a woman struggling for her life had tramped backwards and forwards over them. Sugar and milk had been pounded into the carpet.

The poker lay alongside the policeman's decorative effort with the housemaid's tape. It was heavy, and the end of it, sharpened by constant use, was marked with blood. Bending close, Nosjean saw that fair hairs were clinging to it. There were also traces of wood ash and, turning to the fireplace, he saw the grey remains of a wood fire and logs stacked neatly alongside. A wooden tray lay face down near the hearth with a hole in the centre. Round the hole were traces of the same wood ash that was on the poker, as if Annabelle-Eugénie had used the tray as a defence against the wild swings of the poker. A chair lay on its back and a second one had been flung sideways and smashed the front of the television.

'Looks like quite a fight,' Nosjean commented. 'I'm surprised nobody heard it. There must have been some screaming. Anything missing?'

'Her purse has gone,' the help said.

'Much in it?'

'Could be. She wasn't without money and she usually made sure she had plenty handy.'

'How much do you call plenty?'

'She usually had around a thousand francs on her.'

'That's enough to encourage somebody to break in. Any sign of a break-in?'

'No need. She wasn't in the habit of locking the door during the day. Only at night. I wasn't here then, of course. I only come during the day.'

'Was she alone?'

'Oh, yes. I set the tray for her.'

'Could she have been visited by anybody?'

'She wasn't expecting anyone. She liked to take a nap in the afternoon and it was never certain what time she woke. She was becoming a bit eccentric.'

'Men friends?'

'There'd been a few. She was quite lively in her day. But not so many lately because of her asthma. She suffered from it.' The help shrugged. 'The man she was going to marry was killed on a motorbike years ago.'

'Did everybody know her habits?'

'Yes.'

'Anybody else likely to know them?'

The help couldn't think of anyone so Nosjean began to go through the possibilities.

'Neighbours? How about them?'

'Older than she is.'

'How much older?'

'Sixties. Around there.'

'What about men? Was anyone interested in her?'

'Everybody was interested in her. She was still pretty. The men liked her.'

'How about their wives?'

'The wives, too, as far as I know.

'But *they* wouldn't be worried about stealing her purse, would they?' the cop from Talant pointed out.

'Perhaps whoever did it was less interested in the purse than in Mademoiselle Sondermann,' Nosjean said. 'Perhaps they just took the purse to obscure things a bit.'

'I can see why you belong to Plain Clothes,' the cop said admiringly.

Nosjean moved to the other end of the room. That end had been made into a sort of sun lounge and the floor there was of tiles and was uncarpeted and covered only by two small rugs. Scattered on it were the remains of what appeared to have been a statuette. Nosjean could see parts of the base and the head of a girl.

'What was this?' he asked.

'A statue,' the help said. 'She was very fond of it.'

Nosjean studied the fragments again and gauged the distance between them and the wreckage of the tea tray. There seemed to be no connection between them. The struggle by the tea tray surely couldn't have swayed backwards and forwards as far as this? He studied the floor and saw that one of the tiles was newly chipped – as if a corner of the heavy base had struck the tiles first. Which seemed to indicate the statuette was in an upright position when it had fallen – as if it had not merely been knocked over but had been picked up and deliberately dropped. And if it had, why?

'Was it valuable?' he asked.

The help pulled a face. 'I think so. But I wouldn't know. She treasured it. It was her father's.'

Returning to the area near the tea tray, Nosjean stared hard at the carpet. There was a dried leaf near the hearth and a few twigs and fragments of mulch.

'Could an intruder get in from the back?' he asked. 'Without being seen, I mean.'

'People use the woods.' The help jerked a hand towards the window. 'There's a lot of fallen wood there. We all collect it. It saves buying it.'

'Did she ever have visitors? I mean, during the day?'

'Not really. Only her lawyer.'

'Who's that?'

'Monsieur Lescop. Jacques Lescop. He has an office in the Rue Georges-Guynemer. There's also an architect who came to see her because she was talking about building an extension on the back of the house.'

'Name?'

'Picard. Guillaume Picard. He's not a proper architect. I mean, he hasn't a practice or whatever they call them. He was a draughtsman and he set up on his own. He doesn't design buildings. At least, not big ones. But he does a lot of extensions. Things like that.'

'You seem to know a lot about him.'

'He's my nephew.'

'Ah! Address?'

'Here in Talant. He's only young. But he's good.'

'Neighbours ever visit her?'

'Occasionally. Not really, though.'

'Who did?'

'Chiefly Madame Mahé and Madame Auvignac. Madame Kersta, too, but less so. She's not always well. Nerves.

Madame Auvignac goes in for gardening and she liked to advise Mademoiselle Sondermann on what to do. She never took any notice, mind. She didn't like gardening.'

'What about Madame Mahé?'

'Tapestry. They both went in for it. They were all good friends. They live in the little close down the Impasse. Their kitchens face on to the green and they wave to each other – even call to each other sometimes. They'd know what was going on.'

'Any youngsters live round here?'

'There's Raymond Mahé.'

'Who's Raymond Mahé?'

'He's eighteen. He's the Mahés' son. Occasionally he cut the grass for her. He did it for Dr Kersta, too.'

'Who's Dr Kersta?'

'Dr Robert Kersta. He was her doctor. He has a practice here in Talant. He's had practices all over Europe. He came to see her regularly because of her asthma. He seemed able to cure it.'

'And Raymond Mahé knows the house?'

'I suppose so.'

'Ever been inside?'

'Oh, yes. He sometimes carried logs in and he occasionally brought messages from his parents. She played bridge with them from time to time.'

'This boy. What's he like?'

'All length and no breadth.'

'What does he do with himself?'

'What do you mean?'

'Who're his friends?'

'Other boys of his own age. Girls too. I've seen him with them.'

'Any of them on drugs?'

The help shrugged. 'I wouldn't know.'

'Ever been in trouble?'

'He was once in front of the magistrates for shooting at Leu without a licence.'

'He has a gun?'

'His father has. He shoots at Leu, too. With a friend of his. I don't know his name.'

'This boy. Has he ever threatened anybody?'

'Not that I know of. He doesn't look the sort.'

'What is the sort? Has he ever had words with Mademoiselle Sondermann?'

'Once, when he was little. She ticked him off for being rude. But she seemed to get over it. And so did he. I think his mother made him apologise and she wasn't the type to bear malice.'

As he had been talking, Nosjean had been prowling round the room, nosing into the corners. As he straightened up, the Forensic boys arrived. They were discussing the football scores.

'What was it?' one of them asked. 'A riot?'

'It looks like robbery with violence. You'll find the poker on the floor. Let Prélat have it. I'd better go and see the woman. Perhaps she's come round.'

'What about the room?' the help asked. 'Can I tidy it up?'

'No. Leave it exactly as it is. I'll be back tomorrow. In the meantime, we'll have it sealed.'

When the help had gone, Nosjean turned to one of the Forensic men, and indicated the two lots of scattered fragments, those of the shattered statuette and the broken china from the tea tray. 'Collect it up,' he said. 'But keep the two lots separate.'

'It'll be a job,' Leguyader's man said. 'It looks as though somebody's walked across it wearing clogs.'

'We'll have it just the same.'

The Forensic man stared at the mash of crockery, tea, milk, sugar and biscuits on the carpet and decided it was going to take well into the evening. And he had a date. It was the sort of thing that made police work exciting.

The nurse in charge of the ward where Annabelle-Eugénie Sondermann lay looked like a younger sister of Catherine Deneuve. It bothered Nosjean. There had been a time when people who looked like Catherine Deneuve had always been in danger of getting a proposal of marriage from him.

'How is she?' he asked, glancing at the silent figure swathed in bandages just inside the ward.

'Not in a fit state to answer questions.' The nurse eyed Nosjean speculatively. He was a good-looking young man, brisk and personable, and she thought he looked a bit like Gregory Peck in his younger days. Films were a great leveller.

'Is she conscious?'

'No. You wouldn't be either, with a fractured skull. It'll be a few days before she's fit to see you.'

'Any objection to one of our people sitting near the bed just in case?'

The nurse smiled. 'Who were you thinking of? You?'

nine

France Sport, in the Rue Général Leclerc, just off the Rue de
la Liberté, was a big store. Its windows were full of footballs,
rugby balls, clothes for wearing while exhausting yourself,
clothes for wearing while you were resting after exhausting
yourself, punch bags, sports shoes of every colour and size,
muscle builders, Indian clubs, stationary bicycles, rowing
machines, tennis racquets, inflatable dinghies. Darcy stared
at them contemptuously. The most he conceded was an
occasional go at squash – half an hour of violence with the
chance of a heart attack – then forget exercise for a week.

The fire brigade had disappeared and there was no sign of
the fire beyond a charred shop front and a boarded-up
window. In the window of France Sport, an assistant was
piling tennis balls in a pyramid. From the concentration he
showed, he might have been piling up diamonds.

Léon came from a tiny office at the back of the shop. He
was a tall man, surprisingly unhealthy-looking for the owner
of a sports shop. He also looked nervous and ill at ease.

'Well, you'd be nervous, wouldn't you?' he said. 'With a
fire not twenty paces from your premises.'

'It seems to be out now,' Darcy said.

'It was in the dress shop,' Léon continued. 'Those girls are
always leaving fires on. There was a moment or two when it
seemed to be taking hold and heading for the paint shop next
door. That *would* have had me worried.'

His nervousness didn't improve when Darcy told him why he was there. 'Well, of course,' he admitted, 'I've been expecting you for some time.'

'Why?'

'Well – walloping the boy as I did.'

'So you did hit him?'

'Oh, yes. I hit him.'

'Why?'

'I lost my temper. He was in the cellar. He shouldn't have been.'

'Why not? He said that all he did was go down there to fetch a set of boules he was going to sell.'

Léon licked his lips. 'It isn't as simple as that. They hadn't been processed.'

'How do you process a set of boules?'

'They have to go through the ledgers. They have to go into the IN ledger when they arrive. Everything that comes into the shop has to go through the IN ledger. When they're sold we make a note in the OUT ledger. It's necessary to keep track of stock for reordering. If you don't do that you find you run out of things. That was what it was all about.' Léon seemed anxious to push the point. 'Nothing was supposed to go from the cellar without my knowledge. I'd told him. But he never listened. He was always in a dream.'

It sounded reasonable enough and Darcy didn't argue. Instead he studied Léon. There was a lot of bruising round his eyes that made him look like an elderly boxer who'd tried to make a come-back and failed. Darcy eyed it speculatively.

'Did Roth do that?' he asked.

Léon hesitated. 'Well...'

'Well, did he?'

Léon gave a half-hearted laugh. 'No, he didn't. That was my wife.'

'Been beating her up as well?'

Léon's laugh became a weak smile. 'She hit me with a tennis racquet.'

'Habit of hers, is it?'

'It was an accident. We were fooling about. You know how married people do. It caught me under the eye. Quite a bruise it was.'

'It's a hell of a bruise from an accidental blow from a tennis racquet. A tennis racquet's not all that heavy.'

'The edge is pretty hard.'

'It looks more as if it were done by a fist to me.'

Léon shook his head violently. 'Oh, no. It wasn't a fist. I told you. It was a tennis racquet.'

Darcy didn't believe him and decided he'd have to enquire further.

'This argument with Roth,' he said. 'What was it about? Let's hear your version. Was there more to it than just selling something he shouldn't?'

Léon shrugged. 'No. He was just stupid. He's rather a stupid type. Always thinking of girls.'

'So am I.'

Léon smiled. 'His mind was always miles away. He'd done several stupid things and this time I just saw red.'

'It was an assault. It's a chargeable offence.'

Léon's eyes flickered. 'I have to accept that. Did he put in a complaint?'

'His mother did. She said he'd been beaten up.'

Léon managed a laugh. 'Hardly beaten up. Right hand, left hand, and that was it.'

'What happened then?'

'When I came upstairs, he'd gone. Took his coat and left. Is there anything I can do to put this thing right?'

'You could offer the kid his job back. At a better wage.'

'I tried. He wouldn't come.'

Nosjean was aware of a slight tension in the air when he returned home.

'Are you ashamed of me or something?' Mijo Lehmann asked.

'No, of course not,' he said.

'Well, isn't it about time we met each other's parents? Are you nervous?'

'Yes.'

'What of?'

'Your father.'

Nosjean was nervous of Mijo's father because he had a suspicion that fathers, having got up to a few things in their youth, looked with great suspicion on young men who might be trying to get up to the same things with their daughters.

Mijo laughed. 'My father's all right,' she said. 'He's old-fashioned but he's quite broadminded. He'll understand. What about your family? Don't they wonder why you never go home for meals these days?'

'Oh, they know,' Nosjean said.

'I think I ought to meet them then. Or don't you think they'll like me?'

Nosjean felt his parents would adore Mijo, but it wasn't his parents he was worried about. It was his sisters – Susanne, Emilia and Antoinette. They weren't as clever as Nosjean, nor as good-looking – every scrap of good looks in the family seemed to have flowed past them and gone into the making of their little brother. They all held dreary jobs in the city and he had a feeling that when they saw Mijo Lehmann, who possessed the good looks that had passed them by, the brains they'd never had, and the well-paid job they had never attained, they might dislike her on sight. He knew the way they'd think. A young woman who had ceased to be pure couldn't regain her innocence. God didn't demand that she should, but she could put right the mischief by marriage.

'They've got to meet me sometime,' Mijo urged. 'They'll want to know what we intend.'

'What do we intend?'

'They'll want to know when we're going to get married.'

Marriage wasn't entirely in Nosjean's plans. It wasn't that he wasn't deeply attached to Mijo. It was just that marriage was so final, and he felt he was too young to die.

It bothered Nosjean a lot and even took his mind off the Annabelle-Eugénie Sondermann business occasionally.

The attack puzzled him. For several days he had been checking all the people who had been to see her. They all seemed to have alibis, though young Mahé seemed nervous. That, of course, might be just because he was young and anyway Madame Kersta had seemed nervous, too, and, for that matter, so had her husband. Nosjean wondered how much of it was due to the fact that he, Nosjean, was a policeman – because policemen had a habit of making people nervous – and how much because they knew something about Annabelle-Eugénie Sondermann that other people didn't know. Perhaps, however, they had good reason to be nervous, because Madame Kersta, a faded blonde, had once been mugged.

Madame Auvignac, a large woman with thick legs, was indignant about the way Madame Kersta had been mugged and implied that the police had been sitting around drinking beer when they should have been stamping out crime. Nosjean couldn't imagine Madame Auvignac ever being nervous. Madame Mahé, the tapestry expert, small, neat and precise, also didn't seem nervous. However, all three women swore that at the time in question they had seen the other two appearing in and out of their kitchens across the circle of grass that centred the little close where their houses were situated. Following the modern style, their *salons* were at the back, looking over the gardens running towards the woods between tall hedges, while the kitchens faced north towards the road, and they could always see what was going on.

It seemed very much as Nosjean had first suspected. Somebody had entered the house from the woods, snatched up the poker and lashed out. As the tea things had been upset, Mademoiselle Sondermann had grabbed the tray in an effort to protect herself and the poker had gone through it.

Leguyader's view confirmed it. 'The leaf we found', he said, 'was beech. There are beech trees in the woods behind the house. It was done with the poker because the ash on it's the same as the ash round the hole in the tea tray she used to defend herself.'

Going back to Annabelle-Eugénie Sondermann's house, Nosjean studied the place again. Everything was much as it had been, except that the broken china and the remains of the statuette had been collected and Prélat was going through the pieces in the vain hope that one of them might have on it a fingerprint by which they could identify the attacker.

To get into the house, Nosjean had had to collect the daily help from her sister's house where she lived. She had refused to enter Annabelle-Eugénie's premises alone since the attack. Nosjean turned to her impulsively.

'I'd like to look at the rest of the tea set,' he said. 'To see what it looked like.'

The help produced a cup and saucer. They were of fine bone china and were decorated with pink roses with a gilt edge and fluted sides.

'Pretty,' Nosjean observed.

A few days later Madame Roth reappeared.

'Have you arrested that man yet?' she demanded of the cop on the front desk.

The cop on the front desk was feeling flippant. 'Which man were you thinking of, madame?'

'That one I was talking to one of your detectives about.'

'Which detective would that be, madame?'

'Smooth sort. Fancied himself. Had a mouth full of teeth.'

The man on the front desk recognised the description of Darcy at once. Though having a mouth full of teeth was common to everybody in the Hôtel de Police, Darcy's were most noticeable. Two minutes later, Madame Roth was in Darcy's office.

'I want to know if you've arrested that man yet,' she demanded.

'Not yet, madame,' Darcy said. 'We're making inquiries.'

'What do you need to make inquiries about?'

'We have to ascertain that all the facts are correct.'

'Ask my son.'

'His version doesn't entirely agree with yours, madame.'

Madame Roth uttered what could only be described as a snort. 'He's soft, that's what. He was always soft. Like his father. He has no backbone. It's time you got on with it.'

Darcy drew a deep breath. 'Perhaps I should remind you, madame,' he said coldly, 'that we've been a little preoccupied just lately. There's been a double murder – you probably read of it in the papers – and these things occupy the time of a lot of men. Your son's case is trivial by comparison.'

'Not to me.'

'It seems to be to him.'

'He's a crook.'

'Who is? Your son?'

'No. That Léon.'

Darcy's eyebrows lifted. 'That's a pretty strong statement to make,' he said.

'Well, if he isn't, he has some funny friends.'

'Oh? Who?'

'Well, that type who was killed was one.'

'Which type?'

'The one you're talking about. The one near Lordy. In the car.' Darcy began to take notice. 'Maurice Tagliatti?'

'I don't know what his name was. It was something Italian and unreliable.'

'How do you know he was a friend of Léon's?'

'My son told me.'

'He didn't tell *me*, madame. I think I'd better see Léon and find out what he has to say about it.'

But Léon wasn't available. When Darcy called at France Sport next morning it was closed. The young man he had seen building a pyramid of tennis balls on his last visit was waiting disconsolately for it to open.

'It didn't open yesterday either,' he said. 'I waited until lunchtime but nobody turned up.'

'Who're you?'

'Emile Demoine. I'm the assistant. He took me on after he had a fight with the last assistant.'

'Know where he lives?'

'Haven't the foggiest. He'd better not try fighting with me. I go in for karate.'

The manager of the paint shop next door hadn't seen Léon for some time either and, preoccupied with cleaning up after the fire in the shop alongside, wasn't much interested.

'Know where Léon lives?'

'Out Fontaine way somewhere. It's in the telephone directory.'

It was, and Darcy shot off in a hurry. There was no one at Léon's house. It was a large place and the next-door neighbour informed him that Madame Léon worked in the city.

'They didn't get on,' she said.

'I got the impression', Darcy said, remembering what Léon had told him about the larking about that had resulted in the bruise over his eye, 'that they did.'

The neighbour pulled a face. 'I don't know where you got that story. They never seemed to me to get on.'

The case was beginning to look interesting. There were several varieties of truth – half-truth, more than truth and nothing but the truth – and it seemed that Fernand Léon's didn't belong to the third category.

'Where does she work?' Darcy asked.

'She runs a boutique in the pedestrian precinct. It's called Dorée.'

Dorée might be called a boutique but it couldn't hold a candle to Madame Pel's boutique in the Rue de la Liberté. It was very small, and seemed to concern itself not with the elegant women who patronised Madame Pel's establishment but with brash young teenagers. There seemed to be a lot of bleach-washed jeans and blouses in bright colours, and not much else.

Madame Léon was a brisk brunette who seemed already to have adapted to her husband's disappearance. 'He's left me, I expect,' she said. 'He's done it before. When we were in Aix-les-Bains. He walked out on me for a German woman. He was back within a year but I always expected it to happen again. After all, a wolf doesn't change its clothing, does it? People don't alter, they just become more so.'

She had no idea where Léon could have gone and knew of no woman in particular. 'That doesn't mean he didn't have one, though,' she said. 'I'm surprised he left the shop, all the same. The stock's worth a bit. She must be loaded, for him to do that.'

'He'd got some nasty bruises on his face,' Darcy pointed out. 'He said you caused them.'

'Then he's a liar!'

'He said it was done accidentally, mind you. With a tennis racquet.'

She pulled a face. 'He told *me* he did it falling down the cellar steps when he went to bring up a bottle of wine for dinner. He said he tripped. He might have done. He had two cracked ribs and bruises all over his body. I saw them. He tried to hide them.'

'So it wasn't a tennis racquet, and you didn't do it?'

'No, I didn't.'

'It looked nasty.'

'It was. He had to go to the doctor.'

'Did he now?' Darcy was becoming more and more intrigued. 'Who is his doctor?'

'He didn't go to his own doctor.'

'Why not?'

'I don't know. But he said his own doctor was too far away. He went somewhere else.'

'*I* think he'd been beaten up. Know any reason why he could have been?'

'No, I don't.'

'Or why he's disappeared?'

'Well...' She paused. 'He once got into some funny business in Aix, I know. Perhaps he'd got into some more. He certainly had some funny friends.'

'What sort of funny friends?'

'Well, just lately, anyway. I was in the shop once when they arrived. Big men. Fat men. Wearing smart suits. They pretended to be interested in sport but they weren't the type at all. And when I went in a few days later, there they were again, talking to him. They pretended to be on the point of buying something but I noticed they didn't. I think he was up to something.'

Darcy fished in his briefcase and produced a picture of Maurice Tagliatti.

'That's one of them,' Madame Léon agreed. 'He was the one who was doing all the talking.'

'When was this? Can you remember?'

'July. About the end of July.'

It seemed to call for another visit to Julien Claude Roth. Darcy explained about Léon's injuries.

'What did you hit him with?' he asked.

Roth was indignant. 'I didn't hit him.'

'You're sure?'

'Yes.'

'Somebody did. Hard, too.'

'Well, it wasn't me. I never touched him. I never laid a finger on him and if he says I did he's a liar.'

'As a matter of fact,' Darcy said, 'he didn't. He said his wife did it. Accidentally.'

'I bet she didn't. Not unless she was trying to clobber him for something.'

'Did she try to clobber him?'

'They always seemed to be fighting.'

This, Darcy thought, is becoming a bit of a teaser.

'Ever quarrel with Léon?' he asked. 'Apart from this once?'

Roth shrugged. 'Now and then. He flew off the handle occasionally. I told you.'

'What about? There must have been something in particular that made him nervous. Your mother makes me nervous, for instance.'

Roth grinned. 'She makes me nervous, too. She makes everybody nervous. I think that's why my father took off.' He paused. 'Léon was only nervous when this type came in, though.'

'Which type?'

'A big type. Dark. Fat.'

Darcy produced the photograph of Maurice Tagliatti again. 'Would that be him?'

'Yes, it would. It's the type who was murdered, isn't it? I saw the photo in the paper.'

'What did he talk about?'

'I don't know. They didn't let me hear.'

'What did they do?'

'They went into the cellar.'

'Why the cellar? Why not the office? There is one. A little one. That would be the place to talk business, I'd have thought.'

'Not if you want to keep it private. You can hear everything that's said in there.'

'You think that's why they went in the cellar?'

'It must have been.'

'And what sort of business would Léon be discussing with this Tagliatti type? He's a crook, this Tagliatti. Was Léon a crook?'

'I don't know.'

'Your mother said he was.'

'She thinks everybody's a crook. Even my father.'

'Well, since Tagliatti *was* a crook, this time she might be right and Léon might be a crook, too. Did he ever do anything that seemed crooked to you?'

'Not really.'

'What would he have been crating up in the cellar on those occasions when he worked late?'

'I don't know. I know he had this type called Boileau in the south he did business with.'

'What sort of business was it?'

'It seemed to be sports goods. This Boileau type seemed to sell things in the Middle East and sometimes Léon supplied him.'

t e n

Returning to the Hôtel de Police, Darcy found Pel had just emerged from a conference with the Chief and was in his office studying the reports on Maurice Tagliatti's death. Pel was a great believer in going over reports again and again, feeling that in them somewhere there could be a vital clue. Darcy didn't agree. It worked sometimes, but more often than not it didn't.

He explained what he had discovered. 'There's a connection somewhere, Patron,' he said. 'I think Maurice has been in Léon's sport shop more than once. Why? Were they involved in something together? I think I'd better look up this Léon type and see what his background is.'

The computer didn't fail them.

'Jewellery, Patron,' Darcy said. 'He did time for fencing. There was a jewel robbery at Nîmes. At the home of some big shot. They found some of the loot in Léon's shop. He was in antiques at the time and that's ideal for jewellery, as you know. He seems now to be mixed up in some business with a type called Boileau in Marseilles.'

Pel frowned. Marseilles was noted for its crime. Anything could happen in Marseilles and usually did.

'Let's have him in,' he said.

'Not possible, Patron,' Darcy said. 'He seems to have disappeared. I'd be interested to know where to.'

They didn't have long to wait.

112

That evening it turned colder and the sky clouded over. Because of the cloud, the night was dark – particularly under the trees that overhung the road as the police brigadier from Cloux-les-Bains drove home. His name was Jules Renot – like all names ending in 'ot', a good Burgundian name. He wore no hat, and a checked jacket clashed horribly with the blue of his uniform trousers. He was off duty and had been having a quiet evening in Cloux-le-Petit.

He enjoyed a game of boules or dominoes and, since his wife's mother had come from Lyons to stay with them, he had taken the opportunity to get out of the house. His wife's mother was a Meridionale with an incipient moustache and what Jules Renot liked to call a mouth like a hen's arse. When she was around it was like living with a cat and dog fight because she couldn't stand Brigadier Renot.

Alongside him was one of his constables, Arthur Martin by name. They had served together a long time and often went together to the bar at Cloux-le-Petit in the evening. At that moment, however, they were both scowling and the atmosphere inside the car could only be called 'stiff'. The evening had been a disaster. Martin's interest at Cloux-le-Petit wasn't boules or dominoes but the landlord's daughter, and Renot didn't like her and thought that Martin spent too much of his time thinking about her. To Renot she seemed a little too solid between the ears and too much of a gossip for a cop's girlfriend and he had tried to persuade his constable of this fact.

'She's too slow on the uptake for a chap like you,' he said, trying to put it as gently as he could.

It had started an argument which had grown progressively more bad-tempered as they had neared home. It was even beginning to seem to Renot that visits to Cloux-le-Petit with Martin were likely to occur a great deal less frequently in the future.

The following morning the two men had to go to Maillac. There was a big wedding on there and they were supposed to be keeping an eye on the traffic but, as they sat together in the little white Renault van that belonged to the substation at Cloux-les-Bains, this time wearing their uniform jackets and képis, there was still a great deal of hostility between them. Renot had thought about what he'd said during the night and had come to the conclusion that he'd spoken too hastily. He liked Martin and, after all, it was none of Renot's business whom he fell for. He could marry Dracula's daughter if he wanted, and Renot realised he had been too rude and wanted to put things right.

The morning was cool and the lanes round Cloux-les-Bains were full of early mist which hung about in the hollows, white and milky and thick enough in parts to be dangerous.

'Look – ' Renot tried.

'No thanks,' Martin shot back.

Renot lost his temper. 'I haven't said anything yet!' he roared.

'Well, don't bother.'

Renot had just turned his head for a furious retort when he saw Martin's eyes suddenly open wide. A yell like a train coming out of a tunnel escaped him and, switching his attention ahead, Renot saw in alarm that a large estate wagon was stuck with a wheel in a drainage ditch, its rear end half across the road. With the mist and Renot's attention absorbed by the argument, but for Martin's yell they would have run smack into it.

Drawing the van to a halt, he climbed out. All thoughts of enmity had gone and they spoke as normally as they always did to each other.

'Some bastard had one too many last night,' Renot said.

'It must have been late,' Martin pointed out. 'It wasn't here when we came back from Cloux-le-Petit.'

Renot was on the point of making another attempt to put things rights about the argument they'd had but he changed his mind and commented on the car instead.

'Out with a bit of fluff, I expect,' he said.

'Boss' wife,' Martin added.

'These whiz kids. Must be a whiz kid. Only whiz kids can afford these estate wagons. They guzzle petrol.'

Martin was just ahead of Renot as they approached the station wagon and he suddenly looked alert. 'I think there's somebody still in there,' he said.

The vehicle was an Audi and its awkward position made it difficult to see into it. But it was just possible to see a jacket sleeve, with an arm in it above the edge of the door.

'Still drunk,' Renot said.

'Hang on!' Martin's voice was suddenly crisper. 'He's hurt, I think.'

Then, as they moved nearer, Renot noticed the line of holes in the car door. 'Holy Mother of God!' he said. 'It's another!'

Pel had just appeared when the news arrived. He was never at his best early in the morning and his wife had dropped a hint at breakfast that the garden might need his attention at the weekend. She looked after Pel well but she had her standards. Her view was that boys would be boys and men would be men, but it was a good thing there were girls and women to sort things out after they'd finished making a mess of them; and giving them an occasional spell in the garden was a good way of doing it.

Before leaving home, he had slipped into the Pasquiers' house to check up on Yves Pasquier's silence. The boy had been digging into a tin of dog food and ladling it into a bowl. It had been harder when Pel had been young, he had reflected. Even for cats and dogs. How had they managed to live before all that cat and dog food had been invented?

115

The vow of silence was still holding. Pel, had walked in the garden a little, making sure that it was well remembered, and set off for the Hôtel de Police more than satisfied. There was the usual skirmish with a heavy lorry hurtling down the hill where it joined the main road near Talant, and he had to stand on his brakes and watch the lorry hurtle past like a charging tank, the driver mouthing futile oaths that were soundless above the din. Pel paused to get his breath back. That junction was always tricky – especially to someone who was as indifferent a driver as Pel was. Reaching the office, he laid down his briefcase, smoothed his ruffled feathers and was just trying to avoid lighting a cigarette when the telephone went next door in Darcy's office.

'What!' He heard Darcy's voice rise and, guessing something had happened, gave up the struggle and reached for the packet of Gauloises in his pocket.

'What do you mean, another?' Darcy was saying. 'There's a man out there now? Right. I'll be there.'

As Darcy replaced the telephone with a crash, Pel lit the cigarette and drew a deep gulp of smoke, blew it out, waved it away from his head, had a spell of coughing, then started reaching for spare packets of cigarettes, notebooks and pencils. Darcy appeared in the doorway.

'We've got another, Patron,' he said.

'Another what?'

'Another shoot-up. Estate wagon in a ditch near Cloux-les-Bains, just off the N27. Other side of the bridge. Body inside behind the wheel. Sounds like the same pattern as Maurice's.'

The Audi was tilted at an angle, one wheel down. All the doors were closed and the windows were starred, but they could see a body huddled in the driver's seat. It had slipped forward – they assumed with the jolt as the car dropped into the ditch – and was half under the steering wheel. There was blood about the head and neck and there were bullet holes in the car. Standing nearby was Brigadier Renot from the sub-station at Cloux-les-Bains.

'We've touched nothing, sir,' he pointed out. 'It seemed pretty obvious the guy was dead, so we decided to leave it to you. We thought of telephoning Traffic with the number of the car to get a name but I decided you'd better handle everything your own way. There are ten bullet holes I can see. I reckon three of the bullets are in the driver somewhere – head and neck, I imagine – and there must be around three more somewhere in the car. Four of them seem to have gone straight through. You can see the exit holes on the passenger's side. It looks to me as if another car came up alongside and fired – like the one at Lordy – and the car ran into the ditch.'

Pel was sniffing round cautiously as the cars containing the Forensic boys and Prélat, of Fingerprints, arrived. Doc Minet appeared soon afterwards, to be followed by Judge Brisard. Brisard was itching to ask questions, but, with Pel in a sour mood, he deemed it wiser to wait until he felt like making a statement.

After Minet had pronounced the man behind the wheel dead and the Photographers had finished their work, they eased the body out onto the grass.

'Rigor mortis still present,' Doc Minet announced. 'I'd say some time after ten o'clock last night. It looks as if our little friends who shot Maurice Tagliatti had a vendetta with this one, too. Who is he? Another of Maurice's lot?'

'No, he isn't,' Darcy said bluntly. 'At least, not officially.'

'Do you know him?' Pel asked.

'Yes, I do. It's Fernand Léon.'

They were still standing in a group staring at the car, listening to Brigadier Renot.

'What the doctor says must be about right,' he announced. 'We came down here at around eleven last night and there was no sign of any car then.'

'Dark, was it?' Pel asked.

'Yes. With the trees, *very* dark. We're always careful on this corner because sometimes the kids walk home to Cloux-les-Bains from Cloux-le-Grand. They have a disco there and they come from all the villages around. It's always very dark.'

'Then', Pel asked, 'why aren't the car's lights on? If he was driving through here after 11 p.m. he'd need lights, wouldn't he?'

'Perhaps they *were* on,' Darcy said. 'But headlights would run the battery down in no time.'

'Check them, Daniel.'

Scrambling into the ditch, Darcy reached into the car. The headlights flared, the horn barked, then, as Darcy tried the starter, the car jerked and stalled.

'Battery's not flat, anyway. And the engine was switched off.'

Pel called Leguyader over. 'Bullet holes,' he said. 'There are exit holes on the passenger's side. Four, I make it. Where did they enter?'

Leguyader looked quickly at him then moved back to the car. With a long rod he began probing. A few minutes later he returned. 'The exit holes', he said, 'are directly opposite the entrance holes.'

'In that case,' Pel observed, 'it would seem that it *isn't* the same as Maurice's killing and it might even be that he wasn't killed here.'

Pel's guess was a good one.

'There were two extra bullets in the body', Doc Minet announced, 'that can't be accounted for.'

'There were five altogether,' Leguyader said. 'Three more are embedded in the car and four passed clean through. But only ten shots were fired into the car. So where did the extra two come from? Certainly not from the same gun that made the holes in the car. Those were made by a Kalashnikov AK 47 semi-automatic rifle. The two in the victim's head were from a 6.35 Apex probably. He was shot before the car reached Cloux. It was a put-up job made to look the same as Maurice's.'

They were occupied at Cloux-les-Bains for most of the day, managing on beer, cigarettes and sandwiches. As they returned to the city, the sun had gone down and it was growing chilly. Darcy noticed they were close to Madame Roth's address.

'I think we ought to have another word with that kid, Patron,' he said. 'He seems to know more about Léon than anyone.'

Unfortunately he was out dancing.

'He likes dancing,' Madame Roth snapped. 'Why shouldn't he? He's a healthy boy. It's only just up the road. And they don't dance any more, anyway. They just wiggle their behinds. It's a birthday party for Yvonne Hoss.'

The noise could be heard a couple of kilometres away. The older members of the Hoss family all seemed to be cowering from it in the kitchen of the hired hall. The room where the dancing was taking place was full of enough flashing lights to give the strongest character migraines for a month. Darcy stepped into the middle of the din and, snatching a boy out of it, dragged him into the kitchen.

'Roth,' he roared above the racket. 'Julien Claude Roth. I want him. Find him.'

'He won't come,' the boy said. 'I know. I'm his friend.'

'And I'm the police,' Darcy yelled. 'And I have the power to stop this disco if I have to. Find him, or I will.'

A few minutes later, Julien Claude Roth appeared, blinking in the lights of the kitchen. 'Who wants me?' he said.

They took him out to Darcy's car and pushed him inside. 'Am I being arrested?' he bleated, trying to adjust his eyes to the light.

'No, you're not,' Darcy said. He produced the photograph of Maurice Tagliatti. 'This type you saw in Fernand Léon's shop. Tell us some more about him. When did he start appearing?'

Roth considered. 'June. About then. Then later about the end of July. He came in once with some other types.' The descriptions seemed to match Cavalin and Bozon.

'Anybody else?'

'Yes. Once there was this tall thin chap. Good-looking, with grey hair. He looked like some character out of one of the American soaps on television. They all seem to have grey hair these days. It's fashionable, I think.'

'What did *he* want?'

'I don't know. I was told to get on with my job and they went to the back of the shop.'

'Did you hear what they were talking about?'

'No. They went into the cellar. You couldn't hear a thing when they were down there. The shop used to be a jeweller's and they had the strong room down there. It wasn't a very good one, mind you. Not like a bank's. Perhaps in those days they didn't rob jewellers as they do today.'

'They've learned a lot since then,' Darcy said. 'When was it a jeweller's?'

'1937. About then. Then the jeweller died and the shop changed hands. It was a shoe shop until recently, then the shoe shop moved next door and Léon took the place over for sports goods.'

'Why did he keep boules in the strong room?'

'I don't know. He just did. We used it as a store room really. But he never kept it locked. Not until lately.'

'You didn't tell me he kept it locked.'

'You didn't ask. He started about August some time. But the day the punch-up occurred he happened to go out and when this type came in asking for something special, I thought I'd have a look downstairs. So I unlocked it.'

'What with?'

'There was a spare key in the office. I knew where he kept it. I think he'd forgotten it. I knew he kept all his best stuff down there so when this type said he wanted some good boules for his son-in-law's birthday, I went down and looked around. I thought he'd want me to. But that's when he came back and started yelling that the boules weren't for sale. He played hell. I reckon it was because I'd opened the cellar. I bet he had something in there he shouldn't have had.'

Darcy grinned. 'That's probably not a bad guess, old son,' he said. He turned to Pel. 'It looks as if he was still handling stolen goods, Patron.'

Pel eyed the boy over his glasses. 'Have you been out to Cloux lately?' he asked.

'Not since I was a kid. My father took us one day in his car. I haven't got a car.'

'Know an Audi estate, number 637-RT-25?'

'Sure. That's Léon's.'

'He hasn't been to the shop for the last two days. Did you know?'

'No, I didn't. And I told you, I didn't hit him. I never touched him, so it's not my fault if he's in hospital or something.'

'He's not in hospital,' Darcy said. 'He's not "or something" either. His car was found near Cloux this morning. It was in the ditch.'

Roth stared. 'Well, it's nothing to do with me,' he yelled. 'If he says it is, then he's a liar.'

'He doesn't say anything,' Darcy pointed out. 'He can't. He's dead. He's been shot.'

There was more for them the following day after the Chief's conference.

They were still puzzling about Léon's disappearance when one of Nadauld's men from Uniformed Branch turned up outside Pel's office. His story was unexpected.

'I saw Léon three nights ago,' he said. 'After the fire in the dress shop. He had his car by the back door. It opens on to the Place Franchaud. He was loading cartons into his car. It's an Audi estate. The cartons looked heavy and it was late and I went to see what was going on. I thought at first it was a break-in. But his papers were sound and he had a driving licence to confirm it. Besides – ' Nadauld's man gave a sheepish grin ' – I'm often in that part of the city and I know him well. I was going by the book, that's all. He said he was shifting some stock to his home. And that's what he seemed to be doing. I put it in my report.'

Madame Léon was puzzled. 'He never brought stock home,' she said. 'I wouldn't have allowed it. The shop's the shop. Home's home. I expect he's moved it somewhere else. To Lyons. Or Aix. Or Marseilles. Or Toulon. He worked another shop down there with a friend of his.'

'Name of Boileau?'

'I don't know.' She paused, puzzled. 'On the other hand,' she went on, 'he left a lot of stock behind, and if he'd been opening another shop, surely he'd have taken the lot.'

The new murder had them all baffled. Why should Maurice Tagliatti be in cahoots with the owner of a sports outfitters? Pel was beginning to feel a little desperate at the lack of progress.

'Anything yet from Brussels about Rykx's friends?' he asked.

'No, Patron,' Darcy said. 'They're being a bit slow as usual.'

Pel shrugged. The Belgians were never very quick off the mark. There were jokes by the dozen about their slowness. What would you do if a Belgian threw a hand grenade at you? Take the pin out and throw it back. That sort of thing.

They were still talking round the subject when Leguyader appeared. He was fidgeting as they talked and eventually he began to look as if he would burst. Pel guessed he had discovered something.

'You look like a poodle that wants to be let out,' he said. 'What have you found?'

Leguyader smiled. 'Clay,' he said. 'Modellers' clay.'

'On Maurice's trousers. We know that.'

'I found some more. On Léon's shoes.'

Pel sat up and Leguyader went on cheerfully. 'He wore a shoe with a very distinct pattern on the sole.' He fished in a plastic bag and produced a pair of grey shoes. 'Léon's,' he pointed out. 'You'll notice the sole's designed with V-shaped ridges in it, each about five millimetres deep. They're very marked and distinct, as you can see, and they extend over both sole and heel. My son wears them. They're supposed to stop you slipping. What they really do is pick up mud which later dries out and falls on to the dining-room carpet just when your wife's cleaned it. Clay. Soil.'

'Dog shit,' Darcy added.

Leguyader smiled. 'Dog shit,' he agreed. 'I found two or three patches of this stuff on Léon's shoes. It's modelling clay. He'd obviously trodden on a piece while it was soft, forcing it into the ridges where it set hard. I dug it out.' Leguyader produced a photograph. 'That's it.'

'And it means what?' the Chief asked.

'That wherever Maurice got the splash of clay on his trousers,' Pel said, 'Léon had been there too.'

'So,' the Chief asked. 'Who do we know who uses modelling clay?'

The director of the School of Decorative Arts was very grave but had never heard of Maurice Tagliatti.

'He didn't study here,' he said.

However, he came up with a list of potters he knew, most of them elderly ladies who liked to make crockery.

'Their work's not very good,' he said. 'They haul it round the gift shops with the idea that tourists will buy it. They never do, of course. I wouldn't either. It's always cock-eyed.'

He also knew of a few private pottery classes, and two men, both sculptors – Gilbert Deville, who lived at Perrenet-sous-le-Forêt, and Gaspard Rac, who, he believed, lived somewhere in the same area.

'Let's go and see them all, Daniel,' Pel suggested.

The private pottery classes weren't much help because they never saw anybody but their own members. The old ladies making cock-eyed crockery were under the impression that they were about to be arrested for making pottery without a licence. In the end it left the two sculptors, Deville and Rac.

Deville lived at an ancient barn-like house about ten kilometres from Lordy at the end of a long twisting road that sloped upwards to the old village at Perrenet. The house was on the edge of Perrenet and hidden away among deep shrubbery down a winding drive where the foliage brushed both sides of the car. It was a grey day with drizzle and heavy with shadow so that, surrounded by greenery, it was like being in a goldfish bowl. The garden was littered with white statues that looked like ghosts among the misty shrubbery. Some of them had obviously been there for some time because they had lost their pristine whiteness and gone green, and one or two of them even had convolvulus growing round them.

Deville appeared to be working on a model of a frog about half a metre high squatting on a heavy base shaped like a rock. He was no longer young but he had piercing blue eyes, a mane of shaggy fair hair growing grey, and a tangled mass of beard that hung down on his chest.

'Always intend to shave,' he said. 'But I get absorbed and forget.'

He was wearing a blue labourer's smock and looked as if he'd taken a bath in wet plaster. Dried clay hung from it in globules and there were smears down his front as if he'd wiped his hands there. His trousers were stiff with the stuff, it had got into his hair and on his eyebrows, and in his beard two large pieces clicked together every time he turned his head. The floor and even the walls seemed to be liberally spattered with white dried stone hard blobs and in one corner was a potter's wheel and a large square metal container containing damp clay. Several statues stood about the room, all of them sagging limply as if they'd lost their spines.

'It's the wet application technique,' Deville explained. 'Some call it "Droop". Symbolic. That's how life is, isn't it? Sagging. I do it with wet clay.'

He flicked away a globule of clay from his smock. It landed on Darcy's sleeve. 'Don't worry,' he said. 'You can pick it off when it's dry. Just give it a brush like this.' A big hand reached out and the clay was smeared down the disgusted Darcy's arm. 'Oh, well,' Deville said. 'It'll come off in time. You only have to be patient. I model in paint, too. Like Van Gogh. Put it on good and thick. Use a table knife. Gives depth.'

'Tagliatti,' Pel tried.

'Never touch it.'

'Never touch what?'

'Tagliatti. What is it? An Italian pasta?'

'It's a name. Maurice Tagliatti.'

'Never heard of him. What does he do?'

'He doesn't do anything,' Darcy grated, looking at his sleeve. 'He's dead.'

'That's the worst of dying,' Deville said. 'It stops everything.'

'He was a criminal and he was found in a car at Lordy,' Pel explained. 'Shot. Didn't you read about it?'

'Never read the newspapers.'

'How about the television?'

'Haven't got one.'

'Radio?'

'Bust. It was one a niece of mine bought for me but I made a mess of something I was doing and threw a hammer at it. It missed and hit the radio. I don't take much interest in what goes on outside.'

Pel drew a deep breath. 'He had clay on his trousers,' he said. 'The sort of clay you use.'

'Well, he didn't get it from here, and if it came from here, he must have pinched it. I don't sell it or give it away. I'll have to look into my security. I often forget to lock up at night.' The sharp blue eyes looked narrowly at Pel. 'Why would he want to steal clay?'

'He didn't steal clay.'

'You said he did.'

They were getting nowhere.

'Know anybody else who works with this stuff?' Pel asked.

'A few old ladies making crockery. A few students. An odd studio that works for tourists. Tourists'll buy anything.'

'Whom do *you* work for?'

'I work for me.'

'Where do you sell your work?'

Deville stared at them, a blank expression on his face. 'I never did sell my work,' he said. 'Not until recently. Then this type from Singapore – Japanese or something – turned up. He'd decided he wanted statues for his garden to put among the ferns and the palms and the banana plants or whatever they have there and he decided that what I made was just the thing. Something to do with keeping evil spirits at bay.' Deville paused and clapped his hands. 'Chinese,' he said.

'What about "Chinese"?'

'That's what he was. Chinese. They're great ones for gods and things like that. Like to have shrines in their gardens. Great believers in evil spirits. That's why their roofs always slope up at the eaves.' Despite themselves, Darcy and Pel were listening. 'Evil spirits like to slide down roofs and the bit that turns up suddenly is there to catch them in the family jewels.' Deville grinned. 'I expect all Chinese evil spirits are holding their balls.' He gave a hoot of laughter. 'I expect that's why they have such agonised faces.'

Pel managed to get a word through a chink in the diatribe. 'If Maurice Tagliatti had clay on his trousers,' he asked, 'how would it get there?'

'Easy enough.' Deville flicked his fingers and this time the globule of wet clay landed on Pel's shoe. Deville indicated it. 'Like that,' he said.

'Know a type called Fernand Léon? He's dead, too. Shot like Tagliatti. He kept a sports shop.'

'I gave up sport years ago.'

'He had clay on his shoes. The sort of clay you use. He's mixed up with Tagliatti. They had obviously both been to see someone using modelling clay.'

'They might not have. They might have been buying it from the manufacturers for something else entirely. To seal up drugs, for instance. So the sniffer dogs couldn't smell it.'

It was an idea, Pel had to admit.

Gaspard Rac was a squat hunchbacked man with sour lines on his face, his features covered with black hair that made him look even more evil. He was surly and answered their questions unwillingly.

'Deville's an old fool,' he said bitterly. 'He doesn't know the first thing about modelling. But he's found somebody abroad to sell his work to. He's even got an export licence.'

'Who do you sell to?'

'Anybody who wants to buy. I try to show at exhibitions.' Rac indicated a cubic shape. 'Cupid and Campaspe,' he said. 'I sold that. But the bastard backed off.'

'Perhaps he didn't like Cupid very much,' Darcy said.

'It's a question of how you see them.'

'Know anybody called Maurice Tagliatti?'

'He's the chap who got shot, isn't he?'

'Yes.'

'I heard he was a crook.'

'He was. Ever met him?'

'No. And I don't want to. I think crooks – of any kind – ought to be hung up by their thumbs.'

'How about Fernand Léon?'

'Who's he?'

'He's probably a crook, too.'

Rac stared at them hostilely. 'Look,' he said. 'I don't know what you're after but I don't associate with crooks.'

They went through the same questions and got the same sort of answers, though with a little more coherence. Rac modelled in clay like Deville but he seemed to be no more successful.

'You can buy rubber things these days,' he said. 'Like French letters. You fill them with wet plaster of Paris. When you peel off the rubber, you've got Snow White or Mickey Mouse or Asterix or somebody. Why should people buy statues and models that I've laboured weeks over when they can do it themselves as easily as that?'

eleven

'Whatever it was that Maurice was involved in,' Pel said, 'this big thing he was working on, then Léon must have known about it, too. He must have been part of it. Maurice went to see him at his shop. They talked. The boy, Roth, said so.'

'Jewellery?' Darcy suggested. 'Some big haul Maurice had got hold of that Léon was about to get rid of for him?'

'Whatever it was, somebody else knew about it, it seems, and wanted to be in on it. That's why they tried to kidnap Maurice.'

'So who did for Léon? The same lot?'

'Perhaps not,' Pel said. 'Perhaps somebody different. But somebody who was obviously in the know. They probably even got out of Léon where the loot, whatever it was, was hidden.'

'So where *was* it hidden?'

'In that strong room underneath his shop?'

They stared at each other. 'It occurs to me', Pel said, 'that perhaps we ought to have a look at that strong room.'

Madame Léon had no intention of allowing Pel and his men to enter France Sport on their own and insisted on accompanying them. She seemed to be handling her husband's death with considerable calmness. So far they hadn't seen any tears but had noticed a great deal of cold calculation.

'I could move my stock there from the pedestrian precinct,' she said. 'There'd be more space. It would cost more in rent but there'd be more elbow room.'

She shut up Dorée and walked round the corner into the Rue Général Leclerc with them. Emile Demoine had disappeared at last, and France Sport had a feel of emptiness about it, like an unlived-in house. There was no smell of dust or decay, simply of stale air, of no windows or doors having been opened, of no one having breathed there, of nothing having moved. Madame Léon knew how to switch on and work the till, but there was nothing in it but small change. 'He always took the notes and large denomination coins away with him,' she explained. 'Was it robbery?'

They didn't bother to answer. Instead, they sniffed round the shop, half expecting to find something but not certain what. After moving warily about for a while, Pel turned to Madame Léon.

'The basement,' he said, and she indicated a flight of stairs hidden from sight by a large display of track suits.

They trooped down after her. The basement looked much the same as the floor upstairs, except that the things there were still in cartons and stacked with no pretension to display. There was also a small work bench where minor repairs of one sort or another were made.

'He sent tennis racquets away to be restrung,' Madame Léon said. 'In fact, recently he began to send everything away. He used to have a man who did small repairs for a while but he got rid of him about two months ago.'

'Do you know exactly when?'

'I think it was the end of July or the beginning of August.'

'Let's check if anything big happened about then, Daniel.' Pel murmured. 'A big robbery. A jewel haul. An airport drugs snatch. That might be why he got rid of him. If he had some loot hidden here, he'd prefer no one to know.'

There was a heavy metal door at the end of the basement and Darcy tried the handle. It was not locked and he heaved it open. Inside there were more cartons, most of which seemed to be track suits, and a new stock of football shoes for the coming season. In the deepest recesses of the room there was a clear space where something had been moved. It was about a metre wide and a metre deep and, for all they knew, could have run up to the low ceiling.

'Something's gone from there,' Pel said, turning to Madame Léon. 'Know what it was?'

She had no idea. She had taken no interest in the sports shop and had never intended to. 'Sport's crazy. People drop dead with it.'

'Let's have the dogs in, Daniel.'

The sniffer dogs found a scent at once. It set them all shifting cartons as if there were buried treasure behind them, but all that happened was that they grew hot and dusty, and turned nothing up.

'Well, even if it isn't here now,' Pel said, 'we know they'd used the cellar to hide drugs.'

Locking the place up, they arranged for Prélat, of Fingerprints, to check it over. There had to be fingerprints somewhere, because it was full of glass-topped showcases.

They spent the afternoon checking through records. There were no handy bank hold-ups, no major jewel robberies, no mail snatches, no missing drugs. Prélat appeared at the end of the afternoon, looking triumphant. 'Maurice's dabs, Patron,' he said. 'Just as you suggested. Léon's, too, of course, and a few we identified as belonging to Bozon.'

Pel pulled a face. 'Unfortunately,' he said, '*they're* all dead so we can't ask them how they came to be there. Anyone else?'

'Nobody we're interested in. I expect they all belong to customers. Most of them were on the showcases. I found Maurice's and Bozon's on the door of that old strong room.'

Because he had stayed late at the Hôtel de Police, the following morning Pel was slow getting up. Stumbling to the bathroom, he rubbed his eyes then ran his fingers through his hair. There wasn't much of it and for a moment he was struck by a sudden panic that what there was had disappeared during the night. He stared at himself with distaste. It was the cigarettes, he decided.

After breakfast, all innocence, he wandered into the garden as if to make sure no one had run away with it during the night but in fact to snatch a quick drag at a cigarette. Yves Pasquier was near the hole in the hedge where they usually met.

'When are you going to give up smoking?' he demanded. 'I gave up when I was nine. My father's given up, too.'

'You should both be very proud.'

'My mother says she's going to give up, too. My father says she'll never do it. She won't.'

Pel decided that perhaps they could have a shed erected at the bottom of the garden where it was accessible to both families, so that the outcasts, himself and Madame Pasquier, could go there and smoke themselves silly. Thinking about Madame Pasquier, Pel decided the exile might not be too bad.

Arriving at headquarters, he ignored the man at the desk as he gave him a cheerful good morning. The man at the desk stared at his back and made a rude gesture with two fingers. Darcy hadn't arrived, so that Pel's ill temper deepened. When he opened the newspapers Didier Darras had piled neatly on his desk, the first thing he saw was an article on lung cancer. Thoroughly depressed, he slammed the paper shut. He could feel the malignancies forming in his lungs already.

Darcy appeared a moment later, bright and shining, his teeth glistening, his splendid profile in overdrive, on top of the world and apparently without a worry in his head. 'I've been looking up Maurice in the files,' he said. 'I thought we might have a session on him today.'

'I've got a better idea,' Pel pointed out. 'Let's go out there and tear that house apart. So far we've just asked questions. Let's go and make life uncomfortable for them. I feel like being rotten to somebody.'

It was a grey morning with a suggestion of rain in the wind when they set off. As they drew into the drive of the Manoir de Lordy, the rain was thundering down.

'Like a cow pissing on a flat rock,' Aimedieu said, turning his collar up.

With Aimedieu were Debray, Bardolle, Misset, Cadet Didier Darras and two uniformed men. They were met in the entrance hall by Cavalin who protested vigorously.

'You can't put seals on this place,' he said. 'Maurice wasn't murdered here.'

'You know your law,' Pel admitted. 'But what got him murdered was doubtless being planned here. We don't intend seals but we do have a warrant. I'd be obliged if you'd stay in your office – accompanied', he added, 'by Detective Sergeant Aimedieu here.' Just in case, he thought, the bastard had ideas of destroying anything.

Sidonie Tagliatti arrived as they began to split up and, pink in the face with rage, was escorted back to her room and one of the uniformed cops placed outside the door.

They didn't find much, and certainly nothing to connect Maurice with the scrap of modelling clay found on his trousers.

'Perhaps he picked it up by accident, Patron,' Darcy said.

'I find it hard to believe when Léon had the same stuff on *his* shoe.'

Despite the disappointment, they managed to make life uncomfortable for everybody at the Manoir so that by lunchtime Pel was feeling much more relaxed. He and Darcy took their lunch in the bar at Lordy where the landlord's wife produced wine that tasted as if it were suffering from metal fatigue.

Darcy pulled a face. 'Wonder what they make it with,' he asked. 'It isn't grapes.'

The faux filets were tough enough to be bulletproof and the coffee tasted like being hit in the face with a wet football.

'Oh, well,' Darcy said gloomily. 'If nothing else, it's been a change from the office.'

While his men were going through the house, Pel had a few words with Maurice's wife. She made no bones about the fact that she'd grown tired not only of Maurice's activities, but also of Maurice himself.

'There were other men?' Pel asked.

'Of course there were. You don't think I was going to sit at home twiddling my thumbs while Maurice went off with that stupid secretary, do you? You don't even think he employed her as a *secretary*, surely?'

'No, madame,' Pel said. 'I never did.'

She gave a reluctant grin. 'You knew our Maurice, didn't you, Chief Inspector?'

'I've had a few brushes with him in my time, madame.' Pel paused, trying the 64,000 dollar question while she was in a good mood. 'These other men. Could we have their names?'

She gave them willingly enough. To his surprise, there were only three, one of them a politician.

'I didn't go to bed with them,' she said quickly. 'They were men. A woman needs men. She needs them around her. I suppose you'd say men need women. Maurice certainly did. And I knew he was up to something. All those trips to London he made. He'd spotted that bitch, Vlada.'

'Can you give me dates?'

'No. But I can tell when he turned up here. April 17th. It was my birthday. She was my birthday present. He met her somewhere and offered her a job as a secretary. Secretary, hah!'

'And these men friends of yours?'

'Don't read anything into them, Chief Inspector. I said men need women. We had a few rather sweaty sessions, but I didn't go to bed with them. Not *them.*'

Pel caught the inflexion in her voice. 'With somebody else perhaps?'

'I didn't say that.'

No, Pel thought, but that was what you were thinking. He wondered who the lucky man had been.

'Georges Cavalin?' he tried.

'Him!' Sidonie Tagliatti swung round. 'I wouldn't trust him as far as I could throw him.'

It seemed almost as if she were protesting too much. Pel decided to try Cavalin.

But Cavalin was as indignant as Sidonie Tagliatti had been. 'I wouldn't get fresh with Sidonie,' he insisted. 'Not even if I were interested. It would have been too dangerous.'

'What about now? Now that Maurice isn't around any more?'

'I'm not interested in Sidonie,' Cavalin insisted. 'I'm more interested in the profits from his organisation. God knows what'll happen now he's dead. Sidonie wants to wind everything up. She didn't approve of his activities, naturally. She came from a small town in Provence and small towns are notorious for their morals.'

'What about the children?'

'Away at school. Sidonie insisted. She wanted them as far from Maurice's influence as she could get them.'

'Is that what she said?'

'Yes.'

'To you?'

Cavalin paused. 'Yes.'

'So she at least communicated her secrets with you?'

'She liked to talk to me. She needed someone.'

'And you were a shoulder to cry on?'

'I wouldn't put it that way.'

Pel did. Despite what he said, he suspected that Cavalin had been happily engaged with Sidonie Tagliatti whenever Maurice's back was turned. Was he the other man she had hinted at? It gave them both a good reason for getting rid of Maurice.

Vlada Preradovic seemed to be engaged in packing when Pel found her, and had her head inside a suitcase.

'Leaving?' Pel asked.

'This place gets me down,' she said. 'Without Maurice it's like living in a morgue. I'm off.'

'I'm afraid you can't,' Pel said.

'You can't stop me!'

Pel looked at her mildly. 'Before now,' he said, 'I've put people in a cell to stop them disappearing when I've said they can't.'

She glared at him. 'I had nothing to do with what Maurice did. Or with him being killed.'

'That's something we have to ascertain.'

'I wasn't even there.'

'You might know someone who was.'

'I was going to London.'

'Why not Paris?'

'I don't know Paris. I know London. London's popping. I worked there for a while.'

'Where?'

'For this family.'

'Which family.'

'I was au pair to a Mrs Harding. I looked after the kids. They were horrible.'

'Is that why you left?'

'No. Maurice offered me a job.'

'Doing what?'

'He had to meet people. He liked me to go along.'

'How did you meet him?'

'He turned up at the house one night.'

'When was this?'

'April. I flew back to Paris with him the next day.'

'This Mrs Harding you worked for. How did Maurice come to turn up at their house?'

'I don't know. He was doing some business, I think.'

'What sort of business?' She shrugged.

'He didn't tell me,' she said.

twelve

By late afternoon, they were all beginning to feel low in spirits and the searchers were beginning to mutter. They had been sent into the attics to search in the corners and they were dusty, dirty and had backache from stooping.

The little rooms under the roof were full of broken furniture, trunks, suitcases and hat boxes belonging to the de Lordy family. There were chairs without seats and chairs without legs, wash-hand stands, flowered bowls and jugs in which maids had once carried hot water upstairs for morning ablutions, old paintings, most of them nibbled at the corners by rats, rusting old guns. The cellars were the same, full of iron bedsteads, great iron hinges which had been removed from great wooden doors, picture frames, iron ladles and a crucible which appeared to have been used to melt lead.

'For shot,' Misset observed loudly to Didier Darras. 'For those old guns upstairs. I once met a man who had one. He made his own shot. About a centimetre in diameter it was. He used to stuff powder down the barrel then put more powder and a cap in a little pan. When you pulled the trigger it went bang – a little bang as the powder in the pan went off – then BANG – a big bang as the explosion in the pan exploded the main charge.' Misset looked puzzled. 'He actually used to kill rabbits with it, too.'

Didier indicated a tank of thick moulded glass. Inside it was a bundle of wires. 'What's that?' he asked.

Misset shrugged. 'They use them for arthritis or for injuries to the feet and hands. I once had the treatment. A lorry ran over my foot when I was trying to arrest the driver who was drunk.'

Didier had heard the story – from other sources, which claimed that it was Misset who'd been drunk.

'Perhaps old de Lordy had it,' Misset went on. 'They fill it with water and stick anodes and cathodes in, then they shove your foot in and pass an interrupted low voltage through it. It makes the muscles move.'

As he pushed things aside, trying in his inexperienced way to make a good job of the search, Cadet Darras listened with only half an ear to Misset who, instead of helping, preferred to talk. Anybody else would have told him to dry up but, being only a cadet, Didier Darras didn't have either the authority or the confidence.

Misset picked up a rusting boule from among the rubbish and tossed it up and down in his hand. 'There are always boules,' he said. 'Everybody's got a set of rusting boules in their cellar. I used to be a crack player. I could land the thing within an inch of the jack any time I wanted.'

Didier Darras frowned, wondering how much longer he would have to endure.

'I had a magnificent set once. Made by Favrel and Company at Bonnet-le-Château. That's the place to get your boules. Seventy-four millimetres diameter. Seven hundred and twenty-five grams weight. Cost me ninety-nine francs fifty. And that was a few years back.'

Occasionally somebody appeared from upstairs or from the cellars, with cobwebs in his hair, a smudge of dirt on his face, to ask a question or to produce for inspection something that might have some meaning to Pel.

As they searched, Pel stared at a display of coloured photographs on a desk in the room Maurice had used for an office. Maurice with his children. Maurice on his yacht in

Marseilles. Maurice at St Trop'. Maurice about to ascend the Eiffel Tower in Paris. Usually accompanied by a girl who looked as if she'd been plucked from a film studio. Maurice in nightclubs, wearing evening dress and surrounded by sycophantic aides. Maurice with other men who looked as though they were in the rackets, too. Maurice at race meetings and getting in and out of cars. One of them showed him climbing into a car that was recognisable as a Jaguar.

He was still studying the photographs when Bardolle appeared. Bardolle was a thick-shouldered man, with a voice like a loud-hailer that he'd only just learned to subdue. He'd been a country cop and looked like a yokel but he had a shrewd mind and Pel had grabbed him for his team.

He produced what appeared to be a desk diary. 'I found it in the chest of drawers in Maurice's bedroom,' he said. 'It seems to be for telephone appointments. Telephone numbers and so on. I've been trying a few of them. They all seem to be perfectly normal but there's one here that crops up several times in the last four months. 70421-6666. The entry in the diary just gives a time and then 'G' and the number. It appears three or four times from April onwards but then he stopped using the number, as if he'd got it off by heart, and just wrote down the time and the letter 'G'. I tried ringing it, Patron, but I got nowhere. Enquiries say there's no such number. I wondered if it's a foreign number. Maurice would be able to speak to a Belgian. I got Enquiries to ask. There's no such Belgian number either.'

'A minute!' Pel swung round and snatched up the picture of Maurice outside the nightclub. 'That's a Jaguar,' he said, indicating the car. 'A British car. It belongs to a Geebee. An Englishman. A Rosbif. Let's have it out of the frame. There might be something hidden by the surround. It might show the car number. If it does, we ought to be able to learn who the owner is.'

Bardolle's big hands had the photograph free in seconds. It had been cut down to fit the frame and the car number had been lost. On the back were the photographer's stamps but they'd been cut into, too, and all they could see was:

NOIR

TRAITS

RRIAGES

DUSTRY.

Below in a different colour was another incomplete stamp.

the property of
must not be
acknowledgement

Below that was yet another stamp which, this time, appeared to be complete:

For reorders quote Ref. No. B2835-3

'Taken by a professional photographer,' Pel observed. 'They always stick those things on the back. I expect the first word's his name. Charles Parnoir – Denoir – Renoir – something like that. *Portraits. Marriages. Industry.* To indicate that he does any kind of photographic work from industrial pictures to marriages and portraits. The next one's the stamp they put on to cover themselves for copyright. *This photograph is the property of Charles Parnoir* – or whatever – *and must not be published without acknowledgement.* The last one's in case anyone wants to order extra copies. Go through the telephone directory, Bardolle. Find a photographer with a name that ends like that. When you find him, ask if they've still got the negative. You have the reference number there.'

Ten minutes later, Bardolle returned. 'Got them, Patron,' he said. 'It's the Studio Lenoir, 4, Rue Chanoine-Bordet. They looked up the number. The photograph was taken in April, and they think they ought still to have the negative.'

There was a message waiting for Pel when he arrived at the Hôtel de Police the following morning. *Ring Studio Lenoir.*

'A man called Mariotte just telephoned,' Didier Darras announced. 'He said they'd got the negative you asked for.'

'Telephone him,' Pel said. 'Tell him to hang on to it. I'm on my way.'

Mariotte turned out to be the owner of Studio Lenoir. He was an enormously fat man who seemed to be in a permanent sweat. It wasn't the weather because the day was beginning to show signs of winter, but he seemed nevertheless to be steaming gently.

'What's it all about?' he asked.

'Identification chiefly,' Pel said, giving nothing away. 'Have you got the negative?'

'Better than that. We've got about fifty.'

Pel's eyebrows lifted and he explained. 'We always have a man doing the nightclubs. People like to be photographed having a good time. It's a source of income and we keep a lookout for anybody important and flash them arriving or leaving. We go round the tables, too. Intimate photographs. You know the sort of thing. Funny hats. Paper serpentines and so on. We have the contract to cover this place. Every Saturday night and all big occasions or affairs.'

'Do well at it?'

'On the whole. Some buy. Sometimes they don't want to know. Sometimes, even, they try to buy the film, especially if they're with somebody who's not their wife.'

'Ever tried blackmail?' Darcy asked.

'We could make a good job of it if we did.' Mariotte grinned. 'Of course we don't know who's with his wife or some other dame. We just take the pictures of any likely looking party and get the names from the club management and send them a copy. Some panic. Some don't.'

Pel produced the photograph from the Manoir. 'How about this one?'

Mariotte stared at it. 'Who is it?' he asked. He obviously didn't know Maurice Tagliatti.

'Somebody we're interested in.'

Mariotte began to work his way through a reel of film, holding it up to a spotlight on his desk.

'Here we are,' he said. 'We seem to have only two.'

'Can you print them for me? Quickly?'

Intrigued by being involved in a police inquiry, Mariotte was more than willing. The two photographs had obviously both been taken at the same time, one from the front of the car, showing Maurice with his head out of the passenger's window talking to someone not in the picture, the second from the rear of the car showing that the man he was talking to was a cop who was standing near the driver's door, apparently studying the car's number plate. In this picture, Maurice appeared to be more angry, but the policeman was stolidly uninterested.

Back at the Hôtel de Police, Pel called Bardolle into his office and pushed the photographs at him.

'There's a cop on that one, Bardolle,' he said. 'Find him. It shouldn't be difficult. He's in uniform. See Inspector Nadauld, of Uniformed Branch. He'll identify him. When you've got him, bring him here. Fast.'

The cop was in front of Pel's desk within two hours. 'Brigadier Fourie,' he announced himself. 'They said you wanted to see me.'

'Yes, I do.'

Pel pushed the photograph across. 'Remember this?'

Fourie took a look at the picture and nodded. 'Yes, sir, I do. The car was badly parked. They'd been drinking – not drunk, though – and they were noisy. The driver was sober all right, but his pal made a lot of noise. I got his name. All their names. They're in my notebook.'

'Still using it?'

'Yes, sir.' Fourie started flipping pages. 'Here you are, sir. Disturbance at the Coq d'Or. Owner thought he'd better call us. There was a bit of an argument. Nothing to worry about. Mostly the passenger. They went quietly in the end. I got their names. I put in a report. 'No need for police action.' Passengers: Maurice Target, Naomi Lissac, Julienne-Anne Artois. I know the women, sir. They're on the game.'

'Know who Target really is?'

'Who, sir?'

'Maurice Tagliatti.'

The policeman's face fell. 'Ought I to have pinched him, sir?'

'Not unless he was doing something worth pinching him for.'

'He wasn't.'

'Then that's all right. What about the driver?'

'He was English, sir. Name of Hazard. George Hazard.'

'Any address?'

'He said he was staying with Target. That is, Tagliatti. He gave me his name willingly enough. He spoke French. Not good, but adequate. He could understand me all right and I could understand him. He was sober and was behaving himself. It was Target – that is, Tagliatti – who was noisy.'

Pel called Bardolle in. 'Our friend here, Bardolle,' he said, 'very nearly had his hand on Maurice Tagliatti's collar.'

'I wish I'd known his real name, sir,' Fourie said.

'It doesn't matter. Don't worry. Take a look at these pictures, Bardolle. Maurice Tagliatti. Back and front views. Try Enquiries again and ask them if that number you found could be an English telephone number.'

'Could Maurice speak English, Patron?' Bardolle asked.

'No,' Pel said. 'But the Englishman seems to be able to speak French.'

It took a long time but Pel's guess had been right. When Bardolle reappeared, grinning, Pel had a feeling that the small thing he had hoped to find at Lordy had turned up.

'Harding, Patron,' Bardolle said. 'George Harding. G H T Harding. Address: La Rêve, Spinney Lane, Brookside, Kent, England. 6666 is the number. 70421 is the area code.'

thirteen

Pel was exultant. His hunch that they'd eventually find something at the Manoir had proved right. They hadn't found much. Just a telephone number and a name. But it could lead anywhere.

What had Maurice been up to in London? What was the business he was interested in with George Harding? Who was George Harding, anyway?

Neither Cavalin nor any of the others offered any help. He guessed they were all lying but, apart from thumb screws, he couldn't drag it out of them, because they were all accomplished at it. Sidonie Tagliatti didn't know either, and Vlada Preradovic seemed so dim she probably believed Maurice had been honest. He saw he would have to go elsewhere for his information and decided to try a contact he had in London, Inspector Goschen of New Scotland Yard. Pel knew Inspector Goschen well. He had had to travel to London a few years back and Goschen had put him up for the night. He had learned a lot about the English then. Despite what he'd thought, they knew how to cook, had as many cheeses as the French but didn't talk about them, and ate something called Yorkshire pudding which was served covered with a sauce that was used on everything and was known as gravy. In the hope of getting the dish on the menu at home, he had tried to explain it to his wife but she had attempted it only once.

Calling Cadet Darras, he sent him out for a couple of bottles of beer and a sandwich. What he was going to do was likely to take time and he was going to need all his strength. 'I'm going to telephone England,' he explained. 'And I shall be talking Rosbif.'

In fact, he spoke better English than he would ever admit to, but he still found it hard work. The English were a funny lot. They regarded Paris as the French nation's consolation prize for not being English and had the strange idea that going there meant living dangerously. Their view was about as accurate as their command of French which they failed to understand even when it was shouted at them. Nevertheless, Pel had got on famously with Goschen who not only had a sense of humour but had managed to extract what little Pel possessed, so that they had passed an entertaining hour or two amicably pulling each other's country to pieces.

When the beer arrived, Pel poured himself a glass, took a bite at the sandwich – like most French sandwiches, it was made of ham, lettuce and baguette and needed a very large mouth to encompass it – then, picking up the telephone, dialled the international dialling code, the country code, the zone code, and then the number he required. There was a series of clicks and buzzes then he heard the ringing tone and eventually an English voice. He drew a deep breath, summoning up all his knowledge of the English language, to ask for Goschen. There were more clicks then a wary 'Hello' and Pel asked, 'Is that Inspector Charles Goschen?'

'*Superintendent* Goschen.' The voice came back stiffly.

'Congratulations. This is Chief Inspector Pel.'

'Who?' Apparently Pel's accent wasn't as good as he'd thought.

'Pel.'

'Sorry.'

Pel sighed. 'Evariste Clovis Désiré Pel, Brigade Criminelle, Police Judiciaire. I speak from France.'

There were times when Pel's name had its advantages. Normally, it sat on his shoulders like a lead cloak, but at least you couldn't mistake it and the man at the other end of the line in London caught on at once.

'Got it! Hello! How are you?'

'I am well. And you?'

'Suffering from what you call the English *sang-froid habituel*. What we call a permanent bloody cold.'

The joke was beyond Pel but he struggled on.

'Something I can do for you?' Goschen asked.

'I think there *is* something. It might be difficult to explain. The language, you understand.'

'I speak a bit of French. You speak a bit of English. I imagine we can manage with Franglais. What's the trouble?'

'George Harding,' Pel said. 'G H T Harding.'

There was a long pause. 'I know that name,' Goschen said. 'In connection with what?'

'He's a villain.'

'Would he go in for murder?'

Goschen paused again. 'You bet your life he would,' he said. 'He probably has. But we've never been able to pin anything on him. What's he done?'

'One of our villains has just been murdered. It was an assassination, you understand. Car to car. We have no knowledge of who did it. But we have this name, George Harding. He has a telephone number in Kent.' Giving the telephone number and address, Pel went on. 'It may be nothing, of course. But the name has cropped up. Our man, Maurice Tagliatti, employed as secretary a girl called Vlada Preradovic, who had been au pair to the family of your man, George Harding. They appear to have met while Tagliatti was doing business with Harding. I am interested to know what business your man Harding is in.'

'Everything you could think of.'

There was a long pause as Pel summoned up his courage.

'I think', he said, 'that I need to come and see you.'

To his surprise, Goschen sounded delighted. It always surprised Pel when someone was pleased to see him. He personally wouldn't have given himself house room.

'That will be all right?' he asked.

'Of course. I'll meet your plane. You must stay with us, naturally. The family will be pleased to see you again.'

Would they indeed? Pel began to think there was more to himself than he had ever imagined.

Deciding he needed support, the Chief sent Pel off to Paris in his own car driven by a police chauffeur and clutching an overnight bag and a briefcase containing photographs of the prints taken by Prélat of the car that had been used in the Tagliatti killing, and the artist's drawings of the men who had been inside it. As promised, Goschen was waiting and, as expected, the weather was awful. Goschen welcomed him with a grin.

'Superintendent!' Pel greeted him with what passed with him as a smile.

Goschen gestured. 'For God's sake, let's get rid of this "Superintendent" thing. My name's Charles. What do I call you? Evariste?'

'Not if you wish to remain alive. My wife calls me Pel.'

Goschen grinned. 'Okay, Pel it is.'

They stopped at New Scotland Yard to drop the prints Pel had brought.

'If they're anything to do with Harding, we shall find them,' Goschen said. 'We know all his friends.'

Goschen's family seemed to be looking forward to Pel's arrival. The place was bright and colourful and Goschen's children were intrigued to have a Frenchman in the house again.

'Perhaps if I had two heads it would be even more interesting,' Pel suggested.

The meal, as last time, was better than he had ever dreamed the British could produce, and included the famous Yorkshire pudding.

'I seem to remember you liked it,' Goschen's wife said.

'Indeed,' Pel admitted. 'I even tried to persuade my wife to make it. It came out like cake.'

The wine was also better than he had expected and was served in splendid glasses.

'The English', Goschen said, 'can afford to drink wine so rarely, they make it an occasion.'

Pel shrugged. 'Up to their necks in wine, the French swig Romanée Conti in glasses like cut-down bottles.'

The following morning, Pel accompanied Goschen to New Scotland Yard. He wore what he always wore and felt like something the cat had dragged in alongside Goschen with his smart suit and bowler hat.

When they arrived, Pel was left in a waiting-room while Goschen went ahead; then, eventually, he was waved into another room by a uniformed sergeant with a marked Scottish accent.

'Aye...' Pel caught the tail-end of his announcement before the door closed. 'The wee Frog disnae speak English sae weel.' The sergeant, he decided, didnae speak it sae weel either.

He was shown into an office where a huge thickset man sat at a desk as big as a billiard table. Despite his size, he seemed a little awed to be talking to a Frenchman.

'Chief Superintendent Murray,' Goschen introduced.

Murray sat behind his desk like the Rock of Gibraltar, regarding Pel with suspicion, because for a policeman Pel was small. He was obviously different from Goschen, and regarded the French as quaint, with their strange foreign habits of eating horses and carrying loaves of bread under their arms. He thawed after a while, however. Although he understood some French he wasn't very good at it and, as they started shouting at each other, it required Goschen's smoother approach to get them on each other's wavelength.

The fingerprints and drawings Pel had brought with him had produced no problems. With the name of George Harding already in the air, the officer in charge had known exactly where to look.

'We have them on our files,' Murray said. 'Wayne Braxton, aged thirty-eight, Flat 4, Fulham Buildings, Martlesham. And Thomas Bryan Coy, thirty-one, of Enfield, Middlesex. Both known criminals with records for violence and the use of firearms. Both known to associate with our friend, Harding.'

'And Harding?'

Murray's message was short and simple. 'Harding's a crook.'

'I thought he might be. Maurice Tagliatti didn't associate with people who weren't crooks.'

Murray's report, pushed across the table, had it all. George Henry Tyrell Harding. Aged forty-six. Address: La Rêve, Brookside, Kent. Second address, London. Married. Two children.

Pel's eyes slipped down the list of activities. Harding's record was remarkably like Maurice Tagliatti's. He had driven lorries after he left school, but had somehow got into the property market and made a small fortune and had since gone into haulage and owned a string of shops and land. He had a record which included shoplifting, assault on a policeman, and possessing a gun without a licence.

'Also suspected of the murder of a police informer,' Murray said. 'But we have no information. It was a long time ago, and these days he tries to look respectable.'

Like Maurice Tagliatti, Pel thought.

Harding's line had covered everything you could think of. He had started as a builder's apprentice and had ended up with an estimated five million in the bank. And that wasn't in francs but in pounds and needed to be multiplied by ten to produce a French figure. This was not certain, of course, because nobody really knew. He had a house in Kent worth five hundred thousand pounds, with a swimming pool, a squash court, and all the rest. He enjoyed playing the role of lord of the manor.

Perhaps, Pel thought, that was where Maurice Tagliatti had got the idea.

He skated Maurice Tagliatti's record across. Murray studied it for a while before he made a comment.

'Twin souls,' he said. He sat back in his chair and lit a pipe that filled the room with acrid smoke. In defence – but only in defence, he persuaded himself – Pel lit a cigarette.

'We knew Harding went to Dijon on business in May,' Murray went on. 'And that he was in France about the time your man was murdered. We've been having him watched and he's known to have taken a flight to Paris where he had a hire car waiting. We think his associates were in France, too, at the appropriate times. He's also had some heavy telephone bills lately and seems to be making calls to France. We had a tap put on his telephone and his contact now's a chap called Ourdabi. Know him?'

'We certainly do.'

'Well, whatever they're up to, it isn't finished yet because they're still talking. They're very guarded, of course, and let nothing drop.'

'So what are they involved in?' Pel leaned forward. 'What's this Harding been dealing in? Drugs?'

Murray sat back in his chair and eyed Pel for a long time as if wondering if he could keep a secret. 'No,' he said eventually. 'Not drugs. Gold.'

'Gold?' Pel spoke in awed tones. He had never dealt in gold before. 'Bullion?'

This was big enough to explain Maurice Tagliatti's attempt at an alibi with the disguised Devreux. It was big enough to explain why he was dead.

'You remember the Brinks Mat robbery?'

'Yes.' Everybody had heard about the Brinks Mat job at Heathrow when the crooks had got into a security warehouse near the airport. They'd probably heard of it in China.

'They poured petrol over the guards and threatened to set them on fire unless they handed over the combination numbers of the vaults. They handed them over. They got away with twenty-six million pounds' worth of gold, diamonds and other things.'

'Was Harding behind it?'

'Not that one. Harding set up his own operation. Hung a hand grenade round the security man's neck and threatened to pull the pin and run unless he handed over. He also handed over. They got away with fifteen million pounds' worth of gold bullion. It wasn't discovered until the following morning.'

'What happened to it?'

'We don't know. We've been watching the banks and these days they have to tell us if they get unexpectedly large sums of money that might be from drugs or things of this sort. But there hasn't been a whisper. Perhaps it's in Switzerland. Or in the Middle East. We've checked Germany, Holland, Belgium, Italy and France, and we're working on Scandinavia. Nothing's turned up. We searched Harding's house and we've had surveillance on it ever since, but there's no hint that he's even interested. We have no proof and the gold hasn't been heard of since. We feel Harding masterminded it but he's the sort who doesn't get his hands dirty and he'd arrange for a quick disposal of the loot.'

'With Maurice Tagliatti,' Pel agreed. 'How was the gold moved?'

'It was taken from the warehouse in an airport food van, transferred at some point to another van, and driven out of the airport by one of the service gates and more than likely taken out of the country.'

'By air?'

'We thought of that, of course, and made the necessary inquiries.'

'I expect Maurice fixed it. He'd been to the Middle East and the States. He must have been trying to set up the route.'

'And did he?'

'I don't think so. Or why would he be killed?'

Darcy's reaction was the same as Pel's. He laid down the report Pel had brought back and looked up.

'Gold? And it's here?'

'It must be. Check the hotels, Daniel. For the days before Maurice was killed. We're looking for Englishmen – Geebees.'

Braxton turned up on the books of a hotel in Auxerre and Coy on the books of the Hôtel Central in Dijon where, to their surprise, they also found George Harding's name.

'All nice and handy,' Pel said. 'For when Maurice moved from Lordy.' He lit a cigarette slowly and studied the end of it. 'What do people do with gold when they steal it, Daniel? Do they ever saw a little bit off the end and try to get rid of it to a jeweller?'

Darcy grinned. 'Most of what appears nowadays goes through the Middle East and from there to India which is regarded as a traditional sponge for it. Its value seems to be that it's indestructible and there's no difficulty in changing its identity. You simply melt it down, remould it and put another stamp on it – South Africa, Crédit Suisse, whatever. The basic motive for wanting it seems to be fear. If you have to vanish overnight you can stow enough of it in your pockets to tide you over to easier times. That makes it particularly useful to shaky African dictators. Europe's greatest hoarders are us. The French. It was those two world wars in a generation and all those devaluations of the franc since 1914.'

'It's a convenient way of avoiding death duties,' Pel agreed.

'Doesn't pay to disguise it, though,' Darcy said. 'Some type once did. As saucepans. He painted them black and hid them in his cellar, thinking his family would find them when he died. Unfortunately they didn't like his old pots and pans and sold the lot to a junkman. They never got them back.'

fourteen

While Pel suddenly began to make headway, Nosjean, busy with the Sondermann case, remained exactly where he was.

He sat at his desk and studied two lots of broken fragments in front of him. They were in two neat piles, one the remains of the statuette he had found near the sun lounge, the other what was left of the crockery from the tea tray. But his mind wasn't really on them. It was occupied with Mijo and he was worried because she was still wanting to meet his family. She had been working round to it, in fact, much more persistently of late. 'How about Saturday?' she had asked.

Nosjean wasn't keen on Saturday. He wasn't keen on Sunday, Monday, Tuesday, Wednesday, Thursday or Friday either, because he had a feeling the meeting would be a disaster, anyway. Stilted conversation, long silences, stiffnesses all through lunch of the sort that all the wine in the world wouldn't change. It bothered him as much as the Sondermann case.

Sitting up and thrusting the matter from his thoughts, he stared at the two piles on his desk again. Finally he pushed the remains of the statuette to one side – there was a puzzle there but he didn't know what it was – and concentrated on the pieces of china from the tea tray. There was an explanation for the statuette, he felt, but it wasn't important, and the china was. He began moving the pieces with a pencil, spreading them out until he had separated the parts which seemed to make up the cup, saucer, teapot, milk jug and sugar basin. There seemed to be more left than he'd expected. Puzzled, he headed for Claudie Darel's desk. 'I'd like a bit of help,' he said.

Indicating the broken china, he pointed with the pencil to the portions he had separated. 'That lot', he said, 'makes up the cup, saucer, milk jug, teapot and sugar basin. That lot – ' the pencil moved ' – seem to be the handles. Right?'

'Right. What's the trouble?'

'Well, normally I don't drink out of cups and saucers, I usually make do with a mug. So does Mijo – '

'How's it going with Mijo?'

'She wants to meet the family.'

He had thought Claudie might be sympathetic, but she wasn't. 'It makes sense,' she said. 'It would make her feel more secure.'

Nosjean sighed and Claudie indicated the broken crockery. 'The china,' she said.

Nosjean nodded, coming down to earth. 'How many handles do you make?' he asked.

'Why?'

'I think there might be more than there ought to be and I thought I'd ask you.'

Claudie smiled. 'I usually drink out of mugs, too,' she admitted. 'But I'll have a go.'

Carefully, they began to separate the fragments of pink and white china. Apart from a few missing fragments, they made up the handle and spout of the teapot. That was easy because they were heavier than the rest. The milk jug was easier, too, because that was also thicker. The sugar basin wasn't too difficult, because it appeared to have had a handle on either side, as they discovered by matching the fragments with the sides from which they had broken.

'Just leaves the cup,' Nosjean said.

Claudie poked around a little more then she began to frown.

'That's funny,' she said.

'That's what I thought.'

'There seem to be two handles.'

'That's also what I thought.'

'Did the cup have two handles?'

'If it did, it was the only one in the set that did. I looked at the others.'

'Suppose', she said, 'that we try to put them together.'

Nosjean went out and bought the kind of glue the experts used, and by the end of two hours they had what looked roughly like two cups, each with one handle.

'Two cups,' Nosjean said. 'Not one. That means – '

'That she had a visitor. Somebody she knew well enough to offer a cup of tea to.'

On the Monday morning, Nosjean started staring at the broken crockery again. The weekend hadn't been the disaster he had expected. Mijo had gone down well with his family but his sisters had firmly ruled out the idea of them living together.

'Without a wedding,' his sister Antoinette had decided, 'the union can't be blessed by the Church.'

And that was that. Between them they seemed to have settled his fate. All the same – he cheered up a little – as a fate, with Mijo it didn't look as if it would be too bad.

He dragged his thoughts back to the job in hand, and he suddenly remembered that, quite by accident, in the Tagliatti case they had learned there had been two other people in the car with Maurice when he was killed, not one. His head lifted. There had been two people in the room sitting at the tea tray when Annabelle-Eugénie Sondermann had been attacked, not one as they had originally thought. Had the attacker been there in the room with her all the time?

And the broken statuette? *Why* was it broken? Was it deliberate? Had it been broken out of spite or in a rage? Unlike the china from the tea tray, the statuette had produced fingerprints. But they were useless because everybody in the neighbourhood seemed to have handled it. He could only assume it had been a beautiful piece of work and people had touched it in admiration, as they often did with *objets d'art*.

He thought of the china from the tea tray again. Two cups, and an attacker who was not a stranger to Annabelle-Eugénie Sondermann but someone she knew well enough to ask into her house, for whom she had fetched another cup to offer tea.

After his visit to his home, he had deposited Mijo back at the flat they shared and headed for the Impasse Chévire. His inquiries covered everyone who lived there.

So far he hadn't been able to pin anything on anyone. Young Mahé seemed to have a clear alibi, as did all the other males. Come to that, so did all the women.

For a long time he sat staring at the photographs of the scene of the crime. Eventually, he began to concentrate on that of the battered tea tray on which the china had been standing when the attack had taken place. It had been blown up to actual size and in the centre of the tray was the splintered hole. It looked as if it had been made, as both Leguyader and Nosjean had decided, by someone hitting it with a poker. It was a light tray with a thin wooden base and sides of thicker wood. He studied it carefully. It was possible to see the wood ash adhering to the edges of the hole.

He went in search of Claudie Darel again, to try on her another idea that had occurred to him.

'I thought it had been done by the poker,' he explained. 'I thought perhaps the china was upset because she snatched up the tray to defend herself when she was attacked. As a shield, sort of thing. Now I wonder. It was face-down when I found it. On the carpet, among the broken china. I assumed it was the poker that made the hole because it had wood ash round the edges. Now I'm beginning to wonder if it was.'

Claudie examined the photograph for a moment then she studied her shoe.

Nosjean caught her eye. 'That's what I wondered,' he said.

Once again Nosjean sat staring at the repaired cups. He was almost there, he felt. But young Mahé's alibi seemed sound. So, for that matter, did those of the men who were involved. Dr Kersta had been in his surgery. Auvignac seemed to have been in his office at Métaux de Dijon where he worked. Mahé, who was as neat and small as his wife, had been busy in the large and expensive china shop he ran in the Rue de la Liberté. It was from there, in fact, that Annabelle-Eugénie Sondermann had bought the tea set she'd been using when she'd been attacked. The other men Nosjean had interviewed – the architect, the lawyer – hardly seemed to come into it.

The women?

Nosjean frowned. Madame Auvignac seemed a likely candidate from her size alone. Yet all the women seemed to be in the clear, because all those involved had been able to see each other in their kitchens across the central green of the little close. Madame Kersta had admitted leaving hers for a while – 'There was a short wildlife programme on television,' she had said – but she was prepared to confirm that she had seen Madame Auvignac and Madame Mahé in their kitchens. Madame Auvignac and Madame Mahé had offered the same sort of corroboration for her.

And, if one of them had slipped out, gone down the garden, through the wood and into Annabelle-Eugénie's house and had then sat down to have a cup of tea with her, it would surely have occupied an hour or more, and they had all been prepared to swear they had seen each other in and out of their kitchens at the appropriate time. The most anyone had appeared to be missing was Madame Kersta's quarter of an hour with the television, and a quarter of an hour wasn't sufficient to take tea, half kill Annabelle-Eugénie and return without being missed.

There seemed to be something wrong somewhere.

Nosjean stared again at the two crooked cups he and Claudie had built from the fragments of crockery that had been found. Prélat had been unable to produce any good prints, save one scrappy one belonging to Annabelle-Eugénie which had showed on one of the smaller broken pieces. But that puzzled Nosjean because if someone had taken tea with her, surely there would have been other prints, or parts of prints.

Then, studying the two lopsided cups, Nosjean noticed something he hadn't noticed before. One of them, the one that contained the fragment that bore Annabelle-Eugénie's dab, had the brown stain in the bottom where the dregs of her tea had dried. Tea always left a brown stain and there it was. But what was odd was that the other cup *didn't* show the stain. It was clean and white as if it hadn't been used.

Nosjean swung round and turned his attention to the photograph of the tray again and then, suddenly, the whole thing came together.

fifteen

Pel was going through the papers Murray had given him. It was obvious now what had so occupied Maurice Tagliatti that he had found it necessary to appear to be in the city when he had set off disguised for some destination still unknown. A gold bullion robbery was big enough to account for the Manoir de Lordy, too. That must have cost him a packet, but big, important jobs usually did cost a packet and he had done the job thoroughly, even to having the place redecorated and painted to make it appear the move was permanent, not temporary.

So – was the gold at Lordy? It didn't seem so or they would surely have turned it up in their search. But Maurice had obviously had it and the fact that he'd been well and truly bumped off seemed to indicate that his English partners had been rather more than a little upset. All of which seemed to show that the gold hadn't been sold and was still around, but that Maurice had relied too heavily on his bodyguards and one of them had shopped him.

Cavalin? Sidonie? Vlada Preradovic? One of his men with a grudge? Ourdabi, for instance? Or was it simply that the English partner had found out and produced his professional killers? After all, he wouldn't have had to look in the yellow pages for them. He already knew them well, it seemed. So had Maurice's move to Burgundy been merely to duck out of sight for a while until things blew over? Surely not. Maurice was too old a hand to imagine that someone he'd cheated out of several million francs of loot would just forget it. So what had been going on? Was *this* the explanation for Devreux appearing dressed in Maurice's clothes in the city on the day he died? So that Maurice could disappear in a different direction to organise the moving of the gold?

It seemed pretty obvious now that the gold had been in Léon's shop at some point. But it wasn't there now because they had taken the place apart, and there was that report of the policeman who had seen Léon loading cartons in his estate car to indicate that Léon had got the wind up and moved it.

Pel shifted the papers around for a while then looked up at Darcy. 'Suppose you were moving gold from England to France, Daniel,' he asked. 'How would you do it?'

'Only one safe way, Patron,' Darcy said. 'By air.'

'They seem to have followed that thought up in London and got nowhere.'

'If it came to France, it could be across the Channel in an hour. If it landed here, it could be unloaded and gone within a couple of hours of the robbery.'

'Murray checked all airports. There was no record of any aircraft taking off that couldn't be accounted for.'

'What about small airports?'

'He checked those, too.'

'How about a field – an ordinary field?'

'It would be a heavy load.'

'There are aircraft to carry them, Patron. And there are fields which would be – or could be made to be – suitable. All it needs is flat land. Could it be that some farmer was paid to look the other way? I've been checking the weather for that period. There'd been a long dry spell with wind. The ground must have been rock-hard.'

'Get in touch with the airfields in this area, Daniel. Find out if anything arrived from England on that day.'

Nosjean knew now who had made the attack on Annabelle-Eugénie Sondermann, and it was time to make his move.

Trying to see Dr Kersta, he was put off with the plea that Dr Kersta was busy. Nosjean dug his heels in, however, and insisted, and in the end one of the doctor's patients had to wait instead. Kersta was a tall man with a shock of grey hair that stood straight up from his head like a patch of wheat stubble.

'I thought we'd been through all this once,' he snapped.

'We have, of course,' Nosjean admitted, studying Kersta's neat doctor's fingers. 'But we haven't quite finished our inquiries.'

Having got the doctor to the starting gate, he found him not unwilling but, on the other hand, none too willing either. He seemed to hedge at some of the questions, so that Nosjean began to grow impatient.

'Do you burn wood in your fireplace, doctor?' he asked.

'Yes, of course,' Kersta said. 'We all do. With the woods at the back, it's easy to get. There's always plenty there.'

'What about the ash when the grate's emptied? What happens to it?'

Kersta looked puzzled. 'Is this to do with – with the attack on Mademoiselle Sondermann?'

'Yes, it is.'

'I don't see – '

'I assure you,' Nosjean said, 'it's very important. What happens to the ash?'

'We put it on the garden. It's supposed to do the soil good. It contains potash which is a first-rate fertiliser. We use it a lot. I'm a great believer in wood ash.' Kersta paused. 'Look, what are you getting at, young man?'

It was that 'young man' that niggled Nosjean. He wasn't all that old and he certainly looked younger than he was, but he was no fool. 'Mademoiselle Sondermann was attacked while she was taking tea,' he rapped back smartly.

'So?'

'By someone she knew.'

Kersta's expression changed. 'Oh?' he said.

'Someone who entered her garden from the woods and went into the house. She wasn't surprised because she knew them well. She even fetched another cup and invited them to take tea. Perhaps because she was nervous. She had reason to be.'

'Are you suggesting', Dr Kersta said coldly, 'that whoever attacked her had been sitting down to tea with her?'

Nosjean was silent for a moment. 'That's what it looked like,' he agreed. 'But it isn't what happened. The intruder didn't sit down to tea. It didn't take that long.'

'So it *was* someone from the wood?'

'It was certainly someone who arrived from the wood. You see, there was someone who had been seeing rather more of Mademoiselle Sondermann than he should.'

'Are you trying to suggest something, young man?'

'Mademoiselle Sondermann was popular, doctor. With men as well as with women. She had had quite a reputation when she was young. The habit hadn't left her. And you visited her regularly, doctor, didn't you? Young Mahé has sharp eyes. You had good reason to, of course. For her asthma. But was it always for her asthma?'

'What are you suggesting?'

'You tell *me,* doctor. The layout of your garden is different from the others. You have a flowerbed at the end of it by the wood. You have to cross it to get into the wood. It has a lot of ash on it. Anybody crossing it would get the ash on their shoes. They'd lose most of it as they passed through the wood, of course, but you use a *lot,* don't you? You've just said so. And even going through the wood didn't brush it *all* off. Some of it was still there when the tray was trodden on and it was on the tray when it was found after the attack.'

'Are you suggesting I attacked Mademoiselle Sondermann?'

'No, doctor, I'm not.'

'Surely to God not my wife? Are you suggesting this awful thing was done by my wife? Because she thought I was having an affair with Mademoiselle Sondermann?'

'You *were* having an affair with her, weren't you?'

Kersta gestured irritably, as if that were an unimportant point. 'How could it have been my wife?' he said. 'She was in her kitchen the whole time. She told me. She was even seen there.'

'No, doctor, she wasn't. The programme on television she said she watched was on all right, but she wasn't watching it. She had decided to have it out with Mademoiselle Sondermann. She was determined to protect her marriage. She had found out about you, hadn't she?'

Kersta was silent for a while then he nodded heavily. Nosjean tried to imagine the struggle going on in Annabelle-Eugénie's house. Ground down by the moving feet as they fought, the china gave an indication of how violent the struggle had been. But nobody had heard because the two women had fought in silence, each with her own reason for wishing that nothing should be discovered of the confrontation.

'There was no talking,' Nosjean said. 'Just a sudden explosive quarrel. The tea tray was turned over and your wife trod on it. Her foot went through it. It looked as if the poker had made the hole – but it didn't. It was a woman's high heel. I expect when she saw what she'd done she was horrified and she ran home at once. She was back within minutes and nobody missed her.'

Kersta said nothing.

'She tried to kill Mademoiselle Sondermann because, of you,' Nosjean said quietly. 'It's lucky she didn't manage it. If she had, the charge would have been one of murder.'

Kersta sighed, deflated, and, picking up the telephone, spoke to his receptionist. 'Please cancel all my appointments,' he said. There was a pause. 'Yes, all of them. For the rest of the day and after that, too. I'm going to be rather busy for some time. I may even retire. It's a domestic crisis.'

As he put down the telephone, he looked at Nosjean, a handsome man all concern for his wife and full of remorse for the life he'd led her. 'I'll come with you,' he said. 'I'd better be with her when you see her. She'll need me.'

Madame Kersta sat in a chair in Pel's office, a damp, crumpled heap barely able to talk through her tears. Her husband stood behind her, all attention, helping her with her statement. Most of his concern seemed to Pel to be false and he noticed that he was always quick to interrupt when she began to talk about him.

'Get him out of here, Daniel,' he said quietly. 'I want to talk to her alone with Nosjean.'

Kersta's protest was loud but Darcy put a large hand on his shoulder and propelled him from the room.

Madame Kersta seemed more at ease without her husband, and answered Nosjean's questions willingly enough. She seemed to have given up hope for the future. The chances were that a lawyer would plead a *crime passionnel* and she'd probably get away with it, but she didn't seem to have much faith in a life with her husband.

She admitted the attack on Annabelle-Eugénie Sondermann. 'Yes,' she whispered. 'I did it. She'd wrecked my marriage. I went to see her. But she laughed. I was furious. I picked up that statuette she prized so much. I said, "You smashed my marriage, just as I'm going to smash this" and I dropped it on the floor. Perhaps it was too much. Perhaps she didn't mind about being found out even. But she thought a lot about that statuette and that's what started us fighting.

'She called me names and said I was pathetic and always ill. She and my husband made me ill and I was livid. I went for her. She knocked over the tray and we struggled. Then I picked up the poker. I don't think I realised what I was doing. I think I was really defending myself at first. I hit her with it. More than once, I think.' Madame Kersta seemed to dissolve, collapsing in the chair in a huddled heap. 'I'm sorry. I didn't intend to do it but she was so... so...'

As she became silent, Pel leaned forward. 'Had this affair been going on a long time?'

'Oh, yes.' Madame Kersta sighed. 'Ages. I knew about it, of course. But I thought he'd grow tired. He was never very trustworthy, I suppose. I often thought he was involved with things he shouldn't be, but I was never certain.'

'What sort of things?'

'I don't know. I don't know anything any more.'

That afternoon, Lacocq followed Nosjean in clearing up another of their outstanding cases. Or at least, he was responsible for the arrest.

As Pel was leaving, he appeared in the entrance hall of the Hôtel de Police pushing a man in front of him. The man was well dressed, clean and in a smart suit, but there was a faint look of a ferret about him; there was blood on his shirt and on his face, and a huge bruise on his forehead. Lacocq looked three metres tall.

'Got him, Patron,' he said with satisfaction. 'This is the type who goes round robbing old ladies by pretending to want to buy their property. He reads the papers, finds out what's for sale, and then goes to have a look round the house.'

'He looks a little battered,' Pel observed. 'You, Lacocq?'

Lacocq grinned. 'Not me, Patron. He called at 11, Rue Marc-Béguin. The old dear there, Madame Pliat, keeps a large dog and he said he was scared of dogs so she locked it in the kitchen and proceeded to show him round the house. Upstairs, he tried to lock her in the bathroom, but she's stronger than she looks and she keeps a pick handle handy. She managed to reach it and gave him a couple with it. He went down the stairs on his head, so she let the dog out of the kitchen, and it sat on his chest with its teeth bared while she telephoned us.'

It was a good end to the day and, in addition, though nobody was aware of it, something had occurred that afternoon that was to set in train a series of events that were to start things moving in the Tagliatti case.

Yves Pasquier broke the window of the *salon*. The muddy football, which he had been pounding against the outside wall for an hour, not only scattered shards of glass everywhere, it bounced – complete with mud – across the white carpet, hit the wall of the *salon*, rebounded on to the adjoining wall, knocked over the standard lamp and finally came to rest on the settee.

sixteen

Deciding that her son at home was far more of a problem than her son at school, Marguérite Pasquier telephoned the Hôtel de Police and asked to be connected to Pel.

Misset took the call. 'Who is it?' he demanded.

'Madame Pasquier. Chief Inspector Pel knows me. I live next door.'

'Is it police business, madame?'

'Yes, very much so.'

Misset was skilful at listening in to telephone calls and when he heard Madame Pasquier asking Pel if it were safe for her son to return to school, it set him thinking. One night on duty, he had happened to hear the Chief talking to the Procureur. They were both being very cagey in what they were saying but he had heard the Proc' say something about '...we know the car the killers used was seen before the crime...' It wasn't much, but it caused Misset to remember something he'd heard a week or so before that. Nobody had told him anything but he'd caught the tail-end of a talk Darcy had been having with Pel when he'd barged into his office. Darcy had become silent as soon as Misset had appeared but he'd caught the words '...the boy who saw the car'.

Misset was an expert at putting things together, and he was always prepared to guess at what he didn't know for certain, while Sarrazin, the freelance reporter, was always prepared to accept what he offered as gospel, even when he believed it wasn't. The other newspapermen, Fiabon, of *France Dimanche,* and Ducrot, of *Paris Soir,* were more wary, while Henriot, of the local rag, was always far too concerned with his relations with city people to use gossip, Sarrazin, however, never failed to take a chance.

The day after Marguérite Pasquier's call, her husband appeared in the Hôtel de Police asking for Pel. He was worried.

'I'm a bit concerned,' he said. 'Yves is only a little boy and I'm afraid he might say something he shouldn't. It might slip out. Especially now he's back at school. And if it did and it became known he was a witness to something that led up to a murder, he might be in danger.'

Pel took the matter to the Chief who considered it for a while before agreeing that, with the inquiries beginning to build up and with the lead they had received from London, perhaps somebody *should* be given the job of looking after the boy.

Pel telephoned Pasquier. 'If I arrange for a man to be on duty at your house,' he asked, 'can you feed him and give him somewhere to sleep? Surveillance', he explained, 'usually means three men working in sequence to relieve each other, but three men is a lot when we've got so many inquiries on. We've already got a man living near Lordy as part of a family. If you could agree, it would also be much more efficient because it would mean the boy was never alone. The man's name's Morell and he's young, well brought up and house-trained. He'll give you no trouble.'

Pasquier agreed at once. 'It'll please Marguérite,' he said. 'She's been a bit worried about the possibilities. We'll look after him. He can have the bedroom next to Yves'. It's not very big but it has everything he'll need, and we'll put the portable television in there.'

'No television,' Pel growled. 'He'll be there to keep an eye on the boy, not on the television.'

That evening, Pel drove Morell to the Pasquier house. Pasquier was all for offering him a drink but Morell caught Pel's eye and stoutly refused.

While his room was being inspected, Pel slipped to the bedroom next door to explain matters to Yves Pasquier.

'You've got a guard on you,' he said.

'Me?' The boy's eyes shone.

'You're an important witness.'

'Will I have to appear in court?'

'It's possible.'

'Who is it?'

'His name's Morell. Patrice Morell. He's young. He'll probably play boules with you. He'll escort you to school, remain there waiting for you, and bring you home in the evening. You're to do exactly as he tells you.'

'Does he have a gun?'

'He has a gun.'

'Can I see it?'

'So long as you don't touch it. I don't want him shot by you.'

With the Pasquiers' fears quietened, Pel left Morell with orders to telephone at once if he had any doubts.

The following afternoon, Brochard appeared in the office on one of his regular visits to report. He was still occupied with his surveillance of the Manoir de Lordy, and he was thoroughly enjoying himself. Normally he shared a flat with Debray in the city but they were neither of them good housekeepers and both hated cooking, so that they had to live on odds and ends of frozen food. At the Roblais farm Brochard was fed like a fighting cock. Old Roblais knew what he was up to but, like all hill folk, he kept his mouth shut and didn't ask questions, and since Brochard continued to mend fences that hadn't been touched for years, he saw that he was well fed and watered.

The only snag was the Roblais' daughter, Héloïse. She had noted Brochard at once. Brochard was a good-looking youngster with a sly sense of humour and Héloïse Roblais liked to follow him around, showing him the stables and the quiet corners at the back of the haystacks, offering to help him with fences that were well away from the house. She wasn't bad-looking and had a good figure, but she had knee caps like house bricks and Brochard already had a girl in the city.

From time to time he appeared in the office, on what were accepted by the people of Lordy as his days off. He had been passed off as a cousin and, like the Roblais family, nobody asked questions. When he appeared in the office, nobody asked questions there either, except to comment that he was getting fat. Misset, of course, was always interested.

As Brochard left to return to Lordy, Misset looked up. 'You still on surveillance?'

'Yes. It's infectious. Morell's at it now.'

'Where's he?'

Brochard didn't answer but that evening when Morell reported by telephone, Misset took the call. It was short, to the point and gave nothing away. But Misset was intrigued and tried to probe. Morell's orders were to keep his mouth shut, however, and like everyone else in the Hôtel de Police he knew Misset well enough to say nothing.

All the same, a few cog wheels started churning in Misset's mind. Son. School. 'The boy who saw the car...' 'We know the killers' car was seen before the crime...' Madame Pasquier. All the little snippets Misset had heard began to add up.

When he reached home, he waited until his wife was out of the way, then dialled Sarrazin's number. Sarrazin represented half a dozen newspapers round France and was naturally always eager to be first with information. They talked for a while, exchanging opinions, and Sarrazin sat on the information for a couple of days. He knew Pel and was wary of him, but in the end he telephoned *La Torche,* one of the periodicals he represented, and began to indulge in a long-winded conversation.

Pel was feeling gloomy as he appeared downstairs next day. He was never functioning on all cylinders until he had smoked his first cigarette of the morning.

Finishing his breakfast, he kissed his wife and, clutching his briefcase, headed for his car. He had hardly sat down in the chair in his office when Darcy appeared and tossed down a periodical on his desk. It was *La Torche* and the first thing Pel saw were the headlines.

TAGLIATTI CASE SENSATION. BOY WITNESS IN
DANGER. SAW KILLERS' CAR.

The roof almost lifted.

Sarrazin and *La Torche* had worked hard. Most of the details had come from the records, from the street directories and the office for the registration of births, deaths and marriages. They were short on facts about the reason for the danger Yves Pasquier was in, but they had his name, age and address, his parents' names and what his father did for a living. It was clear from the story that Yves Pasquier had been a witness to something important – although *La Torche* remained vague on exactly what it was – and the facts were being lapped up all the way across France.

Almost before Pel had finished, Henri Pasquier was in the entrance hall demanding to see him. He was livid and it took a lot of diplomacy to calm him down.

'He's my son,' Pasquier said. 'Nothing should have been given to the press!'

'Nothing has been given to the press,' Pel insisted. 'But newsmen have their own means of finding out things – not always honest, I'm afraid. Have no fear, I'll look into it and Morell will be told to be even more alert.'

The news flew round the Hôtel de Police and within minutes Pel was having everybody in and questioning them. Though *La Torche* knew remarkably little, what they had published was enough to direct the limelight on to the Pasquiers' house. Only Pel, Darcy, the Chief and the Procureur knew the full facts, but nothing had been committed to paper so it was impossible that anyone could have seen anything. Those who had discussed the matter went over the conversations they'd had and none of them had said anything to anyone who might have provided *La Torche* with the story. Unable to accuse anybody of anything, Pel called the pressmen into his office but they all blankly denied any knowledge of where the story had come from, and all *La Torche* would say when he spoke to the editor was that the story had come from 'sources'.

They had Misset in, behaving like a dog threatened with a bath. He didn't look them in the eye – Misset believed in never looking authority in the eye in case authority noticed him – but no papers had been lost, no files had been switched or gone missing, no telephone calls had been tapped. Misset had covered himself well and, though Pel had his suspicions, there was nothing they could accuse him of.

There were only two airfields within the city area. One, on the flat land to the south, was partly military with a few Mystère and Mirage jets, but took an occasional short haul liner from other parts of France. The other field was on the N71 beyond Talant, on a flat stretch of land high above the city as you climbed out towards St Seine l'Abbaye.

Darcy had drawn a blank at the southern airfield. All flights were logged and there had been no flights from England. The airfield towards St Seine l'Abbaye was different.

'Sure,' the controller said after a long silence while he looked up the log books. 'There were three that day. A Nord 262 from Luton. Twenty-five passengers. Some sort of archaeological society from Dijon who hired it to take them to England and back. A Cessna F172 from Shoreham. It landed at St Malo and refuelled, then came on here. It dropped a passenger and left for Toulouse. There was also a Centre Est 350 from Gatwick. That's bigger. Short haul, light cargo.'

'That', Darcy said, 'sounds like the one I'm interested in. Is it fast?'

'Oh, yes.'

'What time did it land?'

'Late. We normally close down after dark here, but we'd had a request to stay open. We do if we're asked. It was flying machinery for Métaux de Dijon. They said it was urgent and we arranged for it to be met. They had a van waiting. The machinery wasn't too big but it was heavy. It was transferred in no time and the van left. The machine took off for St Etienne.'

'Who was the pilot?'

'What's he done?'

'Never mind what he's done,' Darcy said. 'I'd just like to talk to him.'

The controller shrugged. 'The log gives Pierre-Paul Genin. He lives in the city. Rue Joigny. He divides his time between here and St Etienne. He'll fly anything.'

Pierre-Paul Genin was tall, handsome, hawk-faced and grey-haired. He was no longer young but Darcy suspected that he was younger than he looked.

'Sure,' he admitted cheerfully. 'I flew the Centre Est.'

Darcy studied him. He had spent some time on the telephone because, like a good barrister, he preferred to know some of the answers before he asked the questions. 'Why?' he asked.

Genin grinned. 'Because they paid me to,' he said.

'Who did?'

'These people who hired me.'

'Which people would that be?'

'They said they were from Métaux de Dijon and that they had to pick up spare parts and would I fly them. Of course I would. A trip like that's better than half-baked little flips round the countryside.'

'What was the machinery?'

'I don't know.'

'Didn't you hear it mentioned?'

'No.'

'Would it interest you', Darcy asked, 'to know I've been in touch with Métaux de Dijon and they say they had no machinery due that day from England. In fact they have no machines at all that would require any spare parts from England.'

Genin suddenly looked wary. 'Well, that's what I was told,' he said.

'Would it surprise you if I told you that what you flew in was probably contraband or stolen goods?'

Genin frowned. 'Yes, it would.'

Darcy hadn't failed to recall what Julien Claude Roth had told him about Léon's visitors. One, he had said, had been tall, handsome and grey-haired and looked like the hero of one of the American soap operas that filled television time. Genin seemed to fit the description exactly.

'What happened?' he asked. 'What were your instructions?'

Genin shrugged. 'I was told to have the machine at Gatwick and to wait.'

'And then?'

'This van drew up.'

'Which van?'

'It was an airport laundry van. At least it had a sign on it that indicated it was.'

'Go on.'

'They unloaded the machinery from it.'

'From a laundry van? Didn't you query it?'

'I was paid to fly,' Genin said. 'Not ask questions.'

Darcy smiled. 'I've checked with Gatwick,' he pointed out. 'No Centre Est 350 left there that day. It couldn't have been Gatwick.'

Genin began to hedge. 'Well, when I say Gatwick, I don't mean Gatwick exactly. Not the airport. I mean the area.'

'Ah! What area would it be? Would it have been a private airfield?'

'Yes.'

'Which?'

'Well, it wasn't an airfield exactly. It was – well – just a field.'

'Where?'

'It was near Billingshurst. That's a town just south of Gatwick.'

'We'd be interested to know just which field.'

'I couldn't tell you. I don't know England. I was given a pinpoint and a map reference and that was that.'

'Are you suggesting that you couldn't fly there again? Didn't you mark it on your chart?'

'Yes. In pencil. I rubbed it out afterwards. You always do.'

'How about your log book? You'd have marked it in that, wouldn't you?'

Genin was beginning to grow red in the face. 'No,' he said. 'As a matter of fact I didn't. Not this time.'

'Why not?'

Genin seemed to be in trouble now. 'Well, they asked me not to. These types who arranged it.'

'Did they say why?'

'No.'

'And you didn't ask?'

'I waited as I was told, then this van appeared.'

'Didn't they introduce themselves?'

'They said they were from Métaux de Dijon, that's all, and the van was unloaded. There were several boxes. They were put aboard and I was waved away.'

'No manifests? No Customs documents? No papers of any kind?'

'I supposed the types who put it aboard had that under control.'

'Any of them fly with you?'

'One. Tall, thin chap.'

It sounded as if it might have been Cavalin.

'And you flew it to France?'

'Yes.'

'So go on. How did you take off? In the dark?'

'These types with the van shone their headlights. There was a car as well.'

'Isn't that difficult?'

'Not to me.'

'You're a good pilot?'

'Fly with my eyes shut.'

'You've done this take-off-in-the-dark stuff before?'

'Yes.'

'Why?'

'What do you mean, why?'

'It doesn't sound very safe. So why do it? Were you carrying something you shouldn't have been carrying? What about when you arrived here in France?'

'It was unloaded. The guys disappeared and that was that.'

'No documents again? Nothing to sign? Nothing at all?'

'No.'

Darcy leaned forward slightly. 'Know a type called Tagliatti?' he said.

'Never heard of him.'

'I suggest you knew you were carrying something fishy.'

'No.'

'How much were you paid?'

'The usual rate for the job.'

'I can check with the bank.'

'Look.' Genin was suddenly very worried. 'I didn't know what was going on. I don't ask questions. I just fly the aeroplane and do what I'm asked. I leave the paperwork to whoever it is who hires me.'

'If what you carried was contraband or the loot from some robbery, you realise you could be charged with being an accessory before and after the fact? You *were* involved in the scheme, weren't you?'

'No!'

'So what did these types who hired you say to you?'

'Look.' Genin was growing very nervous. 'All right, I knew it was something fishy. But it wasn't drugs.'

'How do you know it wasn't drugs? Have you handled drugs before?'

Genin began to look desperate. 'No, I haven't.'

'Never?'

There was the briefest hesitation. 'It wasn't drugs,' Genin said. 'It was too heavy.'

'As heavy as gold?'

Genin stared. 'Is that what it was?'

'It's what we think it was. You, my friend, are up to your neck in a lot of funny things. Stolen bullion. Drugs.'

Genin suddenly took a swing at Darcy. It was clumsy and Darcy dodged the blow easily, kicked Genin on the knee and, as he shouted with pain, hit him in the stomach. As he bent double, Darcy clubbed him behind the head with his clenched fist. When Genin came round he looked a lot less like the hero of a TV thriller and his hands were handcuffed behind him.

'I think we'll go to the Hôtel de Police, my friend,' Darcy said.

'You'll probably have more to tell us there.'

Faced with the evidence, Genin gave up. He identified the field where he'd landed and it was immediately passed to Goschen, who was acting as the French-speaking liaison between the Police Judiciaire and Murray at Scotland Yard.

'It's an enormous field,' he reported. 'It's obviously been prepared. It might even have been used before for other things like drugs because hedges have been removed and the ground rolled flat. It's as hard as iron, a good surface, and perfect for take-offs and landings so long as it's dry.'

'Which it would be. What about the farmer?'

'Hasn't been seen for a long time. Seems he had to go on an urgent visit to the States in early July just after the robbery. Took his wife and family and hasn't been seen since. We're trying to trace him but so far we've got nowhere. Probably deep in the heart of Texas. Got anything there that connects our man, Harding, with the theft?'

'Nothing at the moment. Is he still around?'

'Oh, he's still around,' Goschen said. 'He's the nerveless type. We're keeping him under surveillance. We have a couple of men watching his place all the time. One of these days he'll make a mistake and we'll have him. It's a pity your fly-boy didn't talk.'

It *was* a pity, and doubtless by this time Harding and whoever had murdered Maurice Tagliatti would know he hadn't talked. However, Genin turned out to be a bonus. He was a small-time operator and he had a record – an old one, but a record nevertheless – for smuggling, in the days when it was done from North Africa by fast launch. Since then, it seemed, he had learned to fly, considering it swifter, safer and more profitable. Bardolle was sent to the house where he lived with a girl and, with a little help from the local cops, found heroin in a box at the back of a wardrobe. Genin named names and a few pushers were picked up.

They were able to charge him with flying contraband, with flying to France without having recourse to Customs, with landing contraband, with failing to file a flight path, with smuggling drugs, with possessing drugs and selling drugs, with possessing a gun without a licence, and finally – happy thought – with driving an uninsured car, something they'd discovered at the last minute.

seventeen

It gave Pel enormous pleasure to be able to report to Goschen that they had picked up the pilot who had flown Murray's gold to France.

'Murray'll come over at once to talk to him,' Goschen said.

'No, he won't,' Pel said in alarm. 'It'll get to our suspects and frighten them off.'

'Murray'll howl,' Goschen warned.

'Let him howl,' Pel said. 'If we get our men, you'll get your men and probably your gold back, too. Give us a few days.'

'I'll try to persuade him.'

He didn't entirely, because Murray was on the telephone within an hour and it took all Pel's diplomacy, all his command of Rosbif, all the uses of the Entente Cordiale, to put him off. Murray finally subsided into a grumbling murmur with threats to contact the Foreign Office, Interpol, and the French Minister for Foreign Affairs, but he gave way in the end.

It was very satisfactory from a competitive point of view but, since Genin had suddenly realised that he had said too much about drugs and that it might be to his advantage to say a lot less about gold and had clammed up again, on that subject they were now facing a blank wall once more.

They had Genin's admission that he had flown the gold to France but since Maurice Tagliatti, who had masterminded it, was dead, it looked very much as if they were going to have to start all over again. They still hadn't got the gold and, with Maurice no longer among the living, they were finding it wasn't going to be easy and were just trying to work out the best way to go about tricking someone like Cavalin or Ourdabi into giving something away when Morell telephoned.

It was a few days since he had appeared at the Pasquiers' house and, with his good manners and fresh angelic face, he had won Madame Pasquier's heart. Like Brochard, he was rapidly putting on weight and he had gained an admirer for life in the small boy he was guarding.

'Patron,' he announced cautiously, 'I think the house is being watched.'

'Why do you think that?' Pel asked.

'I've noticed a black Citroën moving up and down the lane in the last day or so. I think it could be some of Maurice's people casing the joint.'

'I think so, too,' Pel agreed. 'Can you see the men inside?'

'No, Patron. Not from the house.'

'Anybody made a move?'

'No, Patron. But I bet they see me taking the boy to school and know who I am and what I'm doing.'

'What about the boy?'

'He does exactly as he's told and keeps his mouth shut. But I think every kid in the school's guessed something's going on. I've seen them nudging each other when we arrive and leave, and the headmaster looks a bit like a terrorist who's been sold a home-made bomb – he isn't sure whether it's going to blow up in his face or not.'

The following day Madame Pel took the day off to work in the garden. She was considering creating a small plot in the English manner. Pel might have liked an English garden but, since English gardens went with English weather, he preferred what he'd got. However, wearing a faded straw hat and humming one of the old tunes she liked so much, Madame busied herself near the gate.

Sur le pont de Nantes
Un bal y est donné.
La Belle Hélène
Bien y aller...

Her eyes bright and alert, she hardly moved during the whole day, despite the unexpected heat, which, in a sudden burst of enthusiasm before the winter set in, soared up into the eighties.

But that evening she sat with Pel in the *salon* looking at photographs he had brought from the Hôtel de Police. She always enjoyed what she called her 'police work'. It never amounted to much but she was shrewd, with sharp eyes, and it made her feel she was sharing her husband's life.

'That one,' she said, pointing. 'He was in the car when it came past this morning. And that one was driving it this afternoon. I noticed that they paused as they passed the Pasquiers' drive to take a good look.'

Pel poured her a weak whisky and water, then poured another, not so weak, for himself.

'Peneau,' he said. 'And Devreux. But Peneau and Devreux don't make plans. They're just heavies.'

The following morning Murray telephoned again from London. As Goschen had warned, he was howling, but he was a good policeman and, like all good policemen, he had decided it might be worth waiting if they could produce a bigger haul of villains than expected and even more worthwhile if they could recover the gold. In the end he became quite friendly.

'By the way,' he said. 'Harding. We've still got his phone tapped. And we picked up a fragment of conversation. It isn't much because they're pretty cagey but it seems to concern some chap called Pasquier. Do you know anyone called Pasquier?'

'Yes,' Pel said. 'I do.'

'It was a very oblique sort of conversation but they seem pretty concerned about him.'

'Who were they speaking to?'

'The Lordy number. This chap called Ourdabi. They talked all round the subject without saying anything but we get the impression that Pasquier could be a problem to them. Could that be so?'

'Yes, it could.'

'They seemed afraid it would lead to them. Think it's worth talking to this Pasquier?'

'I've talked to him already.'

'Who is he? One of this Tagliatti's lot?'

'No. He doesn't belong to the Tagliatti outfit.'

'Who then? A cop?'

'No,' Pel said. 'He's not a cop either. He's a little boy. Aged ten.'

Putting down the telephone, Pel yelled for Darcy.

'Daniel,' he said. 'We have to get the boy away! It's obvious someone's going to try to get at him. That *La Torche* story's put them on to him.'

'Do they read French newspapers in England, Patron?'

'I doubt it. But they do in France. And there are such things as telephones.'

As they made plans, Morell telephoned again. 'No sign of them in the lane today, Patron,' he said. 'But I think they're on the hill opposite. I borrowed Pasquier's binoculars and I can see a car up there and a couple of figures. I also saw the sun glinting on the binoculars *they're* using. I think they've been sizing this place up and they know now what they have to do and they're just waiting their chance to do it. I reckon if I took a day off they'd be in here like a shot. I stayed awake all last night.'

As he put down the telephone, Pel was silent for a moment, suddenly realising that what had happened might provide the breakthrough they had been seeking. Reaching for a pad of paper, he began hurriedly making notes.

'I think', he said, looking up at Darcy over his spectacles, 'that we might provoke our friends into making a move.'

That afternoon, there was a heavy rainstorm to let them know that autumn had really and truly arrived and it turned the ground into a quagmire. It stopped quite quickly, but when Morell's car returned from the village school it sent water flying from a big puddle that had collected outside the Pasquiers' house. Morell and the boy ran through the storm to the front door but the sun was out again ten minutes later as a figure wearing Morell's coat and the cap he affected left the house, climbed into his car and drove away. For once the house appeared to be unguarded.

A little while later, Henri Pasquier's car arrived and the driver went into the house, then Pasquier's wife appeared dressed in a bright pink dress and wearing a blue wide-brimmed hat. Going to the garage, she opened the doors, climbed into her own car and drove off through the big puddle by the front door. The car returned some time later and the same pink dress and wide-brimmed hat were seen heading into the house.

At the substation at Leu, Madame Pasquier, wearing different clothes now, was listening nervously to Pel. Alongside her was her husband, still wearing Morell's coat and clutching Morell's cap in his hand. Between them was Yves Pasquier. Using the door from the kitchen, he had climbed into the rear of Madame Pasquier's car in the garage, where he had been covered with a blanket, then his mother had returned to the kitchen and left the house by the front door, ostentatious in her pink dress and blue hat so she would be seen, and had entered the garage from the front to drive off with him still concealed. She had been firmly convinced that her son had been responsible for the *La Torche* story.

Trying to reassure her, Pel outlined his plans. 'I want you to take your son to your sister's,' he said. 'And stay there. They'll be thinking Morell's gone off duty because they saw him apparently drive away, leaving the house unguarded. So we think they'll try to get into the house tonight and make their attempt to snatch the boy. But he won't be there. Morell will, though, dressed in your husband's clothes, together with another of my officers dressed in yours.'

Out at Leu, still wearing Madame Pasquier's pink dress, Claudie Darel turned on the lights inside the Pasquier house, remaining in front of one of the open windows for some time so she could be seen. Despite the hour, she didn't close the shutters and, wearing Pasquier's dark suit, Morell moved ostentatiously about, even appearing for a brief moment in the garden.

Soon afterwards, Madame Pel got out her car and took away Madame Routy, wearing a red coat and head scarf against the chilly evening, to spend the night with her sister. Depositing her on her sister's doorstep, she then drove to the Hôtel de Police where De Troq', being small and slight, was waiting with a wig and a coat similar in colour to Madame Routy's. Half an hour later the car reappeared outside Pel's house. Pel met them in the hall and indicated the hole in the hedge where he was in the habit of meeting Yves Pasquier.

'You ought to be able to get through there,' he told De Troq'. 'I do.'

Shortly afterwards, he left the house in his car and headed in the direction of the city. At Fontaine, however, he turned off and headed back to where Darcy was waiting.

As the sun began to disappear, Claudie Darel was seen in the window of Yves Pasquier's room, talking loudly to the empty bed as if scolding a child who didn't wish to go to sleep. Then Morell, still in Pasquier's suit, called up the stairs as if he were Pasquier chiding his wife. 'Marguérite *de mon coeur*,' he said. 'Leave the boy alone. He'll go to sleep eventually.'

It all sounded very realistic.

Sitting at one of the upstairs windows in a darkened room of Pel's house, De Troq' watched carefully. Madame Pel stood in the shadows behind him.

'Do you think they'll come, Sergeant?' she asked.

As they talked, De Troq's radio rasped, as if it were clearing its throat. 'Claudie here, Patron,' it said. 'I think a car's just stopped down the lane. It has no lights but I heard its engine and a door closing.'

'Right! Stand by!' Pel's voice came back, calling the silent watchers. 'Daniel! Claudie reports a car. Move in. Are you ready, De Troq'?'

'Ready, Patron.'

'Just tell my wife to keep her head down.'

Going downstairs, De Troq' moved silently into the dark garden and headed for the hole in the hedge. In the next door garden there was a faint brief flicker of a torch. They had no idea whether the kidnap attempt would involve the smashing down of the door or the ringing of the bell. It turned out to be the bell. Faintly, the chimes came over the silence. A light went on in the hall next door, then as the front door opened, a beam of light was flung down the drive. Pel's voice came.

'Go!'

There was a yell from the next garden and Morell's voice. 'Armed police! Drop your guns!'

Stepping through the hedge, De Troq' caught sight of figures in the open doorway of the house and light on the puddle of water in the drive, with, beyond them, a glimpse of Claudie Darel, alongside her Morell, holding his pistol with both hands. There was a flurry of shots and the sound of feet on the gravel of the drive, then a dark shape appeared in front of De Troq', running fast. As he stuck his foot out, the shape went headlong, skating along the ground and throwing up a little bow wave of gravel and mud from the drive. Before he came to a stop, De Troq' was on to him. As De Troq' wrenched his arms behind him, he let out a scream of pain.

Somewhere near the gate there was another couple of shots, then silence. De Troq' hoisted his captive to his feet and dragged him towards the house. Claudie was standing in the doorway, staring at a body sprawled in the puddle in the drive. As Pel appeared out of the shadows, De Troq' arrived. 'There's one here, too, Patron.'

Then Darcy appeared with Lagé. They had Devreux in front of them, and there was blood on his sleeve. 'Just keep your hands up and think pure thoughts,' Darcy was saying. He grinned at Pel. 'Got him as he bolted for the car, Patron. I think one got away.'

The man De Troq' had nailed turned out to be Peneau and, big as he was, he looked disgusted that someone as small and neat as De Troq' had taken him.

Pel glanced round him. He seemed unsatisfied. 'Let's try Lordy,' he suggested. 'We might pick up one or two more. See if you can get through to Brochard.'

Brochard was alert and listening and he answered his radio at once.

'There are only two cars at the Manoir at the moment, Patron,' he announced. 'Cavalin's white Range Rover and Sidonie's Citroën.'

Leaving De Troq' to look after things, the cars went screaming off into the darkness. There were lights on at the Manoir and the front door was open. Prowling warily through the rooms, they found the house apparently empty.

'Upstairs,' Pel said.

The first door they came to was that of Vlada Preradovic. The room looked as though she had packed hurriedly and drawers and cupboards stood wide open. On the bed was a small suitcase, with a few items of underwear draped across it. Everything else seemed to have been cleared.

Pel turned and headed for the apartments Maurice's wife used. To his surprise, he saw the light was on and, as they burst in, Sidonie's head lifted from the pillow. With her was Cavalin.

'What in God's name! – ' Sidonie screamed.

'Get up,' Pel snapped. 'Get dressed.' He looked at Cavalin's clothes piled neatly on the chair alongside the bed. They were tidy, clean and with no sign of mud on the shoes.

'How long have you been here?'

Cavalin managed a slow smile. 'Just as long as it needed,' he said.

eighteen

This time they found out how Léon was involved and why his cellar had been so important; why, in fact, he had cuffed Julien Claude Roth about the head.

In the cellar at the Manoir they found the devices that on the previous search hadn't seemed to Misset to have any connection with what they were investigating. There was the crucible and the ladle, and, when they found traces of what looked very much like gold on them, they sent at once for an official from the Banque de France to come and give them information.

They had no sooner set that operation in motion when Darcy appeared with a set of rusting boules, a heavy plaster cast in two halves, which had obviously been taken from one of the boules, and a wooden box – clearly specially made – into which everything fitted neatly.

Pel stared at them as they were placed in front of the expert from the Banque de France. 'Is that how they make them?' he asked.

'I wouldn't know about real boules,' the expert said. 'But it's a good way to disguise gold.' He was a lean spectacled individual called Munoz and he seemed to be knowledgeable not only about gold but also about all metals and about every kind of metallic process ever invented. 'They must have been nickel-plating them,' he said.

'How?'

'Electrolysis. You learn it in physics at school.'

Having spent most of his physics lessons at the back of the class reading detective stories, Pel had not learned as much as most, and he had to admit it showed.

'Inform me,' he said.

'Well,' Munoz said, 'it's the same as electro-plating table silver. If you connect a spoon made of brass – or a fork, or whatever – to the negative terminal of a battery, and a piece of sheet silver to the positive terminal and immerse them in an electrolyte, the current passes through the silver and out through the spoon or whatever it is. The spoon, the negative electrode, is the cathode and the piece of silver the anode and, as the current flows, the silver is – to put it quite simply – transferred in particles to the spoon, which becomes coated with it until it looks like pure silver. All you have to do then is polish it. It's the same with a bar of nickel and a boule made of gold. Immerse them in the correct electrolyte – nickel sulphate or nickel chloride with a touch of boric acid – apply four volts d.c. and set the appropriate ampage and – hé op! – you have a nickel-plated gold boule.'

'And Maurice,' Pel said thoughtfully, 'having been apprenticed as a youth at an electro-plating plant, would know exactly what to do, while Bozon, who was driving him when they were shot, was a burnisher and would know how to polish up the result. Simple, when you have the facts at your fingertips.'

Munoz gestured at the thick moulded glass tank Misset and Didier Darras had found and discarded. 'They must have been using that. It's about the size they use in schools and laboratories. Manufacturing firms use enormous ones, of course, made of zinc or something. It's quite normal, of course, to electro-plate real boules. They make competition ones of treated steel or special strip steel and build them into a ball and grind them until the weight's right. The ones that aren't stainless they plate.' He gestured again at the tank, then lit a cigarette and offered the pack round. 'We've come across this sort of thing before: casting gold into different shapes and painting it or plating it with nickel or copper. Normally with gold you'd have to plate with copper first because pure metal isn't a good subject, but I don't suppose they bothered because they were only doing it to deceive people for a while.' Munoz smiled. 'Of course, the result would only *look* like chromium-plated boules because the weight would be totally wrong. The atomic weight of iron and steel is 55.85. The atomic weight of gold is 197.2, so that a gold boule would be around four times as heavy as a steel one. You couldn't possibly play with them – not unless you were Superman.'

'Would it be difficult to cast a boule of gold?' Pel asked.

'No.' Munoz was in no doubt. 'Gold's soft. Even a primitive gold beater can beat a gold bar into a film-thin sheet easily enough. They'd grease the boule with soft soap or petroleum jelly.' He fingered the rusty boule Darcy was holding. 'There are still traces on it, I notice. Then they'd pack plaster of Paris round it in the box you have there – a lot of it, to make a thick case. They'd first make a cut-out of the boule, of course, and insert it round the centre of the boule so the plaster would set in two separate halves. When the two halves were hard, they'd fix them together without the cut-out and pour the melted gold into the cast through a hole they'd have made in the top.' Munoz's hand moved to the mould. 'The hole's there. There's another at the side here to let the air out so they wouldn't get a bubble. When the gold set, they'd remove the two halves of the mould, file down the odd bits, cut off the spikes left where the holes had been, and they'd have what appeared to be a boule made of brass.'

They tried their discoveries on Cavalin. He was quite willing to admit they had got their facts right.

'They made several sets,' he said. 'They even plated some of them. But then you turned up to see Maurice and he decided it was too dangerous and shifted it all to Léon's cellar.'

He volunteered nothing else, however. 'I kept well out of it,' he said, urbane and cheerful and with his usual amused smile.

He was sitting at the other side of the table from Pel in the interview room while Darcy stood by the door. 'I wasn't one of Maurice's tame thugs,' he went on. 'I never was. I was office manager and financial adviser. That's all. Chief of Staff, you could say.'

'To a crook.'

Cavalin shrugged.

'Involved in conspiracy, accessory before and after the fact. Before and after a lot of facts.'

'All I did was handle Maurice's business.'

'*And* his wife.'

Cavalin smiled. 'Maurice had the sexual habits of a stoat. He lost interest in Sidonie years ago. He was only interested in Vlada Preradovic.'

'Where is she now?'

'Ourdabi's set her up in a flat in Marseilles somewhere. What did you expect? She's anybody's – a regular *plat du jour.*'

'Did Ourdabi set up Maurice's murder?'

'I shouldn't be surprised. He speaks a little English.'

'Honour among thieves?'

'There's no such thing.'

'And Sidonie?'

'She wasn't involved. You should let her go.'

'We shall at the right time. You know we have Devreux and Peneau? Shapron's dead.'

Cavalin shrugged. 'I warned them something would happen,' he said. 'I happen to have noticed, Chief Inspector, that you're no fool.'

'Where are Guérin, Sagassu and Ourdabi?'

'I haven't the slightest idea. I wasn't involved in that. Ourdabi was told to get the boy. I told him not to be a damn fool. But he fancies Maurice's job. Unfortunately, he doesn't have Maurice's touch. He has no patience. He's clumsy.'

'Did *he* kill Léon?'

'I expect he did. They thought he was about to go to the police.'

'Did Ourdabi know Léon had the gold?'

'No. He thought he was just being used to set up the route to Dubhai because he had a contact in the south who could work it. They'd have liked to know where it was hidden.'

'Who did know?'

'I did.'

'So where is it?'

Cavalin smiled.

'What about the bruises on Léon's face?'

'Devreux. Maurice told him to work him over. Not too much. Just enough to put some spine in him. Maurice had the gold at Lordy but then you turned up, asking questions, and he got the wind up and decided it would have to be moved. He and Bozon had changed some of it into boules but it had turned out to be a bigger job than they'd expected and they transferred everything to Léon's cellar, some of it untouched. But then the kid who worked for Léon somehow managed to get involved and Maurice got the wind up again and Léon began to panic. Maurice told Devreux to give him one, and it was decided to move the stuff again.'

Cavalin smiled. 'That one was a proper balls-up. There was that fire in the dress shop two doors away and for the next day or two there were cops and firemen all over the place. Then the night Maurice decided to do it, one of the uniformed flics turned up and Maurice had to disappear in a hurry and leave it to Léon. Léon almost died of fright. After Maurice was killed, I expect Ourdabi decided he was best out of the way.'

'Did Ourdabi know what Maurice was up to?'

'He knew who to contact to let them know Maurice's plans.'

'What *were* his plans?'

'He was going to pick up Léon and the gold from where they'd moved it and go down the motorway to this pal of Léon's in Marseilles who was going to arrange to get rid of it. That's why he fixed that elaborate alibi with Devreux in his car. Unfortunately, he let Ourdabi know his route.'

Pel lit a cigarette and pushed the pack across. Cavalin accepted one and nodded his thanks.

Pel held out his light. 'Did Ourdabi turn up at the Manoir after the attempt to kidnap the boy?' he asked.

Cavalin drew on his cigarette. 'He'd have been a damn fool if he had,' he said. 'He's gone to ground somewhere.'

'One dead,' Pel reported to the Chief. 'One in hospital with a bullet in his arm. Two in the cells. If nothing else, we seem to be whittling down Maurice's gang. Ourdabi and two others have disappeared, but I dare bet they're not far away and they'll turn up again, because they'll think Cavalin's disappeared, too. They don't know we've got him. We've tried to make it seem as if he's holed up in a hotel somewhere with Maurice's wife. In the meantime, we let Cavalin stew in Number 72 for a while. He's the sort who won't take easily to prison.'

'Does anyone?'

Pel shrugged. 'He'll worry about Tagliatti's wife,' he said. 'I think he'll try to do a deal.'

Pel's guess turned out to be a good one. Within forty-eight hours a message came from 72 Rue d'Auxonne that a prisoner, one Georges Cavalin, wished to have a word with Chief Inspector Pel.

Pel looked at Darcy. 'I'll see him,' he said.

Cavalin appeared during the afternoon. He was handcuffed to two policemen but he was properly dressed and looked clean. The only indication that he might not be enjoying himself was the fact that he hadn't shaved. He didn't waste any time getting down to business.

'I know who murdered Maurice,' he announced.

'So do I,' Pel said. 'Now.'

'They're English.'

'So I understand. I'd like to meet them.'

Cavalin paused. 'I could get them over here for you,' he said.

'How?'

'By telling them where the gold is.'

'Where is it?'

Cavalin gave a small smile. 'I want a deal, Chief.'

'What sort of deal?'

'Immunity for Sidonie. Just leave her be.'

'Is that all? What about you?'

'I'll take what's coming.'

Pel's eyebrows lifted and Cavalin smiled. 'You're looking at a touch of honour, Chief,' he said. 'It's terrifying when you come up against it face to face. Sidonie's not involved and I'll tell the court so if necessary. She made a mistake marrying Maurice when she was young, but that's all she's ever done wrong. We were hoping to disappear. We were trying to scrape up enough money. When Maurice was shot the coast seemed clear.'

Pel was still considering what Cavalin had said when Darcy appeared.

'Patron,' he said excitedly. 'We've got a lead! Brussels has come up with a list of Rykx's pals at last. One of 'em's called Deville. Gilbert Deville.'

'Deville? That old lunatic?'

'He's not so old and he's no lunatic. He's a plasterer. He handles plaster. And plaster's not all that different from modelling clay, I suppose. I made inquiries. He had ambitions to be a sculptor. It seems he became one.'

'Go on. There's more, I suppose?'

'There certainly is. Gilbert Deville did a stretch in Belgium for smuggling heroin into the country inside a pot leg. He claimed he'd broken it skiing and wore a plaster of Paris pot on it. Unfortunately he was knocked down outside the airport by a car and rushed to hospital and they checked his leg while he was unconscious and found the heroin.'

Pel was sitting up straight now and Darcy went on. 'The police questioned him about his pals and where the heroin was going. He wouldn't tell so they asked who'd put the pot on his leg. He said he'd put it on himself but the police doctor said it wasn't possible. He couldn't have done it. It was too difficult and too expert. It had been done by a medical orderly, or a nurse or a doctor.'

Pel was deep in thought. 'Which doctor?' he asked.

'They never found out.'

Pel was quiet for a little longer then he gestured. 'Let's have a look at that statement Dr Dunois made,' he said.

When Darcy produced it, Pel stared at it, frowning. 'He never once says in this that *he* took that bullet out of Sagassu's arm. Not once. He admits it was done in his surgery and that he was there. But the rest of his statement's all "This was done" or "That was done". Never "I did it." Perhaps he *didn't* do it. Get him in, Daniel.'

Dr Dunois looked shabbier than ever and very nervous, and it didn't require a lot of leaning on him before he changed his story.

'Yes,' he admitted. 'It was done in my surgery. I was there. But I wouldn't touch it.'

'Somebody did. Who?'

'They contacted somebody else and he came and did it.'

'And who was that?'

'They paid me to take the rap. I have done. But I didn't do it. I never said I did it. I was careful not to.'

'So who did?'

Dunois' voice could hardly be heard. 'It was Robert Kersta,' he said.

Pel sat silently for a moment then he looked at Darcy. 'Daniel, nip round the corner and see Madame Léon. I noticed as I came in that she's shifting her stock to the shop in the Rue Général Leclerc. See if she knows who treated her husband's injuries when he was beaten up. Because somebody did. It might be interesting to find out why.'

It wasn't far from the Hôtel de Police, and Darcy was there within minutes. Madame Léon was pushing racks of clothes into her husband's former premises as fast as she was pushing out cartons of sports goods.

'I hope you're not expecting to buy any running shoes or a punch ball,' she said. 'I'm getting rid of the lot.'

Darcy grinned. 'Nothing like that. I just wanted to know the name of the doctor your husband saw for those injuries he had. That bruising round the eyes, the cracked ribs, and anything else you noticed.'

She seemed unable for a moment to adjust from her delight in her new premises. 'The injuries,' she said. 'Anything else? Oh! Well, I'm not sure. Kristoff. Kerhays. Kersta. That's it! It was a Dr Kersta.'

Darcy smiled. 'I thought it might be.'

Pel hadn't moved when Darcy returned, but he was suddenly looking very bright-eyed and enthusiastic.

'Let's have Kersta in, Daniel. He seems to be in this deeper than we thought.'

A car was sent and Kersta arrived soon afterwards, looking pleased with himself. His wife was in custody and Kersta had made a big show of caring for her, but it didn't seem to have affected the quality of his life. Doubtless, Pel thought, he had plenty of admiring female patients to offer sympathy.

He sat down, looking handsome and confident of his popularity. Pel didn't waste time.

'You know the name Antonio Sagassu?' he asked.

'Who's he?' Kersta took his time answering.

'He was shot in the arm. You handled it. You took out the bullet, stitched him up, bandaged him, put the arm in a sling and gave antibiotics.'

There was the faintest flicker of concern in Kersta's eyes but it didn't last long. He answered smoothly, indifferently. 'Sagassu,' he said thoughtfully. 'Was that his name? I didn't know.'

'You *did* treat him?'

'Yes. I suppose I did. I certainly treated someone.'

'Why was it done at Dr Dunois' surgery?'

'Because that's where I was called to.'

'Why did you treat him?'

'My dear sir, the man was bleeding and hurt and a doctor takes an oath – '

'He's a crook.'

Kersta didn't pause in his explanation. 'An oath to succour the injured, no matter who they are. I wasn't aware who he was.'

'Didn't you enquire? Weren't you interested in how he came to be wounded?'

'That wasn't my job.'

'Why didn't you inform the police?'

'That also wasn't my job.'

'Not even when a man has been injured in a shooting incident?'

'It was the job of the people who brought him in.'

'Why did they send for you?'

'Why?'

'Yes. Why *you*? Why not somebody else?'

'I suppose because I was handy.'

'Your surgery's a long way from Dr Dunois' surgery. And there are plenty of other doctors – who *would* have informed the police.'

Kersta still looked sure of himself but Pel thought he could detect a slight worry behind his eyes now.

'Didn't you realise that the man was a crook and that something fishy was going on?' he asked.

'No. I didn't.'

'Not even with a bullet in his arm?' Pel was touching on the point again and again, as if probing a painful wound, and it was beginning to bother Kersta. For the first time he hesitated.

'I suppose I didn't think,' he said.

'Not at all?'

'Well, I suppose it must have crossed my mind.'

'So why did you go ahead? You could have refused.'

'I'm a doctor.'

'Even doctors can refuse if the police aren't informed. Why didn't *you* refuse?'

'Well...'

'Well?' Pel leaned forward.

The worry behind Kersta's eyes had increased. 'They threatened me.'

'Ah, now we have it! That would explain it, of course.' Pel was all smiles and reassurance, as if he understood completely. 'A threat can explain a lot,' he said. He leaned forward again. 'A threat with a gun?' he asked silkily.

'No.'

'What then?'

'Well...' Kersta was growing distinctly nervous now. 'They just made threats.'

'What sort of threats? To do what?'

'They threatened to harm my wife.'

'And are you suggesting to me *that* would have worried you? Are you sure the threat didn't concern a plaster of Paris pot you put on the leg of a man called Gilbert Deville in Belgium?'

It was only a guess but it was obviously a good one. Kersta looked startled, then shocked.

'Who...?'

'Who told us? Never mind who told us. But it's true, isn't it? They knew, didn't they? Perhaps they were involved. And they said they'd tell us if you didn't help out with Sagassu's wound.'

It had taken them a long time and the route to their goal had been slow and convoluted. But they'd got there in the end.

'Let's go over and see Deville,' Pel suggested. 'There's a definite link between Maurice, Kersta, Léon and Deville. By his inability to stay in his own bed, Dr Kersta seems to have opened a few doors for us.'

Darcy was careful to make a clandestine inspection of Deville's place for the operation they were planning. After the first few metres, its long drive was surrounded by foliage which had been allowed to become overgrown so that there was no room for two cars to pass. Lagé, who had been watching Rac, the other clay modeller, because Rac had seemed a better bet than Deville for a sojourn in Number 72, had been moved from Jouanot-le-Petit to Perrenet-sous-le-Forêt, and had established himself at the Hôtel des Beaux Arts, a place with bat-haunted outbuildings almost opposite the entrance to Deville's property. He was trying to appear to be a salesman covering the district for a seed firm from Lyons and sat in the bar studying catalogues, pamphlets and small mysterious packages, or outside under the umbrella, a beer at his elbow, with a large notebook in which he kept making notes. When asked by the landlord why he didn't go out and sell, he said he was new to the job and was still getting his act together. It didn't take him long to notice activity at Deville's.

'He went off early,' he reported. 'And returned with a van. He's been loading statues all morning.'

'He's bolting,' Pel said. 'With the loot.'

'He'll be seeing himself sitting in a bar in the States,' Darcy grinned. 'With a luxury flat just down the road and a bird ready to jump into bed with him.'

'He's going to get a nasty surprise.'

'If we block up that drive of his, there's no way he can drive the van away.'

'What about if he tried *running* away. On his own two feet?'

Darcy grinned. 'I've thought of that. Behind the house there's a big meadow that stretches across to the N74. You get into it from the N74 by a broken-down gate, but there's a newish hedge at the back of the house and Deville could climb through and make his way across the field. He might even manage it – except that I'll make a point of being ready for him if he tries.'

As they turned into the winding drive that led to Deville's house, they saw a dark blue van parked by the door. It contained several of Deville's ugly statues, and Deville, his beard trimmed and no longer in the clay-covered blue smock but wearing a smart suit and a butcher's apron, was just emerging with another as they appeared. He stared at the two cars packed with cops for a moment.

'Moving, are you?' Pel asked.

'I'm taking this lot to Marseilles,' Deville explained. 'They're being sea-freighted to Singapore. They'd cost a bit going by air, after all.'

Pel nodded. 'Got them insured?'

'No. I didn't think they were worth it. The arrangement's that they were bought at a good price as originals and, if it's required, they'll be cast in bronze when they arrive. I'm going with them in case.'

Pel mused. 'But they themselves have no value?'

Deville laughed. 'It's only modelling clay. It's only because the Chink in Singapore wanted them I did so many.'

'You were lucky to find your Chinese.' For a while Pel stared at the statues. He was thinking of the one Nosjean had found at Annabelle-Eugénie Sondermann's. Deliberately dropped, it seemed. Well, perhaps it wasn't a bad idea. 'Are they heavy?' he asked.

'A bit.'

'Pick one up, Misset. You're a strong type and you don't use your muscles much.'

Misset got his arms round one of the statues and lifted. It seemed to be of a large toad and was as ugly as most of Deville's models.

'Heavy, is it?'

'Yes, Patron.'

'Lift it higher.'

Deville was watching nervously. 'Take it easy,' he said. 'Those things are valuable.'

Pel eyed him. 'I thought you said they weren't.'

'Well...'

Pel turned again to Misset. 'Go on, Misset. Higher.'

Deville's fists were clenched and he was struggling not to protest as Misset fought to lift the statue higher. 'What is all this?' he asked.

'Don't you know?'

'I think you're up to something.'

Pel smiled. 'Yes,' he admitted. 'We are. Come over here with it, Misset. On to the stone patio.'

Misset struggled to do as he was told, watched by Deville in silent and terrified fascination.

'Suppose you dropped it?' Pel said.

'It'd break, Patron.'

'So it would. Right, drop it.'

'Drop it, Patron?'

'Drop it. Taking care that it doesn't fall on your foot. You're stupid enough.'

Misset scowled and, as a strangled cry was wrenched from Deville, he let the statue go. The base shattered and pieces flew in all directions. As the fragments scattered, Deville stared furiously at Pel then, spinning on his heel, bolted for the back of the house, where he ran straight into the arms of Darcy who had just crossed the field and stepped through the hedge into Deville's garden.

'*Merde*,' Deville said bitterly.

Darcy beamed. 'It's a sentiment that's often expressed when I appear,' he said.

As he marched Deville back to the front of the house, he found Pel examining the statue Misset had dropped. A large piece had broken off the base. Concealed among the broken clay were two golden-yellow boules.

Misset stared at them and raised his eyes to Pel's. 'Boules?' he said.

'Boules,' Pel agreed. 'Now pick up another.'

Misset did so, frowning.

'Drop it.'

This time the broken base revealed a bar of the same golden yellow metal. Along the edge of it were the letters NR and a number, and a stamped seal with the words, *Johnson Matthey, Refiners, Melters, London*.

A glance into the van revealed three wooden boxes containing chromium-plated boules.

'I expect the boules trick was taking too long,' Pel said, 'and some of the stuff was still in its original form that day when we called on them. Maurice must have decided it was safer to get rid of it. I think we've found Murray's bullion.'

That night they contacted Goschen and, without advising him – or anyone else either, for that matter – that they had found the missing bullion, asked him to warn them if there were any signs of activity round Harding's house.

'I take it you're still keeping an eye on the place,' Pel said.

'Oh, yes. Not half.'

With what they'd discovered, they felt they were in a better position to handle Cavalin's request.

'That deal you were after,' Pel announced when he appeared in his office. 'It's a dead letter. We've got the gold and we've got you.'

Cavalin gave a hoot of laughter.

'You knew Deville had it, didn't you?'

'I was the only one apart from Maurice who did know. I was the only one Maurice trusted, and I think that fact will finally have dawned on Ourdabi. He's not a fast thinker. That's why I'm probably safer in jail than out. He doesn't know where the gold went and I expect he's looking for me to tell him. It would have been God help me if I'd still been free. I'd have been short of a few fingernails in no time.' Cavalin paused and looked seriously at Pel. 'I could still get Harding over here for you, Chief. And I would if you'd make it easy for Sidonie.'

Pel studied him in silence for a moment. There was something oddly attractive about Cavalin. He'd been aware of it all along. At first he'd thought it was just his good looks, his intelligence, that set him apart from the rest of Maurice's boys, perhaps just his smile. But there was more to it than that. There was a kind of courage that enabled him to accept punishment so long as Maurice's wife, for whom, it seemed, he had been carrying a torch for a long time, could go free.

He leaned forward. 'Why', he asked, 'would Harding be inclined to listen to a promise from you to tell him where the gold is?'

'Because I went with Maurice to London to make the arrangements.'

'You're guilty as hell then.'

'I didn't touch the gold.'

'Suppose you did get in touch with the London end. How would they know it was you? They'll need more proof than just a voice.'

'There were code words.'

'How do you know?'

'I used them. We always used them when we talked on the telephone.'

'Would they come if they thought you could lead them to the loot?'

'You bet they would.' Cavalin smiled. 'There's a hundred and fifty million francs' worth of gold bullion. They'd surely take a risk for that. Especially as I expect they're beginning to worry by now that it'll disappear altogether if they don't get their claws on it soon. They offered Maurice fifteen million francs to hide it but he decided he preferred the whole lot. If I told them I knew where it was, they'd come all right – if only to grab me. They'll decide I know where it is and they'll try to snatch me, as they tried to snatch Maurice, as a guarantee of getting it.'

Pel sat brooding. He would have liked to get Harding and his associates to France. He had a feeling that there weren't many people close to Harding. Perhaps just the two who'd done for Maurice. A tip would certainly bring them across the Channel, but he didn't trust Cavalin and he was not unaware that several of Maurice's much-battered gang were still around – Sagassu, the Corsican, Bernard Guérin and the

Humphrey Bogart type, Ourdabi. Two of them weren't much more than heavies, but Ourdabi had the look of a man with a cold ruthlessness who wouldn't miss a trick.

Cavalin watched him. 'I'd need protecting,' he said. 'Harding and his friends aren't going to enjoy it.'

'You'd be protected all right,' Pel said grimly. 'Have you got any ideas? They won't walk into a trap.'

'I could arrange to meet them on the road from Leu to Perrenet-sous-le-Forêt on the corner below Lordy. I could be waiting there. In my car. They know it. It's the Range Rover you've got. I'd be alone. I'd suggest that I arrange for them to drive past me and then that I start up and follow them, pass them, and lead them to the gold at Deville's where I assume you would already have made arrangements.'

'Do you think they'll fall for it?'

'Yes. The way they'll see it, there'll be no waiting, and the road from Lordy to Perrenet's open all the way and no place for an ambush. The way I'll suggest, there'll be no hanging around and, if they're suspicious, all they'll have to do is keep going. Besides, they'll think they've got me. Me, Chief, not the gold. Me. Once they're round the corner, they'll stop and try to grab me.'

'How do you propose to avoid that?'

'By moving fast. Round the corner, the road widens into a sort of lay-by and they can't block it if I don't give them time. And if I get in front they won't be able to pass me because the road twists too much. All they'll be able to do is follow, and before they know what's happening, I'll be turning down the drive to Deville's place. They'll not notice they're inside it until it's too late. It starts as if it's a road but then it narrows suddenly and once in you can't turn round without going to the end. They'd have to follow.'

'And then?'

'Then it's up to you.'

Pel studied the man at the other side of the table. 'What about you? How do we know that once you're behind the wheel of the Range Rover, *you* won't bolt?'

'You can have a man in the back. An armed man. That ought to be enough to guarantee I'll do as I'm expected to do.'

'Suppose Ourdabi's around to make sure you don't get away with it?'

'I have to take a chance on that.'

'You're taking a lot of chances.'

'Yes. But that's another reason why I'll be happy to have one of your men in the back. In addition to being able to shoot me if I run, if Ourdabi turns up, he'll also be able to shoot *him*.'

nineteen

'I don't believe in deals,' the Chief observed grimly.

'Neither do I,' Pel admitted. 'But if it brings in everybody we're looking for instead of just a few odds and ends who don't matter, it's worth it.'

'What sort of deal have you in mind?'

'We could arrange to look a little lightly on Cavalin. He hasn't been involved in murder as far as we can find out.'

'He was involved in handling Tagliatti's business.'

Pel agreed, but there was something about Cavalin – his sense of humour; his loyalty to Tagliatti's wife, perhaps; the fact that he was willing to help so long as she went free. It was against all his principles of dealing with villains, but after listening to his arguments, the Chief threw up his hands.

'Very well! Go ahead.'

The deal with Cavalin was concluded and the code word, Nabulione Buonaparti, was passed over.

'Not Napoleon Bonaparte,' Cavalin said. 'The name he was born with. Not many know the original. They consider him a French hero. Actually he was more of an Italian shit like Maurice.'

'You're taking a chance, Patron,' Darcy said as the office emptied. 'Harding will pass on the information to Ourdabi.'

'I wonder if he will,' Pel said. 'You heard Cavalin say Ourdabi has no patience and that he's clumsy. Harding tipped him off to get rid of young Pasquier and look what a mess he made of it. Harding might prefer to act on his own this time. After all, the gold was his. He lifted it. He won't want Ourdabi muscling in.'

Darcy was still worried and Pel tried to calm his fears.

'It's not normal police procedure,' he agreed. 'But the outcome of a weak case depends on retaining the initiative. And that means making sure the other side dance to your tune.'

'This is different, Patron.'

'It's legitimate so long as there's a risk to the interests of justice and our investigation. Every cop knows the time comes eventually when he has to justify his actions. The risk's self-evident and if he makes a mistake he lays his career on the line. There are plenty of lawyers willing and eager to make money by impeding the law.'

'Won't New Scotland Yard demand that we deport Maurice's lot for their airport robbery?'

'I'd rather they deported Harding and *his* lot for *our* murder. It would look better in our statistics than in theirs. You know what they say, Daniel: when the firemen give a ball, it's always the same types who do the dancing. It's like that with us. We're the ones who take the responsibility. I'll chance it.'

Cavalin had been rehearsed in what to say by Darcy, with De Troq', who spoke English, sitting in to check that he was saying what he was expected to say. Then he spent a sweating hour with Pel, Darcy and De Troq' alongside, arranging a rendezvous, while they listened in on a loudspeaker.

The conversation started warily in slow French. 'I want to speak to Monsieur Hazard,' Cavalin said.

There was a pause then a brisk voice came. 'This is Hazard. Who's that?'

'This is Nabulione Buonaparti. I know where the goods are.'

There was a long silence then one word. 'Where?'

'I can't describe it. You'd have to come and I'd lead you there.'

As Cavalin had suggested, a rendezvous at the bottom of the hill at Lordy was offered and a time two days ahead.

'How do I know this is genuine?' Harding asked.

'You know who I am. I'll be sitting in my Range Rover. If I'm not there when you appear, it'll mean something's gone wrong and you can just drive on.'

There was a long pause, then, 'Let's hear the rest of the story. What's the drill?'

'You drive up from the direction of Leu. Go straight past me as if you don't know me. That will give you a chance to identify me and for me to identify you. As soon as you've passed I'll follow and pass you and lead you direct to where the goods are hidden. It's not far.'

'How do we know the cops aren't in on this?'

'Haven't you asked Ourdabi?' This was one of Pel's questions to find out how much Ourdabi knew. The answer came promptly and grittily.

'To hell with Ourdabi! He couldn't run a whelk stall. What he wants and what he gets are two different matters.'

'Where is he now?'

'I don't know and I don't care. It's you I'm interested in. What about the cops? I want something better than this.'

Cavalin paused. 'I'll be coming from Talant,' he said. 'I'll stop at the corner below Lordy. You'll be able to see into the Range Rover as you pass, and make sure there's nobody in it but me. As soon as you've passed, I follow you round the corner and lead the way.'

'All right.' Harding seemed satisfied.

'You'll need something solid to carry the stuff.'

'Right.'

'You might need some help.'

'I'll bring Coy and Braxton. What's your interest?'

'A share.'

'We don't share. The stuff's ours.'

'I'm not asking for Maurice's share. Just enough to get me to Brazil. I want out.'

There was another long pause then Harding's voice came again. 'What's the guarantee that this isn't a set-up?'

Cavalin drew a deep breath. '*I'm* the guarantee,' he said briskly. 'If you think it's all a phoney, all you have to do is what you did to Maurice.'

The conversation ended abruptly, as though the man at the other end had simply replaced the receiver.

Pel looked at Cavalin. 'Think he bit?' he asked.

Cavalin shrugged. 'If he turns up,' he said, 'he did. If he doesn't, it didn't work.'

Pel was still doubtful.

Cavalin explained. 'The corner at Lordy's overlooked by bushes and trees,' he said. 'They won't want to hang about long but they'll slow down alongside me for a second to make sure the Range Rover isn't full of flics. There's a tarpaulin in the back, though, so, as Harding's lot vanish round the corner, one of your people dives out of the bushes and into the back of the Range Rover. I'll have the door unfastened ready. He gets under the tarpaulin – a matter of seconds – and I follow Harding. I pass him, going fast, and lead them to Deville's. I shall be moving at speed from the moment your man's inside because if I don't get in front of them they'll grab me. That's what they want. It would be a much surer way of getting the gold than simply following me.'

'All right,' Pel said. 'Suppose it goes according to plan?'

'In that case, as I say, I shall be arriving at Perrenet very fast indeed. Because of that, they'll be moving fast, too. So your people had better make sure they move even faster.'

'And your share? They'll not put a cheque in the bank before they get the gold. And they certainly won't put one in afterwards. You haven't mentioned that part yet.'

Cavalin's smile came again. 'Are you kidding yourself, Chief? They won't be expecting to pay up. As soon as they get their hands on the gold, they'll expect to get rid of me.'

Pel stared at Cavalin. 'You'll take that chance, too?'

'Yes.'

'For Sidonie?'

Maurice Tagliatti's black Cadillac had been found in St Seine l'Abbaye but they still had no idea where Ourdabi, Sagassu and Guérin were. Pel guessed that they weren't far away, with their ears to the ground, waiting to see what would happen. As far as they could tell, they had no idea that Cavalin was in police custody and he suspected they were watching the Manoir de Lordy for him to return to pick up his belongings.

Then Murray telephoned. 'What have you been stirring up?' he demanded. 'There's been a lot of activity at Harding's house. His wife's away and the lights were on all night. Two cars appeared and left, driven by Coy and Braxton. We've got a tap on the telephone and we heard Harding ordering three separate seats on a flight to Paris from Gatwick. He's just left. We assume the other two seats were for Braxton and Coy.'

'Check the hotels Daniel,' Pel said, putting the instrument down.

Bardolle was keeping an eye on the Hôtel Central in Dijon. Harding seemed to be a creature of habit and, sure enough, Bardolle was on the telephone just as they expected.

'He's here,' he reported. 'Together with the other two. A grey van's also turned up. I checked. It's hired.'

Replacing the telephone, Pel turned to Darcy. 'Is Nosjean in position?'

'Any time now, Patron. Brochard reported that a green Renault was prowling round the corner at Lordy last evening. He thinks it might have been Harding's lot casing the place for a set-up. Nosjean keeps well back in the wood and will continue to do so until an hour before Cavalin's due to arrive.'

They started to place their men in position well ahead of time. Still doing the rounds of the Roblais family's fences and hedges on the south side of the farm, Brochard was warned to keep his eyes open. He was pleased to do so because Héloïse Roblais had taken to turning up at his side in the evening with so much make-up on her face it looked as if it had been spread with a trowel. She was clearly determined to get him somehow.

Darcy's men were placed in the outbuildings round Deville's studio, all with good viewpoints over the drive. The blue van which had called to collect Deville's hideous statues had vanished and in its place was another one belonging to the police. A policeman in a blue smock and bearded to look like Deville was visible inside the house.

'Everybody in position?' Pel asked.

'Everybody,' Darcy reported.

'Who's riding with Cavalin?'

'Morell. He knows exactly what's happening. There'll be five men on the corner when Cavalin appears. Nosjean has orders to put a bullet into Cavalin if he shows any sign of trying any tricks.'

'Has Cavalin been briefed?'

'He knows the score. He'll be led from Talant by an unmarked police car which will restrict his speed and he'll be followed closely by another so he'll not be able to slip away. As he stops on the corner at Lordy, the two cars move on towards Perrenet as if they just happened to be going in the same direction. As they leave, Cavalin will be covered by Nosjean's men. He has instructions to stop exactly opposite them and if he doesn't they have instructions to let him have it. They'll shoot the tyres out for a start. After that...' Darcy shrugged. 'He knows the spot because I've taken him over the ground, and they can't miss because I've had the two front windows of the Range Rover removed – just in case they have to shoot at *him*.'

'Has everybody had plenty of opportunity to study the pictures we have of Harding?'

'Everybody. And Bardolle's joined Lagé at Perrenet. They're watching the entrance to Deville's place. Lagé has his car and it'll be their job when Harding's lot enter the drive to follow at a distance so they'll be bottled up inside. Once in the drive, they can't get out without going to the house to turn round. We'll be waiting.'

'Have we heard from Brochard?'

'Not for some time. Perhaps he's busy.'

twenty

Brochard was indeed busy. He was in the attic of the Roblais farm watching Ourdabi.

He had discovered that much the best place from which to watch the Manoir was not from the boundaries of the farm but from the attic. He had taken to it originally in defence from Héloïse Roblais because her suggestions had started to become quite outrageous. She had even offered to help him clear the sluices of the dam in one of the lower pastures.

'It'd mean taking your clothes off and getting into the water,' she pointed out.

'Not likely,' Brochard said, looking for any excuse. 'That's hard work. I'd be flat on my back.'

It didn't work. 'I could be flat on mine if you prefer it,' she'd offered.

Brochard had even been tempted – after all, it was easy enough to die a virgin – but he was terrified of Pel if he fell down on the job and he had managed to fight her off and begun to seek somewhere he could be nearer the safety of the rest of the family. The attic had seemed perfect and he was there now with old Roblais, his son, Gilles, and Héloïse, who was sulking in a battered armchair with a sagging seat. Brochard had just discovered that Ourdabi had turned up at last and he could even see him, with Guérin and Sagassu, whose arm, though out of a sling, still seemed to be stiff. They were on the high ground just behind the Manoir and just below the Roblais farm and he had been obliged to admit Roblais and his son into his confidence to get a better view of what was going on.

Ourdabi held a pair of binoculars and was staring towards the Manoir. Near him stood a big black Citroën.

'What are they looking for?' Roblais asked.

Brochard wasn't sure but he suspected that, having assumed that Cavalin had gone into hiding after the fiasco at Leu, they were waiting for him to return to lead them to the stolen bullion. Brochard had been well briefed and he could think of no other reason for the interest in the Manoir.

Then he noticed that Roblais was rooting around among the junk that filled the attic, pushing aside an old-fashioned cradle, a broken pram, a three-legged sofa oozing stuffing. As he straightened up, Brochard saw he had a telescope in his hand.

'It was my uncle's,' he said. 'He went to sea. Can you imagine? Going to sea from Burgundy! It's about as far from the ocean as you can get in Europe. He became a captain. Sailed out of St Nazaire.' He indicated a crude painting of a windjammer on the wall. 'That was his ship. We got his belongings when he died.'

Brochard eyed the telescope. 'Is it powerful enough to see into the Manoir?' he asked.

Héloïse gave a sour chuckle. 'It was powerful enough for us to see what old Lordy got up to in the maids' bedrooms,' she said. 'I watched him many a time.'

Nosjean, Lacocq, Debray, Morell and a man from Uniformed Branch had been in the copse at Lordy all night. They were cold and in a bad temper and more than willing to shoot Cavalin. Given a chance, they'd have shot anyone. As the Range Rover drew to a stop, the two escorting plain cars – both supplied by Traffic and driven by policemen – moved on, as if they were driven by perfectly innocent travellers who had just happened to be moving in the same direction.

The leading car continued at its steady pace and the following car drew out, swung round the Range Rover and headed up the winding slope towards Perrenet. It all looked very normal.

With the Range Rover's windows missing, Nosjean called out to let Cavalin know he was there. 'No tricks,' he said. 'We have rifles with telescopic sights on both sides pointed straight at you.'

Cavalin's face twisted in a smile. 'No tricks,' he agreed. 'You hold the ace.'

'Any sign of them?'

'No. Any sign of them last night?'

'There are indications they've been around – at least, I expect it was them, looking for signs of a set-up.'

They waited in silence for a moment. 'Perhaps they won't come,' Cavalin said quietly.

'They'd better,' Nosjean said. 'Or the Old Man will explode.'

'He explodes easily?'

'You bet he does, so one false move and we give it to you.'

'Could you do it?'

Nosjean shrugged. His attitude to crooks, like Darcy's and that of every other member of the team, had been drilled into him by Pel. 'I don't have a conscience about that sort of thing,' he said.

With the end of the telescope poked from the attic window, Brochard was staring towards the Manoir. The place sprang into immediate vision, then, as he directed the telescope towards Ourdabi, Brochard saw him point and Guérin snatch the binoculars from him. They were staring towards Perrenet. Something had caught their attention and Brochard pointed the telescope in that direction.

'Let's have a look,' Gilles Roblais asked.

'Hang on!' Brochard's voice rose. 'They're leaving! Something down there's caught their attention. Hold it!' Brochard became excited. 'I've got it. It's Cavalin's Range Rover. He's just come up from Leu.'

Among the bushes on the corner, Nosjean tapped Morell on the shoulder.

'Ready?' he asked.

Morell nodded and laid down the rifle he'd been holding.

'As soon as they round the corner, you've got three seconds to get into the back of the Range Rover. Cavalin's got the door ajar.'

'What if they don't go round the corner? Suppose they stop this side?'

'In that case, you'd better be quick to pick up that rifle again.'

'What are they driving?'

'We think a grey van. I – hold it! Something's coming!' Nosjean peered through the foliage. 'It's a van – a grey van. This must be them. They must have been watching from the hill back there and seen Cavalin arrive. They haven't wasted time.'

Brochard wasn't worried when Cavalin didn't reappear from beyond the trees and bushes on the corner below him – he knew the plan – but suddenly he saw the men who were watching the Manoir begin to head down the hill to the house, then stop, point and start to retrace their steps towards the black Citroën.

He guessed they'd seen Cavalin and, realising that he wasn't about to turn up at the Manoir, as they'd obviously thought, they were going down the hill to pick him up. The whole plan was suddenly in jeopardy.

As he watched the road winding away up the slope towards Perrenet, Brochard saw it was quite empty. But then, labouring up from Leu to the corner where he'd seen the Range Rover he saw a grey van of the type that delivered goods to shops.

Through his mirror, Cavalin was watching the van approach.

'They're taking no chances,' he called softly to Nosjean.

Crouching in the undergrowth, Nosjean and the others were well placed to see what happened. Cavalin sat bolt upright in the driver's seat of the Range Rover, an easy target, apparently studying a map. The rumble of the approaching van increased and they saw it lift slowly over the brow of the hill towards the corner. Cavalin started the engine of the Range Rover.

As the van drew alongside, they half expected a blast of fire to destroy him, and Nosjean had to admire his nerve as he sat motionless as the van slowed. There were three men in the front and, as it passed, he saw them staring into the rear of the Range Rover. The pause was only momentary, however, then the van moved on. As it rounded the corner, the rear door of the Range Rover flew open and Morell took a flying dive inside. As the door clicked shut, the Range Rover began to move.

Its speed building up rapidly, it rounded the corner on two wheels. Though he couldn't see, it wasn't hard for Nosjean to guess that the Englishmen in the van had been caught off guard, and, judging by the slamming of doors and the roaring of engines that followed, he assumed that Cavalin had managed to pass them and was now in the lead.

'Right!' he said. 'It worked. Let's get on with it!'

But as they ran through the trees to where they had parked their car, they saw a black Citroën hurtle down the hill from Lordy and swing with swaying body on to the Perrenet road to join the chase.

'For God's sake,' Nosjean gasped. 'That was Ourdabi! Where does he come into it?'

When Brochard took another look from the attic, the black Citroën had gone and so had the watching men. Then he spotted the white Range Rover come into view on the road to Perrenet. It was moving fast and was followed at a distance by the grey van he'd seen labouring up the hill from Leu. Then, as it vanished behind a stretch of hedgerow, he saw the black Citroën containing Ourdabi and the others appear by the corner where he had first seen the Range Rover and watched it turn on to the Perrenet road.

Reaching for his radio, he called Darcy.

'Brochard here,' he said, 'Ourdabi, Sagassu and Guérin have turned up. They're on their way to join the fun.'

As Guérin swung the big Citroën on to the road after the Range Rover, Ourdabi was startled to see a grey van between himself and his quarry.

'Where did that damn thing come from?' he snarled.

'Must have been coming up the hill from Leu,' Sagassu suggested.

'Knock it off the road,' Ourdabi snapped.

'*Merde*, no,' Guérin said. 'Something might go wrong!'

'Pass it!'

'I can't,' Guérin said. 'The road's too winding. Don't worry, though, it straightens out after Perrenet. I can pass him then.'

The atmosphere at Perrenet was tense when Brochard's message arrived.

Keeping below window level, Darcy moved towards where Pel was crouching.

'Message from Brochard, Patron,' he said. 'Ourdabi, Guérin and Sagassu are on the way here, too. They're in a black Citroën.'

What passed for a pleased smile moved across Pel's face. 'All the lot at one go,' he said.

'I've also just picked up Lagé at Perrenet. The Range Rover's just come into view. It's being followed by a grey van. Which, judging by what Brochard says, is being followed in its turn by a black Citroën which must be Ourdabi's lot. They obviously don't know who's in the grey van and they're trying to get in on the act.'

Waiting in Perrenet outside the bar, with a bock of beer and a pile of pamphlets each, Lagé and Bardolle appeared to be arguing about seeds. Lagé had taken Darcy's message calmly and two or three minutes later the white Range Rover appeared round the corner followed closely by a dark grey van. Both were travelling fast.

Bardolle glanced at Lagé and they were piling the pamphlets neatly on the table as the Range Rover passed them. Soon afterwards, the van passed and they quietly sank the last of their beer as the two vehicles vanished in the long winding drive leading to Deville's house.

'Why didn't you pass him?' Ourdabi was still urging as they entered the outskirts of Perrenet.

'Damn it, I couldn't,' Guérin yelled.

They had seen the Range Rover higher up the slope over the top of the grey van that had appeared so unexpectedly in front of them. Then both vehicles in front had vanished round the corner into Perrenet, and as Guérin swung the Citroën after them they saw only an empty road to the next corner. Both vehicles had vanished and the Citroën slid to a stop.

'You've lost them!' Ourdabi snarled as the brakes shrieked. 'They've gone!'

Sagassu was silent for a second. 'They must have gone round the corner there,' he said. Then his voice rose. 'No!' he yelled. 'Cavalin's heading for Deville's place! It's here in Perrenet! That's it! That's where the gold must be! Deville worked for Maurice on that cocaine haul.' He gestured wildly. 'Those statues he makes! He has an export licence to send them abroad. I bet the stuff's hidden inside them.'

Ourdabi gave a shout of triumph. 'Name of God, I think you're right! That's where Cavalin's vanished. That's the entrance right there. By those trees!'

As the big Citroën passed them, Lagé looked at Bardolle. 'That was Ourdabi,' he said. 'What's he doing here?'

As they started towards where Lagé's car was parked, they saw the Citroën vanish after the other vehicles into the drive to Deville's house. As they disappeared down the drive after them, two cars containing Nosjean and his men came whooping up from the corner at Lordy to add weight.

Cavalin had no idea that the van that was following him was being followed by another car containing Ourdabi and, since the Citroën had breasted the hill into Perrenet after the van had turned into the drive behind the Range Rover, Ourdabi had no idea that between him and his quarry was a vehicle containing men as desperate as he was.

'Here they come!' Pel said as they heard the sound of the Range Rover's engine.

Cavalin brought the Range Rover swiftly up to the front of the house and turned with a swish of flung gravel to stop alongside the blue van the police had parked there to make it look as if Deville was still in residence. Almost immediately, the grey van containing Harding came into view and soon afterwards the Citroën containing Ourdabi.

'Got them,' Darcy said.

Almost immediately also, however, it occurred to four different sets of people that something had gone wrong. Harding's head was turning swiftly to right and left to get a picture of what was happening. Judging by his expression, he had decided it was a trap. Seeing the Citroën behind him with three men in it, he immediately assumed they were police and leapt from the car, shouting, 'Cops!' Swinging towards Cavalin, he lifted a hand holding a pistol. 'You bastard,' he roared. 'It was a set-up!'

He was livid with rage and, realising that something unexpected had happened but not certain what, as Harding pulled the trigger, Cavalin flung himself down in his seat in the Range Rover. Instead of hitting Cavalin, Harding's shot passed through the skin of the vehicle and hit Morell just under the right shoulder.

'Holy Mother of God!' he yelped.

Seeing Lagé's car coming up behind them, Ourdabi had decided that the grey van which had appeared in front of them as they had dived down the winding drive, when they had thought it had continued on through the village, was also part of a set-up and that *he* was the target. His reaction was the same as Harding's.

'Cops!' he yelled.

Harding and the two men with him thought it was a warning to drop their guns, and as both sides opened fire, Harding went down immediately, as did Ourdabi. Trying to retreat, Braxton fired at Guérin just as Sagassu started to fire at Lagé and Bardolle, and Guérin began to fire at Braxton and Coy. For a moment or two everybody seemed to be firing at everybody else, with the police trying to get in shots from the windows at a lot of men jumping about like fleas on a hot plate. Caught in the crossfire and with Morell wounded in the back of the Range Rover, Cavalin revved the engine and jerked forward and round the corner of the house. Bumping over the rough ground of a flowerbed, for safety he smashed through the hedge into the field beyond.

'Mother of God,' Morell yelled in agony. 'Stop! Stop!'

By the time Nosjean's cars were brought to a stop in the drive by Lagé's car which had been halted by the flying bullets ahead, five of the six men involved in the gunfight were on the ground, with the sixth, Sagassu, screaming for

mercy with his hands in the air as if he were trying to claw
his way up to Heaven.

'Good God,' Darcy said. 'Everybody's shot everybody!'

As they ran outside, Harding was in agony with a bullet in
his hip, Braxton was huddled in a groaning heap in the
bushes, Guérin was sitting with his back to the off rear wheel
of the Citroën, clutching a shattered knee. Ourdabi and Coy
were dead.

'Who shot which?' Darcy asked.

It had been like a Keystone Cops sequence, with one
vehicle after another arriving at full speed. First Cavalin, then
Harding, then Ourdabi, followed by Lagé and Bardolle, and
finally Nosjean's two carloads. It had been almost farcical –
but for the shoot-out. Each assuming the others were the
police, Harding's group and Ourdabi's group had both
opened fire with everything they'd got and at a range where
they could hardly miss. As they discussed the matter, it
seemed the police hadn't shot anybody because they hadn't
had a chance. Then, as they counted noses and moved
vehicles, it suddenly dawned on them that the Range Rover
that had started the fuss was missing.

'Cavalin!' Pel yelled. 'Where's Cavalin!'

At Pel's shout, heads jerked round and they immediately
spotted the hole in the hedge where Cavalin's heavy vehicle
had crashed through.

'He's got away!' Darcy yelled.

'Mother of God,' Pel stormed. 'What was Morell doing?'

Several men scrambled through the hedge and started up
the slope, Darcy in the lead. As he reached the top, Pel saw
him stop, stare, then turn round and start galloping back.

'He drove straight through the gate at the other end on to
the road,' he snarled. 'You can see his tyre marks all the way.
There are bits of gate everywhere. He must have gone across
that meadow like shit off a shovel. Those damned Range
Rovers are built for it.' He was scrambling into a police car

as he spoke and, a second later, with Bardolle trying to get inside with him and shut the door as it moved away, he shot off down the narrow winding drive, removing a wing mirror from the indignant Lagé's car as he tore past.

Two hours later, with the ambulances beginning to crowd the forecourt of Deville's house and the ambulance men trying to clean up the mess, Darcy came back, scowling, followed by Bardolle driving the Range Rover.

'The bastard's given us the slip, Patron,' he said furiously. 'By God, it was quick thinking! He knew we'd be issuing a description of the Range Rover and he's already switched vehicles.'

'What about Morell? Why didn't he stop him?'

'Morell's in hospital. I drove him there. He was in the back of the Range Rover all the time. But he'd got a bullet under his right shoulder blade. He got it when the shooting started so it wasn't ours. He couldn't move his arm or even get himself upright. He managed to get one shot off but, with Cavalin driving like a kamikaze pilot and the Range Rover bouncing all over that field, it went through the roof. You can see the hole. He thinks he passed out as they smashed through the gate on to the road. Later on, he says, he remembers Cavalin saying he was sorry he'd inconvenienced him but that he'd telephone the police as soon as he could, and warn them where to find him.'

Even as Darcy spoke, one of the walkie-talkies squawked and Cavalin's message arrived via headquarters.

It was all over. They had the gold back. Not all of it. But most of it. A million francs' worth was still missing, but insurance would cover that and nobody was complaining and the newspapers were assuming that Maurice had used it for petty cash.

Goschen appeared to collect the gold and it turned out to be quite a celebration, with brandy in the Chief's office and

Goschen staying at Leu where Pel was childishly pleased to show off his new wife, his new home, and his new better manners.

'The gold hadn't been sold,' he said. 'It was sitting in a shop here in the city. Having stolen it, Maurice didn't know what to do with it and decided to make it into boules and hide it in Léon's strong room. When Léon panicked, he moved it to Deville's place, because Deville really did have a customer in the Far East who wanted statues for his garden. He even had an order and Customs and Excise export papers. It couldn't have been better.'

Suddenly everybody was doing all right. Nosjean was a hero in the eyes of both Mijo Lehmann and his family and even Morell hadn't come out of it all that badly. His shoulder still hurt a bit but he was in hospital with Catherine Deneuve's double keeping an eye on him and was knee-deep in fruit, flowers, chocolates and get-well cards from the Pasquiers. Even Misset was doing all right and appeared in the Hôtel de Police pushing in front of him a scruffy-looking individual with about three days' growth of beard.

'Soscharni, Patron,' he announced. 'He's decided to give up scribbling in books he disagrees with. He's decided to spit in them instead.'

When the full story of Maurice Tagliatti's murder appeared in the newspapers, names were mentioned and Henri Pasquier found his clients were more interested in what he knew than in his accountancy, Madame Pasquier discovered she had become remarkably popular with the housewives at Leu, as had her son, Yves, with his schoolmates. Despite the pictures of him in the press – they make me look as if I've been struck by lightning,' he said – Pel kept a low profile. He believed in low profiles. High profiles were bad for the police. However, he did finally make a point of supplying Yves Pasquier with an answer to his query about boules.

'The general view at the Hôtel de Police', he said gravely through the hole in the hedge, 'is that there's a lot to be said for boules. Some people appear to put a lot of money into boules.'

There was a snag, of course. There always was, and the final word came a few weeks later. It was a telephone call and Pel recognised the voice at once as Pépé le Cornet's. He sounded as if he were making a conspiracy.

'Thought you'd like to know, Chief,' he said quietly. 'Carmen Vlaxi's moved in.'

'Moved in where?'

'Everywhere Maurice moved out. The word went round that Cavalin was running things but, for your information, what's left of Maurice's organisation's now fallen completely apart. That left a vacuum with Vlaxi sitting in the middle of it. He just took over. Just thought you'd like to know.'

As the telephone clicked, Pel stared at it. You got rid of one and almost immediately there was another to take his place. You couldn't win.

All the same – there was always something to lighten a policeman's heart – Maurice's mob was no longer around to trouble them. Maurice was dead. Several others were dead, too, and the rest, including Harding, were in prison. With the aid of the police in Marseilles, they had even picked up Boileau, Léon's contact who had been arranging the route for the gold to the Middle East and, in addition to everything else, he had turned out to have been handling drugs. Vlada Preradovic had vanished back to London and Maurice's children had been removed from the expensive school they had been attending, and soon afterwards Sidonie had boarded an aircraft with them for the United States.

Only Cavalin had got away. He had ridden off into the sunset and they had found a trail of abandoned and stolen cars all the way to Marseilles. From there the route led to Italy and finally to Milan airport where it had completely

disappeared. They learned nothing until a telegram arrived a few weeks later.

It came from Buenos Aires and was addressed to Pel. It was signed *Georges Cavalin* and the message was brief. *Arrived safely,* it said. *Sidonie sends regards. Nicely provided for. Maurice didn't use the million for petty cash. I did.*

MARK HEBDEN

DEATH SET TO MUSIC

The severely battered body of a murder victim turns up in provincial France and the sharp-tongued Chief Inspector Pel must use all his Gallic guile to understand the pile of clues building up around him, until a further murder and one small boy make the elusive truth all too apparent.

THE ERRANT KNIGHTS

Hector and Hetty Bartlelott go to Spain for a holiday, along with their nephew Alec and his wife Sibley. All is well under a Spanish sun until Hetty befriends a Spanish boy on the run from the police and passionate Spanish Anarchists. What follows is a hard-and-fast race across Spain, hot-tailed by the police and the anarchists, some light indulging in the Semana Santa festivities of Seville to throw off the pursuers, and a near miss in Toledo where the young Spanish fugitive is almost caught.

MARK HEBDEN

PEL AND THE BOMBERS

When five murders disturb his sleepy Burgundian city on Bastille night, Chief Inspector Evariste Clovis Désiré Pel has his work cut out for him. A terrorist group is at work and the President is due shortly on a State visit. Pel's problems with his tyrannical landlady must be put aside while he catches the criminals.

"…downbeat humour and some delightful dialogue."
Financial Times

PEL AND THE PARIS MOB

In his beloved Burgundy, Chief Inspector Pel finds himself incensed by interference from Paris, but it isn't the flocking descent of rival policemen that makes Pel's blood boil – crimes are being committed by violent gangs from Paris and Marseilles. Pel unravels the riddle of the robbery on the road to Dijon airport as well as the mysterious shootings in an iron foundry. If that weren't enough, the Chief Inspector must deal with the misadventures of the delightfully handsome Sergeant Misset and his red-haired lover.

"…written with downbeat humour and some delightful dialogue which leaven the violence." *Financial Times*

MARK HEBDEN

PEL AND THE PREDATORS

There has been a spate of sudden murders around Burgundy where Pel has just been promoted to Chief Inspector. The irascible policeman receives a letter bomb, and these combined events threaten to overturn Pel's plans to marry Mme Faivre-Perret. Can Pel keep his life, his love and his career by solving the murder mysteries? Can Pel stave off the predators?

'...impeccable French provincial ambience.' *The Times*

PEL UNDER PRESSURE

The irascible Chief Inspector Pel is hot on the trail of a crime syndicate in this fast-paced, gritty crime novel, following leads on the mysterious death of a student and the discovery of a corpse in the boot of a car. Pel uncovers a drug-smuggling ring within the walls of Burgundy's university, and more murders guide the Chief Inspector to Innsbruck where the mistress of a professor awaits him.

TITLES BY MARK HEBDEN AVAILABLE DIRECT
FROM HOUSE OF STRATUS

Quantity	£	$(US)	$(CAN)	€
THE DARK SIDE OF THE ISLAND	6.99	11.50	15.99	11.50
DEATH SET TO MUSIC	6.99	11.50	15.99	11.50
THE ERRANT KNIGHTS	6.99	11.50	15.99	11.50
EYE WITNESS	6.99	11.50	15.99	11.50
A KILLER FOR THE CHAIRMAN	6.99	11.50	15.99	11.50
LEAGUE OF EIGHTY NINE	6.99	11.50	15.99	11.50
MASK OF VIOLENCE	6.99	11.50	15.99	11.50
PEL AMONG THE PUEBLOS	6.99	11.50	15.99	11.50
PEL AND THE TOUCH OF PITCH	6.99	11.50	15.99	11.50
PEL AND THE BOMBERS	6.99	11.50	15.99	11.50
PEL AND THE FACELESS CORPSE	6.99	11.50	15.99	11.50
PEL AND THE MISSING PERSONS	6.99	11.50	15.99	11.50
PEL AND THE PARIS MOB	6.99	11.50	15.99	11.50

ALL HOUSE OF STRATUS BOOKS ARE AVAILABLE FROM GOOD BOOKSHOPS
OR DIRECT FROM THE PUBLISHER:

Internet: www.houseofstratus.com including author interviews, reviews, features.

Email: sales@houseofstratus.com please quote author, title and credit card details.

Please allow for postage costs charged per order plus an amount per book as set out in the tables below:

	£(Sterling)	$(US)	$(CAN)	€(Euros)
Cost per order				
UK	2.00	3.00	4.50	3.30
Europe	3.00	4.50	6.75	5.00
North America	3.00	4.50	6.75	5.00
Rest of World	3.00	4.50	6.75	5.00
Additional cost per book				
UK	0.50	0.75	1.15	0.85
Europe	1.00	1.50	2.30	1.70
North America	2.00	3.00	4.60	3.40
Rest of World	2.50	3.75	5.75	4.25

PLEASE SEND CHEQUE, POSTAL ORDER (STERLING ONLY), EUROCHEQUE, OR INTERNATIONAL MONEY ORDER (PLEASE CIRCLE METHOD OF PAYMENT YOU WISH TO USE)

MAKE PAYABLE TO: STRATUS HOLDINGS plc

Cost of book(s):————————— Example: 3 x books at £6.99 each: £20.97

Cost of order:————————— Example: £2.00 (Delivery to UK address)

Additional cost per book:————— Example: 3 x £0.50: £1.50

Order total including postage:——— Example: £24.47

Please tick currency you wish to use and add total amount of order:

☐ £ (Sterling)   ☐ $ (US)   ☐ $ (CAN)   ☐ € (EUROS)

VISA, MASTERCARD, SWITCH, AMEX, SOLO, JCB:

☐☐☐☐☐☐☐☐☐☐☐☐☐☐☐☐☐☐☐☐

Issue number (Switch only):

☐☐☐

Start Date: **Expiry Date:**

☐☐/☐☐   ☐☐/☐☐

Signature: _____

NAME: _____

ADDRESS: _____

_____

POSTCODE: _____

Please allow 28 days for delivery.

Prices subject to change without notice.
Please tick box if you do not wish to receive any additional information. ☐

House of Stratus publishes many other titles in this genre; please check our website (**www.houseofstratus.com**) for more details.

TITLES BY MARK HEBDEN AVAILABLE DIRECT
FROM HOUSE OF STRATUS

Quantity		£	$(US)	$(CAN)	€
☐	PEL AND THE PARTY SPIRIT	6.99	11.50	15.99	11.50
☐	PEL AND THE PIRATES	6.99	11.50	15.99	11.50
☐	PEL AND THE PREDATORS	6.99	11.50	15.99	11.50
☐	PEL AND THE PROMISED LAND	6.99	11.50	15.99	11.50
☐	PEL AND THE PROWLER	6.99	11.50	15.99	11.50
☐	PEL AND THE SEPULCHRE JOB	6.99	11.50	15.99	11.50
☐	PEL AND THE STAG HOUND	6.99	11.50	15.99	11.50
☐	PEL IS PUZZLED	6.99	11.50	15.99	11.50
☐	PEL UNDER PRESSURE	6.99	11.50	15.99	11.50
☐	PORTRAIT IN A DUSTY FRAME	6.99	11.50	15.99	11.50
☐	A PRIDE OF DOLPHINS	6.99	11.50	15.99	11.50
☐	WHAT CHANGED CHARLEY FARTHING	6.99	11.50	15.99	11.50

ALL HOUSE OF STRATUS BOOKS ARE AVAILABLE FROM GOOD BOOKSHOPS
OR DIRECT FROM THE PUBLISHER:

Hotline: UK ONLY: 0800 169 1780, please quote author, title and credit card details.
INTERNATIONAL: +44 (0) 20 7494 6400, please quote author, title, and credit card details.

Send to: House of Stratus Sales Department
24c Old Burlington Street
London
W1X 1RL
UK